A LADY Can Never Be TOO CURIOUS

MARY WINE

sourcebooks
casablanca

Published by Sourcebooks Casablanca, an imprint of Sourcebooks, Inc.
P.O. Box 4410, Naperville, Illinois 60567-4410
(630) 961-3900
Fax: (630) 961-2168
www.sourcebooks.com

Printed and bound in Canada.
WC 10 9 8 7 6 5 4 3 2 1

For Deirdre Sargent. A Queen, an author, but most importantly…a true friend. A gem among pebbles, may you always know how brightly you shine…

One

Great Britain, 1843

"You are going to be caught one of these times, Janette."

"Don't lecture, Sophia," Janette begged. "I get too much of that from my father. Sometimes he turns red because he won't stop long enough to draw breath."

Sophia choked back a giggle. "Well, he isn't the only one who thinks the Illuminists are uncivilized. Besides, we well-brought-up girls must be...mindful of appearances."

Sophia lost the battle to remain prim-looking and dissolved into laughter.

"Their Solitary Chamber is anything but uncivilized. Look at those arches, just like the Romans built," Janette remarked in a hushed tone to keep her words from drifting to where Sophia's father was minding his shop in the front of the house. "Doesn't it drive you simply mad to not know what goes on in there?"

Janette leaned on the windowsill, trying to gain a glimpse of what the large building kept so secret. On the outside, it was an imposing structure more suited to ancient Greece than England. Smooth columns held up the three-story roof, and all the doorways were constructed with arches. It was only the front of a four-block enclosure. No one outside the secret Order really knew what was inside, but there were plenty of rumors.

Wild sexual indulgence…

Strange science experiments…

Satanic rituals…

But the members coming and going looked normal enough. Even if their vests were constructed with additional pockets and the females among them were often seen openly wearing the pantaloons style so scorned by upper society.

"I don't find it as fascinating as you do. So where's the science circular? You only come to see me when you want to buy one without your father knowing."

"At least your father doesn't mind your reading them."

"So long as I do so in the back room," Sophia remarked drily. "Society is unforgiving of ladies who try to expand their minds. Such drivel."

Janette shrugged off her shawl. It was rolled lengthwise to contain the circular. Unrolling it, she began scanning the articles.

"Isn't it fascinating, Sophia? Look at this one; it's about currents of electricity being used. There's a lecture next Tuesday in the Solitary Chamber. How I'd like to see that with my own eyes."

Sophia scoffed. "It will cost you every friend you have to experience it."

Janette looked up at her friend. "Including you? Would you shun me if I challenged the exam to

become an Illuminist?" They were bold words, but
a little jolt of excitement went down her body when
she said them. Her father's insistence that she remain
meek and obedient was overly constrictive, but what
annoyed her was the expectation that she refrain
from education. Her mother had secreted tutors into
the house to instruct her. The circular in her hand
was nourishment to her ravenous mind. Yet she
was forbidden to discuss the tantalizing data because
it wasn't considered ladylike. There were times she
feared being crushed by the rules of her society.

"Well, perhaps not me," Sophia muttered. "But
my father would most likely insist on your using the
back door if you started wearing one of those gold
lapel pins of the Illuminist Order. Our esteemed
clientele might find another designer if we had any
Illuminists in the main salon. You wouldn't want
my father to have to resort to producing clothing
like a factory worker, would you? He must maintain
appearances or lose his clients."

And there was the bitter truth—the definite
boundary between the Illuminists and society. You
were either one or the other. "There are no demon-
strators today. Perhaps everyone is ready to begin
accepting the Illuminists since the Queen has spoken
well of them," Janette offered hopefully.

"The Queen is young," Sophia remarked.
"Everyone will listen to her with smiles on their faces,
but it will not stop the calls for the Illuminists to be
run out of the city. People fear the unknown. The
Constables are always here hassling the members on
their way up those steps."

"They keep their secrets; that much is true." Janette went to join her friend, but she stopped before she made it to the summer porch.

"When did your father start making cycling pantaloons?"

One of the wardrobe cabinets was slightly open. Hung up in a neat row were several pairs of the controversial women's wear.

"Father didn't make them. I did," Sophia informed her. "You aren't the only one who likes Illuminist ways. They are quite comfortable."

Janette looked at the makeshift dressing room formed with curtains near the back door. A full-length mirror stood next to it. "I want to try on a pair."

"Your father would have a brain seizure." But Sophia sounded excited.

"He would." Janette held the pantaloons up in front of her and stared at her reflection in the mirror.

There was a swish of fabric as Sophia pulled out a coat with a peplum attached to it. "You will need this, or you'll be shocking even to an Illuminist in naught but pantaloons and your corset."

Janette took the pantaloons and coat into the dressing room and heard the curtain close behind her.

She was behaving wickedly.

No, that wasn't true. She refused to believe a piece of clothing might be the cause of her moral corruption. She unbuttoned her dress and reached down to release the waistband on her petticoat so she could step out of it. She contemplated the pantaloons for a moment before shaking them out in front of her and lifting one foot. They slid easily up one leg and then the other.

She turned to the coat and slid it off the hanger. The pantaloons felt slightly strange, but the brush of air against her lower legs was pleasant.

"These must be heavenly in summer," she murmured.

"Don't become too enamored, Janette. You know your father detests anything to do with the Illuminists."

Janette pushed her hands into the sleeves of the top and pulled it closed over her corset. "How could I forget? I have to hide my science circulars in my shawl. You've no idea what it takes to keep the upstairs maid from discovering them in my room, but I'm not giving them up. Privately, I shall keep my mind as sharp as I please."

Sophia laughed, and Janette pushed the curtain open while working the last of the coat buttons closed. Excitement turned her cheeks pink as she hurried to see her reflection. The long mirror showed her more of her shape than she'd ever seen. She turned to look at the back view. The coat's peplum fell to just above her knees, and the bagginess of the pants didn't allow her knees to show at all. The cuffs of the pantaloons fit easily around her calves, allowing several inches of her stockings to be seen before her boots began. Both pieces were made of caramel wool.

"You might as well try on the hat while you're at it, Janette."

Sophia offered a top hat, only it wasn't made of wool or beaver silk as Janette expected. Nor was it in a size a lady normally wore.

"Why is it so large?"

"Illuminists consider function more important than fashion. This hat was ordered by a woman who claimed the kid leather would fail to conduct something or other."

"Electricity," Janette supplied while sitting the hat on her head. It sat comfortably around her forehead, exactly like a man would wear his hat.

"I never thought cycling pantaloons would feel so free."

Sophia failed to hide her amusement. "I warn you not to get accustomed to the feeling. Both our families will see us shipped to the Highlands before allowing either of us to set one foot outside without a dress on."

Janette walked to the door of the summer porch and looked at the yard beyond as if she were inside a prison cell and what she saw was impossible to reach.

"I'm going outside," she decided. The fear of discovery was beginning to bother her. Was she truly a coward?

"Janette, Scotland is cold, you know, and it rains all the time."

"I'm just going to feel how the hat works in the sun."

Sophia followed her but stopped in the doorway. "You are beyond hope."

Janette stepped farther out into the sunlight, the brim of the leather hat shading her eyes.

"Come back in, Janette. My father might check on us."

"Must I?" she teased.

Sophia surprised her by raising one eyebrow in a very daring way. There was a hint of a challenge in her eyes Janette couldn't recall seeing before. "By all means, walk up to the Solitary Chamber doors and see if they allow you inside."

Janette shot her friend a look full of mischief, encouraged by the bold nature of her suggestion. "That sounds like a challenge."

"Maybe it is," Sophia answered. "But like all challenges, it comes with a consequence. If my father catches us and informs your father of what we have been about, we shall find ourselves in the draftiest castle they can rent to lodge us and not just Scotland: they will likely send us to the Highlands."

"In that case, you should change into a pair of pantaloons as well. You shouldn't suffer in exile with me without having some of the fun."

Sophia laughed, rolling her eyes. She reached inside for something and reappeared with a similar top hat on. This second one was made of kid leather dyed a deep red.

"The clothing is fun, I admit." Sophia stepped into the sunlight while adjusting the hat to shade her eyes. "And so functional, unlike fashion with its ridiculous ideas about tight lacing and overly large petticoats. Not that I mind a pretty ball gown, but honestly, I would like to fit through the door of the carriage without having to bend my skirts."

It might yet be more fun…

Janette turned to look at the Solitary Chamber building. She reached for the latch on the back iron gate before her common sense reared its head. She knew she was acting impulsively, but she felt there would never be another chance for her to attempt to satisfy her curiosity.

Never, which meant she'd have to live with the knowledge that she'd acted the coward when opportunity was upon her.

No…she would be bold. It felt absolutely necessary. The need raced through her veins as her heart accelerated. Maybe Sophia felt the same urgency, because as she made her way through the gate, her friend never called her back.

Within moments, Janette stood on the opposite side of the street. The columns looked taller now. She climbed the steps, tipping her head back to investigate the construction of the roof. The portico was covered in brilliant paintings—perfect images of the solar system and other things she'd never seen before. But were the paintings of fact or fiction? Fact. She knew she was in the place of facts. Satisfaction filled her and left goose bumps along her arms because it was so intense.

Someone cleared his throat.

Janette jerked her attention down to discover a doorman standing inside the building with the door open for her.

"Good afternoon."

The doorman didn't even blink but remained at his post. He looked straight ahead, never focusing on her. Excitement renewed its grip on her. Janette wasn't sure if she forgot to draw breath or not, but she walked through the forbidden doorway.

The doorman shut the door behind her and walked to a small booth. He stood there, facing the wall, but when she peered closer, she could see he was watching through some sort of window. It wasn't transparent, but she could clearly see outside.

Fascinating…

"The experiments have already begun."

She straightened abruptly as he spoke without looking at her.

"Yes, thank you."

It was difficult to turn her back on the window set into solid stone. She wanted to look through it and discover its secrets, but the doorman's words tempted her to see how much further she might go.

The hallway was lit, but instead of the green glow of gaslights, a muted white light glowed from behind frosted panes of glass. She reached out and touched one gently and found it cool. There was no smoke or soot either.

Astounding.

Voices drifted into the hallway from a large archway ahead. A few more steps and she could make sense of the conversation.

"So we know the conductive capabilities of Deep Earth Crystals…"

Janette entered under the arch and froze.

"We also know that Deep Earth Crystals respond to one another…It is this reaction that allows us to harness their energy…and produce steam for power…"

The lecturer was in the center of the room. A table stood behind him lit by huge panes of frosted glass that glowed brighter than a full moon. Each was held by a large copper stand with gears built into them so the light could be aimed in different directions. Like a lamp that might be moved to aim light in any direction.

But what was a Deep Earth Crystal? And how could it respond?

She took a step sideways into one of the rows of seats ringing the stage the lecturer stood on and sat down. Excitement gripped her as she leaned forward to hear the rest of the lecture. A sound rose from those watching as the man pulled a large crystal from a case.

"Impressive…yes…but remember…size does not dictate the potency of the conductive properties."

He set the crystal down and plucked what looked like a folded leather apron off the table. Once he flipped it open and pushed his hand into it, it was clear it was a glove, made of leather reinforced with sturdy canvas. Janette leaned forward, eager to see why he needed such protection from rocks. He lifted a dome such as she might expect to see on a breakfast service tray, and beneath it lay a small crystal.

It was no thicker than a broom handle and only about six inches long, but he handled it with great care, reaching out his gloved hand to pick it up while holding his head back, as though the crystal were molten metal.

"Here we have an excellent example of the true power of—"

The moment the smaller crystal came closer to the large one, the room filled with a sharp whine. The lecturer stiffened, fighting to maintain his grip on the smaller crystal. His assistants lunged forward to help him, but the smaller crystal broke his grip and went sailing up into the seats.

The whine decreased as it arced through the air and left the other crystal behind. The Illuminists watching in front of her ducked, and the crystal landed neatly in her lap.

Janette picked it up before thinking, and the pulse of electricity began shooting through her body. It was deeper, almost harmonic. She swore she could hear the delicate sounds of music, and the crystal itself felt warm against her palm. It felt completely correct to hold it, and satisfying in an unexpected way, as though she'd never truly been complete until this moment.

"Madam…*madam!*"

Janette was startled out of the strange euphoria by the lecturer's frantic voice. He'd rushed up the aisle but stood staring at her.

He suddenly smiled, and crinkles appeared near his eyes. "I wasn't informed we had a new handler in our midst. When did you arrive?"

The rest of the audience all stared at her.

"Well…just now." She stood, and those closest to her shifted back, their attention on the crystal she held. "Would you like me to place this somewhere for you?"

Four assistants were clustered around the lecturer. They wore leather overcoats and had leather hoods on their heads with a pair of goggles pushed up above their eyes. One of them leaned in and whispered in the lecturer's ear, pointing at Janette. The lecturer's eyebrows rose.

"You will need to come with me." A deep voice issued the command from behind her.

Janette felt a tingle race down her spine. The newcomer had a voice edged with steel, the solid sort of authority that announced a man who was accustomed to being obeyed. She turned to discover the owner of the voice standing only a single pace from her. She had to look up because he was tall with broad shoulders.

He was attired in a double-breasted vest and overcoat—just as proper as any gentleman—but there was something in his dark eyes that was very uncivilized. For all that they were surrounded by others, she felt like she was alone with him.

And that knowledge excited her.

Definitely wicked…

The sensation was unsettling, and for some odd reason, she sensed that he knew exactly how he affected her. It was in the narrowing of his eyes and the thinning of his lips—tiny little details she shouldn't have noticed but did.

"My apologies, Professor, for having your lecture interrupted by a trespasser," the newcomer said. "I will remove her."

"Mr. Lawley, she is still holding the crystal…If you touch her…the current…ah…" The lecturer's warning came too late. Janette barely felt the man close his grip around her upper arm when he growled and released her.

"I did warn you, Darius. That's a level-four sample she's holding. Because she's a Pure Spirit, the current is going straight—"

"Enough. She's heard too much already. She is not an Illuminist."

Darius Lawley offered the professor a frown. When he turned his head, Janette was treated to the view of some sort of device covering his ear. Several copper and silver gears were visible, and the men behind him wore similar devices. These men didn't look like the other Illuminists attending the lecture. They were burly, and their expressions, hard.

Like constables.

Darius jerked his head back toward her the moment she moved. There was sharpness in his eyes, but what she sensed most about him was the fact that he was dangerous. He was unlike any man she'd met. Her world had always been full of gentlemen whom she trusted to remain at a polite distance.

This man was nothing like that. He'd boldly touched her, and that brief connection felt somehow... intimate. Yet she wasn't offended. The surge of excitement was only growing stronger as she contemplated leaving with him.

"If you please, miss, give the crystal to Professor Yulric." His voice was deep and raspy, setting off a ripple of awareness that traveled down her length in spite of how perfectly polite his words were.

"Yes, quite right. Hand it here. It's quite volatile, you understand." The professor shuddered. He extended his hand with the protective glove still in place.

"I find the lecture quite amazing. I'd like to remain to learn more about the crystal."

"Illuminists only," Darius informed her. His expression tightened, his lips sealing into a hard line.

She sighed before turning her hand over so the crystal dropped into the professor's waiting palm.

"Clear a path...Clear the way..." Professor Yulric hurried down the aisle, and the crystal began to whine as he neared the other one. "Remove the male, for heaven's sake, or we'll have another uncontrollable reaction."

"The what? Did you say male? As in gender?" Janette asked, too curious to contain her question.

"Nothing," Darius informed her quietly. "You do not belong here."

He reached past her and grasped one of her shoulders and neatly turned her around so the sight of Professor Yulric was lost. It was done with such a light touch she stood slightly shocked.

"But I want to see——"

"I've no doubt you do, but you have snuck inside our chambers, which I cannot allow. Please come with me."

She really couldn't refuse; after all, he was correct. She followed him, and his men fell into step behind them.

Confusion needled her as they went right past the doorman. Her expectation that she would be tossed unceremoniously out onto the front steps vanished as Darius continued on, granting her the opportunity to see more of the forbidden building.

It should have alarmed her; instead, she felt another jolt of heat stab into her. She didn't care at all if the situation was proper, it was exciting.

"Where are you taking me?"

"To my office."

He lifted his hand to touch the device in his ear. Almost in the same instant there was a groan as a door ahead of them opened. Darius led her through it, and the door closed behind them with a solid sound.

The room they had entered was quite big for an office and had a large desk like one she would expect to find in a police station sitting in the middle of the floor. Darius walked around to sit behind it as his men took up positions behind her. There was no chair in front of the desk. The criminal stood, while the detective sat.

Darius considered her from head to boot toe with a razor-sharp gaze. "Ladies who practice deceptions often discover themselves far from their comfortable parlors, Miss…?"

"Miss Janette Aston."

How wicked such a simple suggestion seemed coming from him. Her cheeks felt like they were blazing, yet fear hadn't arrived to dampen her enjoyment of the moment.

Bold women come to no good end, her father was fond of telling her. But at the moment she felt more alive than she ever had. In fact, she wanted to match the man in front of her.

"You needn't be so sour. I haven't hurt anyone." She swallowed to clear the huskiness from her tone. "You are not an officer of the law."

"Here, I am." His voice returned to its formal tone. "And before you demand to see my superior, I will tell you I am in command of the Guardian personnel in this Solitary Chamber. You shall deal with me, Miss Aston."

There was a flicker of heat in his eyes, a hint of enjoyment that made his statement more personal. A twist of excitement went through her belly, shocking her with just how affected she was.

"I see." Apprehension tried to rise inside her, but she shook it off. "Surely you can see the compliment in my desire to attend one of your lectures."

He raised a dark eyebrow, appearing too rakish by far. There was a hint of something in his eyes that sent her eyelids fluttering. It was pure response. She failed completely to control it, and it undermined her determination to meet him with boldness. His gaze settled on the blush staining her cheeks.

"Tell me, does it concern you to be here unescorted?"

He waved a hand, and the two men behind her turned to leave. Amusement glittered in his dark eyes, rubbing her temper enough to help her recover her poise. The man was clearly toying with her.

And she was enjoying it…

But she shouldn't. She folded her hands primly.

"Mr. Lawley, I simply cannot stand for this… well…this—"

"Lack of formality?" he supplied in a tone rich with suggestion. "You have willfully entered my world. Do not be so naïve as to think I will conform to your high-society ideas of what my behavior should be."

Her mind was happy to offer several ideas of just what he might be suggesting too. She shook her head to dispel her wild imaginings. Boldness might be fine to toy with, so long as she wasn't facing a man such as this one. She could not trust him or her reaction to him. The Solitary Chamber truly was another world, and she felt the change dramatically.

Yet there was something about him—something she felt more than had evidence to support—that made her believe he was only trying to play on her fears.

"I really am not a rabbit to be frightened off with any hint of impropriety. If that were so, I'd have stopped reading your science circulars years ago, or likely never begun, given my father's disapproval of anything to do with your order. I find the circulars fascinating."

His head cocked to one side as he studied her. "Brave words, easily spoken when you clearly believe your behavior will never be found out by anyone in your corner of the world. Perhaps I should keep you here and send a message to your father to come and collect you."

"How unkind of you to threaten me like a child." The man was trying to unnerve her. It should have bothered her; instead, she was beset by the need to stand firm in the face of his threats.

"If you want to be treated gently like a lady, you should remain in your dress and petticoat."

Maybe she was tired of being treated like a lady…

Her thoughts shocked her, making her struggle to find the correct words to reply. There was too much expectation in his tone, and part of her truly wanted to surprise him. "I never thought the title *Illuminist* implied your kind were not honorable."

"Really?" He stood, and she felt her breath quicken. His devil-may-care attitude fascinated her when it should have sickened or shocked her at the very least. She needed to find her discipline—and quickly.

"You are amusing yourself at my expense. Even if you persist in accusing me of wrongdoing, you shouldn't try to frighten me like some dockside bully." She nodded, satisfied with her reply. At least she sounded confident, even if it was pretense. Even an Illuminist couldn't see into her thoughts.

And yet there was a flicker of something in his dark eyes that hinted that he knew just how unsteady she felt. But she maintained her composure, staring straight back at him, and he abandoned his playfulness.

"And what, pray tell, would you have to say if you had discovered me in your kitchen, Miss Aston? Would the excuse that I was curious as to the pattern of china you keep be sufficient to appease you?"

He was mocking her, his voice deep and rich. But she felt a prick of guilt.

"There is a difference between walking up to a door to see if it would be opened and discovering you in my home," she muttered. "Your man opened the door for me. Go and deal with your doorman for allowing me in without one of your pins."

"He only did so because you are a—never mind."

"I am a what?" She looked at the gold pin on his lapel, noticing the crystal in it for the first time. "Is my ability to handle crystals the reason I was allowed in? What does that make me?"

His expression became stone-hard and impossible to read.

"You are being childish to assume we keep such strict membership requirements if there were nothing inside this building worth keeping secret."

There was a note of truth in his words, but part of her was still insanely captivated by the rogue who'd been teasing her. He'd retreated behind a socially acceptable demeanor now, and she found it disappointing.

"I suppose you are finished now with teasing me about doing your worst. Do you truly believe I was impressed?" The words tumbled out before her better judgment intervened.

Surprise lit his eyes, and the corners of his mouth

twitched up. The smile transformed his face, making him too pleasing by far once again.

"You are nowhere near ready to handle my worst, Miss Aston. But you are accurate in your assessment. If you weren't so young, you'd recognize that as a warning and not a compliment."

There was a dark promise in his voice. His gaze settled on her lips for a moment, one that lasted longer than was proper. She needed to escape from the room before she did something…impulsive. It was so odd to discover how volatile her nature might be when she was paired with a man who didn't condemn her for her boldness. Part of her was sure he was encouraging it, pushing at her boundaries to see where her limits were.

Wicked…and dangerous, for a woman was worth little without her good name. "You have a good point, but I cannot claim I am truly sorry for trying your door personnel. I did not choose where I was born any more than you did," she stated quietly. "Yet it is time I departed before my friend worries enough to summon the local constables."

He shook his head, enjoyment glittering in his eyes. "You were not kidnapped, so I highly doubt your friend will be quick to report where you are."

"A moment ago you were insisting that I do not belong here, and now you dangle the idea that no one shall miss me in front of my nose?"

He was like a cat with a mouse, so confident of his superiority. Her temper rose, burning through the haze that clouded her rational thinking.

"You shall press that ear device of yours immediately

and open that door for me." She slapped her hand down on the desk to ensure he understood how intent she was.

Darius jumped the moment her hand made contact, and he reached out to capture her wrists, but he only locked his fingers around one of her hands. Her other hand made contact with the smooth surface of the desk, and when it did, the entire thing lit. A soft whine filled the air, and she felt the current travel through her.

Darius released her with a muffled word that sounded very much like profanity.

"Remove your hand." He sounded annoyed, which pleased her because it placed them back on even ground.

"Are there crystals inside this desk?" She lifted her hand when his expression tightened with determination to maintain his secrecy. "Why does it pain you to touch me when I'm in contact with those crystals?"

Science questions were wonderfully devoid of stimulation, at least the physical sort.

She directed her attention to the desk. Darius reached out and boldly cupped her chin, lifting it so their gazes fused. Her skin flushed uncomfortably hot, her poise deserting her in an instant. Sensation rippled across her skin. She was stunned by just how much she enjoyed his hand on her. So delightful, but wicked nonetheless.

"You're being quite forward," she said, but her tone lacked true conviction.

"You are hardly sputtering with indignant, puritan outrage," he muttered. "In fact, you sound…breathless."

Now his toying was much more personal and dangerous. Her belly twisted with something that felt like excitement, but her common sense warned her to avoid any further discoveries. He wouldn't be condemned in his world, but she would be in hers.

"I'm agitated." She stepped back to remove herself from his touch. "But you clearly don't recognize civilized emotions."

"Because I'm an Illuminist?" he offered too quickly.

"Because you are clearly no gentleman, as your behavior proves." Her father would have approved of her words, but part of her cringed. She was acting the prude when her thoughts were anything but proper. "Why are you being so presumptuous? You judge me, sir, far more than I am guilty of having preconceived notions about your character."

Darius came around the desk, his large body capturing her attention. An insane rush of heat washed down her body as he came closer. She became more conscious of the lack of skirt hiding her legs. He was the first man to see so much of her form, and she felt her cheeks burning as he loomed over her. The man never averted his eyes, like a gentleman would have, but surveyed her from head to toe without hesitation.

Did he like what he saw?

"Miss Aston, I am responsible for security here, and I don't have time to teach curious girls lessons their nursemaids should have."

He wasn't attracted to her one bit, which made her a fool. "You are free with your judgments sir."

"Perhaps, but I assure you I am very skilled at keeping this Solitary Chamber secure."

Now he was formal, and she believed him. Duty was something he held very dear; she could see the devotion in his eyes. He reached up and tapped the device covering his ear. She witnessed it glow. Only in a tiny portion, but the light was unmistakable. The door opened with a soft sound behind her.

"I will return once I've questioned the doorman," he said. "By all means, continue to think of me as no gentleman. I find the blush on your cheeks…charming."

Outrage banished the shame flooding her. "Why, you…rogue."

The door closed behind Darius, but not before she witnessed the satisfied smirk on his lips.

Ill-mannered, gutter hound!

Insufferable man. She wasn't going to waste her time on thinking about what he thought of her.

But you're still disappointed he is quite out of reach.

Oh stop already.

She couldn't possibly be interested in seeing him again. No. She would deny such feelings, because otherwise she would be doomed to weeping in her bed.

Illuminists and ladies did not mix. Ever.

"You seem to be failing to impress our guest, Darius."

Darius made it to the observation room adjacent to his office to discover Lykos Claxton watching Janette.

"She lacks a sense of self-preservation. I was attempting to motivate her to stay at her friend's tea table. I'm sure her father would want it that way." He wished he agreed more with his better judgment, but his tone betrayed just how little passion he had for doing the correct thing when it came to Janette Aston. She tempted him, and that was dangerous ground.

Lykos peered at Janette through the wall screen. "You managed to bring a blush to her cheeks and spirit to her voice. No simpering at all. Interesting."

Darius didn't care for the tone of his comment. His comrade was an outstanding guardian, but his second love in life was the art of seduction—a skill he had polished to a high shine with the help of his handsome face. Fair hair and blue eyes added to his appeal with the gentle sex.

"Why are you here, anyway? I can handle a single trespasser by myself. If you don't have enough to keep you busy at your posting, I'm sure the council would be happy to assign you someplace that can keep you from wandering away from your post looking for afternoon diversion."

"For a look at a Pure Spirit, I'd sit through tea at Buckingham Palace, boring conversation and all. But that little bit of womanhood isn't hard on the eyes, even if blondes aren't my favorite."

Darius frowned, recognizing the tone of his friend's voice. Lykos knew how to seduce women far too well. "She's a Pure Spirit, for all the good it will do us. Her family is upper-crust, not an Illuminist-accepting bone in their bodies."

"Why so skeptical? Those cycling pantaloons give me hope." Lykos nodded. "She won't be so hard to entice into the order. If she found the courage to step out in those, she's not the model lady her family wishes." He flashed a grin at Darius. "Maybe I'm being too rash about those golden locks."

"What's this?" Professor Yulric came around the corner, his thoughts spilling from his lips in the same moment his mind formed them. "Have you convinced the girl to train for the exam already? Excellent." He beamed at them, rubbing his hands together excitedly.

"No, I haven't even broached the subject, and you both know she must ask. It's a rare young woman who is willing to take such a drastic step in changing her life."

The professor's hands stopped, and he stared at Darius like a child being denied a favorite toy. "But we simply cannot allow such a unique discovery to slip away. Need I remind you that the number of Pure Spirits has been greatly reduced due to the nefarious habits of the Helikeians? If she is discovered and refuses to participate in their evil, she will be killed."

"I am well aware of the Helikeians' thirst for Pure Spirits, Professor. That does not in any way grant us the right to act as they do and keep Miss Aston simply because we are aware of her secret origins."

"But can we allow her to return to the outside world when her secret is undeniably exposed now?" Lykos asked. "All it will take is one undetected spy among those at the lecture, and the Helikeians will take her the moment we allow her to leave. You admitted as much this morning."

Darius didn't care for the hard truth in Lykos's words. In fact, there was very little about the day he did like. Miss Aston was in more trouble than she might ever suspect. But there was something about the way she had stood up to him that made him want to resist dismissing the situation as something beyond his control.

That was the true reason he needed her to leave his world. His emotions were boiling dangerously, and his duty required complete control.

"Yes, I agree with Mr. Claxton," the professor said. "It is simply too great a risk to allow the girl to return to her father's home." The professor began rubbing his hands again. "I cannot wait to begin instructing her."

"You mean to say…you eagerly anticipate being able to use her abilities for your work," Darius said.

Yulric's eyes widened. "Well, yes."

"That makes you no better than a Helikeian."

The professor frowned. "Now, see here—"

"Professor, the girl has a family, and unless you would like the duty of strong-arming her into a room for the night, legally I have no grounds to keep her here, nor do I have a personal desire to imprison her. She has not asked to challenge the exam, and she is not the offspring of an Illuminist, even a disgraced one, so you both know none of us can put the question to her."

"Damned law," Lykos replied. "I don't suppose the lot of you would care to look the other way while I break that legal noose Parliament insisted on passing to keep us from growing in numbers?"

"The one you need to worry about is her," Darius answered while studying Janette. "It would be unwise for us to assume she's willing to walk away from her family and shield us from reprimand. That little dove will no doubt sing loud and clear if we break the law, landing us all in prison."

"Unless she is motivated by the need to keep her afternoon adventures secret from her family," Lykos countered.

Darius shifted his attention to his friend. "However passionate we both are, neglecting honor has never been a failing either of us have been guilty of. We've both sworn to uphold the law. We break our Oaths of Allegiance if we put the question to her."

"True," Lykos admitted. "Frustratingly so."

Darius discovered himself staring at Janette again, his jaw aching as he ground his teeth. He was tempted, but honor was not optional. If it were possible to will another person into doing something, Janette would have turned toward them and voiced the demand to challenge the exam. Instead, she continued to investigate his desk, blissfully ignorant of the law that bound his hands. Parliament wanted the knowledge the Illuminist community had, but they also wanted their high British society untainted. Recruiting was strictly prohibited, and even now, when Janette had walked through the doors of her own will, he couldn't ask her if she wanted to join.

Part of him was happy about it—pleased that he wouldn't be faced with dealing with her. She had too much raw magnetism, and she was also in possession of an uncanny sense of perception. In short, she could see past his hardened exterior too well. That was something he couldn't tolerate.

The professor's shoulders slumped. "That is terribly disappointing. Very tragic…and such a loss…"

The man walked away, still babbling. Lykos suddenly started chuckling. Darius turned to see his comrade watching their subject again. Janette had returned to his desk and placed her hands firmly on the surface.

"She's a curious one." Lykos cut him a sidelong glance. "About a lot of things." His words were coated with suggestion. "If she were my sister, I'd have to hit you for how much of a knave you were with her."

"So hit me," Darius remarked. "I enjoyed it, so did she," he added with a wolfish grin.

Lykos smothered a bark of laughter. "It's about time a member of the fairer sex made a hole in your rough exterior."

"Don't start, Lykos," Darius said. "She's a lady, and the last thing I need is another lady anywhere near me. One look at my true nature and she'll have nightmares."

"Or heated fantasies." His friend became serious. "Let Miss Aston go if you must, but don't fail to admit to yourself that you're interested—besides, maybe you should court her. That's the only other way around the law."

"Neither of us would make it past the butler, much less into the parlor."

It irritated him to discover he admired her tenacity enough to toy with her. To what end? She would return to her father's house, where an Illuminist like himself wasn't welcome. No matter how bright the blush staining her cheeks, she'd turn her nose up when her family pressed her to choose him or her standing in society.

He was an Illuminist, and he'd never leave the order. The last thing he needed was another lady of society looking down her nose at him. Better to be done with it quickly, no matter the fact that she was a Pure Spirit. At least she'd be blissfully ignorant of her loss. He wouldn't be so fortunate.

He'd know what she could have been, and for the first time in a very long time, he was going to lament not being able to get to know a lady better.

❧

She couldn't see the crystals, but she could hear them.

Janette moved around the desk and bent over to look beneath it. The top was a good inch thick, like a baking pan, with room beneath the frosted glass. Once she stood in front of it, symbols appeared on the top. They were vaguely familiar, and she leaned closer to study them.

"Did you open the drawers of your friend's wardrobe to discover that ensemble you're wearing while she was fetching the tea service?"

The door had opened, and she'd been too absorbed to notice. Janette quickly removed her hands from the desktop, the hair on the back of her neck rising with apprehension. Just the sound of his voice and her thoughts shifted back to her fascination with Darius Lawley. She forced herself to draw a deep breath before facing him, but it didn't steady her as much as she'd hoped.

"No, I did not. Sophia knows very well that I am wearing her creations." At least her voice came out steady. "When are you going to stop insinuating that I'm some sort of criminal?"

Darius closed the space between them. Beneath her corset, her nipples contracted in response. Her mouth went dry, the pure wickedness of the response stunning her.

"What would that leave for us to discuss except improper topics?" His voice was low and suggestive, but his eyes were guarded again, almost as though he didn't consider her worthy of his attentions.

"Somehow, I'd always thought of an Illuminist as someone more interested in spending their time on facts instead of useless gossip."

He drew in a stiff breath, all hints of playfulness gone. "Your friend will no doubt be looking for you, Miss Aston. However, it is my duty to warn you not to be so foolish as to believe no one else shares your curiosity about what is inside this chamber." He walked toward her. "Has it occurred to you that someone might be willing to harm you to learn what you now know about Deep Earth Crystals?"

He half turned and extended his arm toward the door. At the same time he touched the device covering his ear, and the door opened.

"My doorman will not make the same mistake twice, Miss Aston. Do the wise thing and stay where you belong. Only members are allowed inside our walls."

"But…would it be possible…to attend a lecture…"

He tapped the gold lapel pin on his vest. "We share our knowledge only with those willing to announce their loyalty to us."

But there was a flicker of something in his eyes; it looked like hope. The man appeared to be waiting for her to jump at his offer. He tapped his lapel pin several more times, and she ended up staring at it.

Did she dare?

"It is not your intelligence I question, Janette, but your ability to sever emotional ties. Something society will require of you if you join our order. Think about that before you take any action." His tone was harder than any he'd used before, setting off a desire to understand him.

"Do you regret becoming an Illuminist?" She was being intrusive but couldn't seem to feel ashamed. Something flickered in his eyes that betrayed a deep pain, and she discovered herself battling the urge to console him.

"Not enough to regret my choice. I am proud to be an Illuminist and a guardian of our order."

Now that she was looking closer at the pin, she could see a pair of crossed swords on the top and a crystal set into it.

"Guardian…So you are a constable?"

"Closer to a Knight of the Garter. My duty doesn't end at shift change. To become a guardian is a lifelong commitment."

She could see there was dedication in him and even something she might describe as nobility. For certain, she had heard the word *honor* used by the men of her father's acquaintance, but Darius was the first man she'd met who seemed to embody the quality.

"As a guardian, it is my duty to escort you off our property."

He reached out and secured her upper arm in his firm grip while pressing on the ear device. They passed through the door and into the hallway.

"You had to leave someone behind who you cared

about, didn't you? It was a lady. That's why you were taking such delight in needling me."

Surprise registered on his face, shining through the stern expression of duty, but it vanished almost as soon as it appeared.

"Don't meddle in my personal affairs, Janette. Unless you plan to become an Illuminist, we will remain strangers." He was warning her now, but it was a personal one—and yet the man was dangling a temptation in front of her nose too. It felt like he was daring her to try living as an Illuminist.

To try living near him…

"Perhaps I will," she countered. "But I must say, you handle me far too much for someone who continues to insist we shall never cross paths again."

He froze, his dark eyes glittering. The grip on her arm tightened, just a fraction, betraying a reaction from him.

"My world is more concerned with facts. We do not spend our time worrying about propriety, since it changes so often."

Just for a moment, his expression transformed into something she might honestly label roguish. The hard, judgmental security man had been vanquished, and in his place was a man who sent heat surging up into her cheeks once more. She looked away, without really thinking. It was pure response, an instinctive need to shield her innermost thoughts from him. The reason was simple; he was far more capable than any young swain she'd tried flirting with.

"Yet apparently you lack the courage to see your course through," he accused softly. "You appear quite maidenly with your eyes cast down."

She snapped her head back around. "I did not lack the confidence to walk past your doorman."

"Yet you lack the nerve to witness what your barbed words kindle."

His face hadn't returned to the cold expression, but there was definitely judgment reflecting from his eyes. "I believe I understand you very well, Janette. You long for something you know comes with consequences. Reaching for it will cost you the security of the position you currently occupy." He retreated behind a carefully controlled expression once more. "A facet of reality we all encounter at some point in our lives. The difference between us is how we both meet the moment of decision."

"I stand before you, proving I am not some timid mouse, sir." Boldness sent her chin up in defiance. "I am not afraid to seek out what I desire."

One dark eyebrow rose, and the challenge returned to his eyes. "But do you have any idea what it is you desire, Miss Aston?"

"Yes, I believe I do—"

He tugged on her arm, and she ended up against the man. For one moment, their bodies were firmly pressed together. She was sure her heart stopped for several beats.

"As you already noticed, I am not a gentleman." His hand smoothed down her back in a long stroke that sent enjoyment through her. "Tease me, and I will be happy to respond. Pretense is not practiced here, and I'm interesting in doing more than kissing the back of your gloved hand."

She hoped so…

She shocked herself with how quickly such an impulse took control of her. It just erupted inside her mind, destroying all other principles instantly. She needed to regain her composure immediately.

"I was not teasing you. I was making my point." She pressed her hands against his chest, but the man was immovable.

He chuckled. Amusement sparkled in his eyes, but so did passion. She stared at the raw emotion, fascinated by the thing that had been only whispered rumors until that moment. Understanding dawned with a ripple of awareness that threatened to buckle her knees. Instinctively, she knew exactly what she was looking at, and her body responded with need so sharp she gasped.

"You were testing me, Janette?"

She had been. The knowledge stung, but it also tore away the veil of innocence blinding her. She'd risen to his bait because she wanted to be closer to him. She'd wanted him to reach for her. The knowledge was scalding, and yet she enjoyed the sting. Sensation was rippling across her skin, awaking nerve endings she hadn't noticed before. It was dark and inviting—like his eyes.

"I didn't realize…" she murmured.

His gaze focused on her mouth, and the delicate skin of her lips tingled. She wanted to know what his kiss felt like, tasted like. Wanted it so bad she began rising up onto her toes…

She mustn't…

"But I do now." She forced the words out and moved back, startled by the level of sensation coursing down her body. It was wild and intoxicating, making her both dizzy and keenly aware of every tiny detail. Part of her wanted to move back into his embrace, and that had her moving toward the door because the urge was so contrary to everything she had ever been taught.

Ladies did not seek the kisses of gentlemen.

Darius was no gentleman…

The fact that he offered no words of apology for their embrace confirmed it. A gentleman always took responsibility for improper situations—at least in her world. He was trying to frighten her, she was sure of it, but the knowledge only made her want to rise to meet his challenge.

If she tasted his kiss, she would never forget it. Somehow, she was sure of that fact, and it sent her back a few more paces. Hunger glittered in his eyes, and she allowed herself only a moment longer to study it.

"Good-bye, Mr. Lawley. I have enjoyed the afternoon."

Surprise appeared in his eyes, pleasing her. She took one last look at him before stepping out into the sunlight. Impulses should always be tempered with reason. Even when thinking was the last thing she was interested in doing—along with behaving like a lady.

Two

"YOU FOLLOWED HER HOME," LYKOS STATED.

Darius stiffened as his friend emerged from the shadows. The alleyway had plenty of doorways for hiding in, and a few shadowy figures chose to move on when it was clear Lykos was his friend. Together, they were far more trouble than the possible gain to be had from robbing them.

"You're making an assumption. I might well be returning from a number of different errands."

Lykos fell into step beside him. "True, but you are avoiding answering, which means I'm correct. You followed her home. How noble."

"It was the right thing to do. She doesn't know she's a lamb crossing woods filled with wolves."

"Maybe. Perhaps *calculating* is the better word, because I believe you did it to gather information that just might be employed to assist you in seeing the fair damsel again."

Lykos offered him a grin Darius recognized too well. "Don't let the fact that I sometimes consider you a friend allow you to forget I do not like being teased about the topic of the fairer sex."

"I wasn't teasing when I said you need to move on from the fair lady in your past."

Darius refused to rise to the bait. "What makes you think I haven't? I believe you observed me flirting with Miss Aston just this afternoon. No better evidence of my having moved on."

"Point taken. Which makes me wonder if it isn't time for you to emerge from your self-imposed mourning. Seems rather fitting, considering the pair of you were never married," Lykos continued.

"I have no interest in signing dance cards at some overcrowded event where the matrons can point at me and condemn me for being an Illuminist. Neither do you, so stop trying to annoy me." And tempt him with the promise of seeing Janette again. The tie needed to be severed before he went too far and found out what her lips tasted like. Before she encountered his darker side. Ladies never suffered a man like him well—he had the scars to prove it.

Lykos grinned smugly. "Ah, but you do have an interest in ensuring Miss Aston returns to her life among the unenlightened without any grime associated with us clinging to her ankles."

"What exactly do you mean by that?" Darius stopped and aimed a hard look at his comrade. "She is not my responsibility."

The moment the words were out of his mouth, he cursed. Lykos's grin widened until his teeth flashed.

"You know me too well. It was my door personnel who made the mistake of allowing her in and thereby exposing her to possible detection." He resumed walking. "I do feel responsible for her."

"I'm glad to hear you say that."

Darius lifted an eyebrow suspiciously. "Why?"

"Because tonight Mrs. Brimmer is holding a social gathering to which Miss Aston has accepted an invitation. Professor Yulric is not quite ready to abandon all hope of discovering a way to lure Miss Aston to our cause." Lykos held out a sealed envelope. "The good professor procured an invitation, and I believe he promised you would attend. I suspect he is hoping you will change your mind about courting the fair Miss Aston and bringing your blushing bride back to where he can claim her as his student."

Darius glared at the envelope. For just a moment, he suffered the impulse to smile, which annoyed him even further.

"And did the professor make it an official request that I attend?"

Lykos smirked. "Indeed he did. Insisted I set off after you immediately, so you wouldn't chance missing the event." His friend patted him on the shoulder. "How is your waltz these days?"

"Deplorable." Darius paused to read the invitation in the light of a streetlamp. "Even you will likely perform better on the dance floor tonight."

Lykos lost his smirk, and Darius felt his lips rising at his friend's expense for a change. "I'm sure the professor would want us to take the matter very seriously, considering she is a Pure Spirit," Darius observed drily. "What sort of friend would I be to exclude you from a matter so vital to our order?"

"A good one," Lykos growled before shrugging off his ill humor. "Mrs. Brimmer's husband's factory

benefits from our inventions a little too much for her
to turn her nose up, even if many of her neighbors
do. I believe she's hoping to gain an edge against the
competition by issuing invitations to Illuminists. It
would be callous of me to ignore the lady's attempt to
charm my brethren."

It was risky. The Helikeians blended into society
very well; no one knew that better than Darius did.
Anyone might notice their interest in Miss Aston, but
the Professor was on the council and had the right to
command a Guardian in cases of Pure Spirits.

"You can escort Decima," Darius suggested smugly.
"She'll be delighted."

Lykos choked, earning a grin from Darius.

He forced himself to consider the saving grace of the
invitation. Watching Janette among her high-society
compatriots would no doubt place her in a position to
join them in their disdain of his Illuminist allegiance.
Once she sneered at him or turned her back on his
offer of a dance, he'd be able to sever the connection
he felt. The fact that he didn't like the way that made
him feel sent him home in search of his evening attire.
He would pay her court and recall just what happened
when he forgot what ladies thought of him.

❧

The Brimmers' home was impressive, and the lady of
the house knew how to ensure her neighbors were
talking about her party the next morning. The ballroom was lit with Illuminist lamps, the lack of smoke
welcome. Servants kept the long buffet table looking
as though no one had touched it, while butlers offered

drinks in crystal goblets. But tension filled the guests as Illuminists were admitted.

"I simply cannot believe it," her father sputtered.

Janette bit her lip to maintain her silence. Her father removed his spectacles, cleaned them with a hand-kerchief, and put them back on before squinting at the Illuminists standing so calmly inside the Brimmers' home.

"We should leave immediately," he announced firmly.

Janette's mother gasped. "We will do nothing of the sort. Mr. Brimmer does plenty of business with you, and we cannot afford to upset his wife. She might well complain, and who knows how tender their relationship is? Appearances, dear, we must maintain appearances."

"Perhaps you're correct, my dear," her father grumbled. "I know little of how to deal with the sensitive side of women's emotional natures. I much prefer our civilized union, but I understand there are many couples who embrace a more emotional condition. We shall stay."

Janette almost wished her father would order the carriage brought around.

Coward.

She didn't care for just how true her inner voice was. Forcing a smile onto her lips, she called upon every ounce of self-discipline she had to look across the room at Darius Lawley.

The man could look like a gentleman when he chose to, she noticed as she drew in a deep breath. But that didn't ensure that he'd act like one.

Is that a fact or a hope?

She felt heat rise to her cheeks as her thoughts ran wild. All because of Darius Lawley, once again. He triggered something inside her, something she discovered she liked too much.

She tried to focus on his attire to bore herself. He was dressed in a formal black overcoat and pants. His vest was the only garment setting him apart from the other guests. Instead of formal white silk, his was a robin's-egg blue. He was accompanied by another man and a woman, both wearing their Illuminists pins proudly. Darius still wore the ear device, and there was more than one guest attempting to look at it without being caught staring.

Oh no, not a one of them might commit the sin of looking curious about the Illuminists. Such an action was unforgivable among high society. Fools.

The woman looked the most uncomfortable, as if the dress she wore was something she found cumbersome. It was very similar to Janette's, with a fan-type front formed with smocking and a full skirt held out with a taffeta petticoat. She flipped her blond curls back when she felt them on her collarbones, but she'd pinned her gold Illuminist pin to the front of her dress to ensure no one missed it. For the moment, her dance card dangled from her wrist, no gentleman reaching for it.

"Do you see who is here?" Janette asked as Sophia arrived.

Sophia hurried up, her petticoat rustling from moving too quickly. An older lady turned and looked down her nose at them.

Janette wrapped her fingers around her friend's wrist—their hands hidden by the volume of their skirts—and tugged her down into a curtsy.

"Good evening, Miss Garret."

"Ladies should never scamper like nursery-age children." Miss Garret delivered the slight in a tone full of arrogance.

Sophia tugged Janette away. "Sour old spinster."

"And you said I'd be the one getting us sent to the Highlands," Janette whispered. "Be overheard saying things like that and we should go home to pack our trunks tonight."

"Go home? So early?"

Janette gasped as Mrs. Brimmer turned around to peg them with a shocked look. "I simply will not hear of it. In fact, you two are exactly who I require at this moment. You shall assist me in breaking the ice that seems to have formed. I have been planning this event for a year, and I will not suffer this tension, I tell you."

"Of course," Janette muttered. Mrs. Brimmer frowned at the evident lack of enthusiasm in her tone.

"Come now. You two are young and full of vigor, much too young to be prejudiced." She snapped her fan shut against her gloved hand. "At least I was more open-minded when I was your age. I shan't have my guests glaring at one another. No, indeed, I shall not. Why do your parents insist on trying to act as though they did not court during a time that was so much more fun?" Mrs. Brimmer actually winked. "We had summerlong parties in the country, flowing gowns, and none of these long stays. Those cotton gowns would let the summer breeze right up your legs." Her eyes twinkled with something that looked a lot like naughtiness. Janette found herself staring at the woman because that sparkle was in such contrast with the prim and formal-looking hostess Mrs. Brimmer presented in her evening matron gown, which was buttoned precisely at her neck. She lifted a hand that sported a white glove, and motioned to Janette and Sophia. "Follow me."

Janette hung back. Sophia gave her a jab in the ribs, but Janette still refused. "That's him. Darius Lawley."

"You'll just have to suffer through it. We can't be frozen here when Mrs. Brimmer turns around. She'll be insulted," Sophia warned. "So come on."

Janette stepped forward. Sophia was correct; they didn't dare insult the woman by refusing her request, but Mrs. Brimmer was heading straight toward the Illuminists. Janette felt the assembled guests turn their attention to her and Sophia. If Mrs. Brimmer noticed, the formidable lady never allowed it to show. She maintained her perfect poise and unhurried pace until she was standing in front of her Illuminist guests.

But the twinkle in her eyes brightened, betraying just how much she enjoyed playing with her guests' priorities.

"Good evening, Miss Decima. I am delighted you could attend. Gentlemen, may I present Miss Sophia Stevenson and Miss Janette Aston, two ladies of keen intelligence. I have complete confidence in their ability to recognize what suitable gentlemen you both are." Mrs. Brimmer didn't raise her voice, but she didn't need to. The conversation in the room had almost stopped as she made her formal introductions. She turned to Sophia and Janette.

"May I present—"

"Janette has made Mr. Lawley's acquaintance

already." Sophia's eyes widened when she realized she'd spoken her thought aloud.

"She has? How fortuitous." Mrs. Brimmer tapped her fan against her gloved hand. "Mr. Lawley, would you do me the honor of starting off the first dance set with Miss Aston?"

"Quite delighted, Mrs. Brimmer."

Darius offered her his hand, but there was a flicker of challenge in his eyes that made Janette hesitate. She recalled too well her lack of ability to maintain her poise when she was near him. Sophia jabbed her in the side with a sharp elbow to jolt her into action. Darius clasped her hand, and the connection sent a tremor across her skin.

Fans opened as they passed, whispers filling the room. She and Darius stood alone in the middle of the dance floor for a moment that felt endless. At last someone cleared their throat, which prompted other men to offer their hands to the nearest lady before Mrs. Brimmer was offended. Silk petticoats rustled and heels hit the floor too hard as couples rushed to join the dance set.

The musicians struck up a lively tune. Janette curtsied and moved forward for the first close turn of the dance. A shiver shot down her spine the moment she tipped her head back to maintain eye contact.

"You might at least wipe the smirk off your face," she snapped. "I'd have danced with a leper to avoid displeasing Mrs. Brimmer."

She swept away, grateful for a chance to catch her breath. But when the steps called for her to be turned about with him close behind her, he took the opportunity to reply.

"As would I." She gasped as his words teased her ear. "But you're dancing with an Illuminist, somewhat the same in your father's eyes." His tone wasn't dark and teasing, but somewhat expectant.

"Do you ever get tired of warning people? I thought you felt returning to my father was the best action I might take."

The steps took her away, and his demeanor changed. A flicker of amusement entered his eyes and his lips curved, but the expression wasn't pleasant. She faltered when it came time to move close to him once more. Her feet felt stuck to the floor. Darius covered her hesitation, cutting in with a longer step to make sure he was flush against her back for the next turn.

"Yes, but you cannot stand in the middle of the road, Janette. I doubt your father will have anything nice to say about our dancing together."

"I agree." She felt satisfied for some reason. Oh, her father would no doubt be quite angry with her, but the look of surprise on Darius's face was worth it. "You really need to accept the fact that I am not frightened of you."

Or of being near him. She should have been, or at least wise enough not to rock the boat. Instead, she discovered herself rising to the challenge in his eyes.

"And you should accept the fact that we are from two very different worlds," he countered before turning her once more.

It wasn't right that he looked as if he expected to be slighted—or maybe she just didn't care to be so predictable. She liked thinking that, among his brethren, women didn't need to be mindless ducklings who always simpered when in public. She liked even less the fact that he was pointing out what her father expected of her. The man was an Illuminist; she craved something different from him. It was like a thirst she couldn't seem to quench.

The music finally rose to signal the end of the dance. Janette slid into her starting position before sinking into a curtsy. The room filled with soft applause created by gloved hands.

"Thank you, Mr. Lawley."

She noticed her father shaking his head with disapproval. Her mother stood by his side, fanning herself at a frantic pace. But there was also something in her mother's eyes that looked very much like approval.

"My pleasure, Miss Aston." He took her hand but didn't kiss the back of it. Instead, he looked like he was attempting to solve some sort of puzzle. "I believe I need some air after dancing with you," he added quietly.

Mrs. Brimmer overheard him from her position on the edge of the dance floor.

"The gardens are a feast for the senses. Go and enjoy them." She waved them off, casting approval on them with her smile that dared any of her guests to condemn their actions. Janette saw her father start after her, but Mr. Brimmer stepped into his path and her father was forced to stop and offer his host a formal bow.

The Brimmers were old blood but maintained their fortunes with new industry. The rest of the guests might whisper, but no one dared comment aloud because future business deals might not appear if the Brimmers were offended during their party.

Janette knew she would be on her own with Darius Lawley, just as she had been before. A bolt of excitement shot through her as he placed her hand on his forearm.

"Still unwilling to offend your hostess?" he asked quietly, but not so much so that she didn't hear the expectation in his voice. The man certainly did think he knew a great deal about her.

"What I'm unwilling to do is back down from the challenge you insist on directing at me," she informed him through a smile she'd practiced in front of her mirror.

"I am not a toy for you to satisfy your need for amusement with," he admonished her softly.

Some of her anger faded. Again, she heard expectation in his tone.

"I believe I could fairly accuse you of the same thing—you mentioned the garden." Her heart accelerated as they neared the open doors and the garden beyond came into sight. "Well, I am not so timid, sir."

There was only one reason a couple retired to the garden during a dance...

"You don't lack spirit, Miss Aston. But it would be in your best interest to refuse me."

His hand rested on top of her gloved fingers. She could feel the steel-corded muscles of his forearm, and his grip wasn't gentle either.

"Why do you want me to?" She tightened her grasp on his forearm.

His eyes narrowed. "I will take you into the garden, Miss Aston. But are you quite certain you want to continue this game? It is sure to be the topic at every breakfast table in town."

He slowed his pace, giving her ample time to jerk her hand away while still in full view of the guests.

"I refuse to give you the satisfaction of believing I cannot suffer the gossip of being alone with you while my peers know it. Besides, it would be quite rude."

He guided her down a stone walkway and around a corner so that they disappeared from the sight of the guests. That was when he gave her a look at his true emotions, his expression now one of frustration.

"But that leaves you to deal with me alone, yet again. I find your choice interesting."

"At least I do not feel as upset by that fact as you sound, Mr. Lawley."

The night air teased her cheeks, cooling them and reminding her that she was blushing. He continued on, not stopping until they were far enough away that the music became only background noise. The air was still warm enough for the jasmine to be blooming, and late-season roses also added their sweetness to the air.

Once out of sight of the ballroom, Janette pulled her hand away. "Is it necessary to sound so annoyed with our circumstances? I believe you are the one offering me insult. Perhaps you are the one truly worried about being the topic at breakfast? Are your Illuminist brothers going to condemn you for spending time with me? Will holding your head high be difficult among the members of your Order tomorrow?"

Maybe she was mad to take such a bold approach with him, but his constant warnings awakened a reckless need to do so. In his world, women could speak their minds, and she wanted to make sure he noticed she was up to the task of having a logical discussion with him. The man would not find her wits lacking.

"If you believe I'll begin muttering polite topics any matron behind us would approve of, simply because I was raised a lady, you are going to be disappointed."

He folded his arms across his chest and studied her. The pose was considered common in polite society, but it drew her attention to how muscular he was beneath the fine wool overcoat. He really was an overly large man; she doubted her head would reach his chin, and his jaw was lean, telling her he was very physical. It also drove home just how annoyed he was with her for not slighting him.

"I'm warning—"

"Yes, yes," she interrupted. "As you have done before. But I will not believe it was necessary for me to reject you to protect myself."

He chuckled, but the sound had a sinister quality. "Your education is lacking, Miss Aston. I would have thought your mother would have instructed you on the dangers of being alone with an Illuminist."

"Your being an Illuminist doesn't have anything to do with it."

Yet her mother had warned her of exactly that on many occasions. *Walk out with an Illuminist, and your reputation will be tarnished…*

He cocked his head to the side. "I know what the polished upper crust thinks of me. I've seen their sneers often enough."

There was his expectation again, the firm belief that she would look down her nose at him. She refused to give him the satisfaction—even if he was correct.

Trouncing back into the ballroom would please her father enormously.

"Then by all means, return to the party before someone thinks you brought me out here for a moonlit kiss." She turned her back on him, suddenly as frustrated as he appeared. "I wouldn't dream of sullying your reputation by having our names linked over breakfast tables tomorrow."

Disappointment raked its claws across her emotions, killing the excitement that had been twisting her insides. It was bitter, indeed. All her senses felt heightened, her lips more sensitive as though they longed to feel what his kiss was like.

What you want is to flirt with a man who will not act like a gentleman...

"You have no concept of what you're saying, Miss Aston."

She turned back around to face him, her temper sizzling. "I see you're intent on punishing me like some child who needs reprimanding. If that is how you see me, please depart." It stung—in spite of her determination to banish him to a place in her mind where his opinion might have no importance.

"An incorrect assumption on your part, Miss Aston," he insisted. "I've noticed just how much of a woman you are."

His leisurely position had given her a false sense of security. To her surprise, Darius closed the gap between them and pulled her against his body in a fluid motion that was lightning-quick.

"My interest in you is rapidly growing beyond my ability to ignore it. This opportunity to kiss you, too tempting to resist. Yet if you are intent on reminding me that you are a woman, there is no reason for me to restrain myself."

She flattened her hands against his chest, but that didn't stop him. He angled his head and pressed his mouth against hers before her skirts had finished swishing. She tried to shove him away and pull her head back, but he captured her nape, cradling it in one large hand to keep her in place for his kiss.

The few kisses in her past paled in comparison. Darius pressed his lips over hers but began teasing her lips with his. The kiss didn't end after a brief press. He continued to slide his mouth across hers, pressing against her lips until they parted and their mouths fit together more completely.

Sensation poured down her body. She felt it pooling in her belly as excitement flared up. She moved in his arms, not necessarily in an effort to escape, but following his lead, moving her lips in unison with his. She heard him pull in a deep breath, and it made her bolder. She rose onto her toes to make sure her lips were fused with his, and his kiss became harder, more demanding.

She liked his embrace. The hardness of his body and the way his hands moved her to suit his desire. He continued to kiss her with a skill that sent delight racing through her. He teased her lips with the tip of his tongue, just a tiny stroke along her lower lip, before he sealed her mouth again with his. She shivered, surprised to feel her passage yearning for something more.

The desire was there inside her, shocking but too

real to ignore—twisting every principle she had while, at the same time, urging her to seek out his bare skin. It was instinct, something rooted deep inside her, and it felt like it was ripping at the fabric of her being in an attempt to break free. The scent of his skin further fueled her rising desire.

"We must stop…" she murmured.

"No," he growled softly.

She reached up and depressed the device covering his ear. It let out a sharp whine. He reached for her hand, giving her the opportunity to escape his embrace.

"Yes," she insisted, but her breathing was harsh, and she noticed his was too.

"Damn us both, Janette. I didn't need to know what you tasted like. It will be damned hard to forget."

Yes…it will…

There was a promise lurking in his eyes that she retreated from. The more she considered it, the farther back she moved. It wasn't Darius who frightened her; it was her reaction to him. When combined, they created a reaction that threatened to be unstoppable. What surprised her was the realization that she was equally responsible.

"I shouldn't have…kissed you back." But she'd enjoyed it so much, it was an effort to maintain a distance from him.

He cursed, the profanity rolling across his lips without hesitation. He was so contrary to what she'd been raised to desire in a man, but her flesh burned for him. It was dark and wicked, but too hot to control.

"You should have sneered at me, Janette; I need you to be exactly what I expect of a high-society lady."

For just a moment, she let the burn of her desire warm her. She could be his equal, step back into his embrace and do all the things her flesh was urging her to. "Being a lady doesn't mean I have to be prejudiced, Darius. I'll judge you on your actions alone."

One corner of his mouth curled up, making him look like a rogue. "So judge me, sweet lady. I await your decision."

Tension drew her body tight. She felt poised on the top of a wall, her answer some manner of test from him. There was something inside her that didn't want to fail, didn't want to be what he expected. She pushed aside all the lectures from her parents and heard instead the words Mrs. Brimmer had spoken... *too young to be prejudiced*. Was that all it was? This division between Illuminist and high society?

"Nothing to say, sweet lady? Or should I say, not enough courage to speak your mind?"

It wasn't the smugness in his tone that needled her, but the bitterness.

"You are bold, and I believe I enjoyed it too much." Her words came out in a husky whisper she didn't recognize as her own voice. She'd never sounded so sultry before.

"You did," he concurred, his voice deep and edged with satisfaction. She witnessed the truth shimmering in his eyes before she turned her back on him and ran. It wasn't Darius she fled, but the certainty in his dark gaze—the flame of desire that she wanted to move closer to until she surrendered to the heat his kiss unleashed. She felt more alive than she ever had, as though she had just been waiting until this moment for her life to begin. If she didn't run, she was going to forget why kissing him back was a bad idea.

But he wasn't a gentleman, and she was a lady. He might ruin her and return to his Solitary Chamber, where she might never see him again. So she proved him correct about one thing: she lacked the courage to stay anywhere near him. She ran right to the front of the house, and her father's butler noticed her immediately from where he waited with the other servants.

Why had she never noticed how some men were considered better than others? Across the well-manicured lawn stood the personal escorts of everyone inside. They had their collars turned up to keep the wind from biting into their necks while they passed flasks of whiskey between them.

All the while waiting on their betters.

The idea stuck in her throat, but she climbed into the carriage when it was brought around, because it offered escape.

Coward.

She didn't dispute it.

❧

"I cannot begin to express how disappointed I am."

Janette stood by the breakfast table as her father eyed her.

"Indeed, I believe I have always been quite clear on my view of Illuminists, and still you accepted one as an escort."

Heat rose to her cheeks, but it wasn't from shame. Janette bit her tongue to hold back the tart response she wanted to make.

"Howard, really. Mrs. Brimmer would have been offended if Janette had declined the dance," her mother reminded him. "You know very well the Brimmers are controversial in their views on Illuminists interacting with society."

"*Controversial* is too mild a word to describe that woman's tendencies to ignore decent behavior. How dare she select my daughter for her atrocious public demonstrations? Well, she shall not change my thinking. Not one bit!"

Her father hit the tabletop. The breakfast dishes clattered, and Janette stared at his closed fist in shock.

"You see what this has pushed me to? Physical outbursts! The calling card of the low-bred who do not have enough intelligence to rise above common brawling."

Howard Aston stood and threw his napkin down. He pointed at his wife, who had taken to hiding her gaping mouth behind her napkin.

"You made a promise to me, madam, one I will see you keep. I insist upon it. Those Illuminists are endowed with a cheap sort of intelligence that has its uses and place. They are uncivilized. I am a gentleman, and you shall recall that marrying me lifted you above the station you were born to. I will have respect and order in this house. The Illuminists shall not be spoken of or acknowledged by any member of this family."

Her father stomped from the room. The serving staff did their best to look as though they were not listening. Janette stared at her mother.

"Mother, what did he mean? What station did he lift you from?"

"Oh dear." Her mother stood, her chair scraping the hardwood floor because the butler hadn't anticipated her action. The man ran to catch the back of her chair before it fell over, but her mother sat back down.

"I never thought…"

"Mother, please tell me. Is that why I've never met any of your family? Father believes them beneath us? Why?"

Her mother looked at her before drawing in a stiff breath that she held a long moment. When she blew it out, she stood again.

"Janette, you shall have to put this morning completely out of your mind."

"But—"

Her mother held up a single finger. "Yes, wipe it from your thoughts and never speak of it. Your father is correct. It is best you concentrate on ensuring you recall that having your name linked with an Illuminist will only bring distasteful encounters with your father. We shall have no contact with Illuminists. The matter is not open for discussion."

Janette found herself standing in the breakfast room with the stunned butler. They locked gazes for a moment before they both looked away out of habit. But Janette wasn't so confident of her place in the world. Not since meeting Darius Lawley. Two days ago she'd accepted that the Illuminists were people of a lower station than herself. But today she discovered herself questioning the teachings of her father.

And her mother? She was hiding something. Janette walked through the house, feeling very much as she had when trespassing at the Solitary Chamber. As if she did not know where she was or what might happen next.

Maybe she should seek the man out again.

෴

"Miss Janette, your father requests you in the parlor."

The downstairs maid offered a quick curtsy before hurrying back to her duties. Her apron was still pristine and her cap perfectly pressed well into the afternoon.

Appearances.

Her father was demanding when it came to the staff maintaining the standards he expected of them. That maid had several aprons all hung neatly in a closet at the end of the upstairs hallway in case she needed to change. Even being in the middle of her workday didn't allow for her to look rumpled. Wasn't an apron worn for the purpose of keeping dirt off one's dress?

It was something Janette wouldn't have questioned the need or wisdom for before her encounter with Darius. Appearances were maintained for the betterment of everyone in the family, yet now she wondered if being honest wasn't more important. This realization vexed her. Why wasn't she questioning the useless actions and prejudices surrounding her? It was astounding to consider how much effort was wasted on things with so little meaning.

So did that mean Darius Lawley was a more noble man than the gentleman her father claimed to be?

"Ah, there you are, Janette." Her father gestured her into the parlor. "I've a friend to introduce you to. This is Dr. Nerval."

Janette curtsied without thinking or taking the time

to look at the doctor. When she raised her attention to the man sitting in the red leather armchair, a chill traveled across her skin. She'd never seen such cold eyes.

The doctor studied her from head to toe. Standing behind him was a plump matron in a stiff, full-length apron. It crisscrossed her chest, and she wore a white handkerchief hat like a nurse, only it lacked the red cross.

"Turn around," the doctor instructed.

Janette looked at her father to find him nodding. Turning her back on the doctor unnerved her. She felt her heart beating faster while she attempted to keep her motions controlled.

Dr. Nerval clasped a cane with both gloved hands. It was a wooden one with a glass knob topper.

"Dr. Nerval has graciously called upon us to assist us in overcoming last night's unfortunate incident."

The doctor was an old man with deep folds around his mouth. All of his hair was white, and his thick sideburns too. He was perfectly groomed, every hair in place. His clothing was just as pristine, but what bothered her was the way the matron stood so still. She looked straight ahead, never turning her head to whoever was speaking. Obviously, the doctor shared her father's views on people knowing who their betters were.

"Take my cane, please, Miss Janette."

He grasped it around the wooden neck and extended it toward her. Apprehension tingled down her nape, but there was nothing overly strange in the request. Janette wrapped her hands around the glass knob and felt the current run through her.

Crystal. Deep Earth Crystal.

The rhythmic hum began playing in the back of her senses, and she looked down at the knob topping the cane. The doctor took it back, his grasp surprisingly strong for how aged he appeared.

"You were correct to summon me, Mr. Aston. Your daughter requires purging immediately."

Janette spun around to look at her father. "I am quite well, Father."

Dr. Nerval stood and tapped his cane against the floor. "She is not. My dear girl, you have no idea what manner of sinister infection has latched its teeth into you."

"It was only a single dance. I couldn't very well refuse Mrs. Brimmer, Father. It would have shamed you." Tension pulled the muscles along her neck tight. She wasn't even sure what she was fighting to avoid, only that she wanted nothing more to do with the cold-eyed doctor. His spectacles did nothing to shield her from it.

Her father looked undecided, but the doctor stepped between them.

"You must listen to me, Mr. Aston. This sort of thing can easily grow into something unstoppable without treatment. Considering your wife's unfortunate history, you cannot afford to hesitate. Send her tomorrow morning for treatment."

The matron opened the parlor door for the doctor, and he strode out. He turned to look at her before leaving. Janette felt the chill race down her back once more. This time there was a look of satisfaction in his eyes that horrified her.

"Tomorrow morning, the clinic. Do not go soft."

"I shall not disappoint you, Doctor."

Janette felt the walls of the parlor closing in. What had once been a favorite place now felt as cold as a prison cell. The butler closed the door behind the doctor, and her father remained facing it, giving her nothing to look at but his back.

"Father, you cannot mean to send me to that clinic. I hear they do the most brutal things there."

He turned on her, determination etched into his expression.

"Nonsense you no doubt heard over a tea service. Dr. Nerval is a highly esteemed member of the scientific community. His clinic will provide you the treatment necessary to keep you from tumbling into the insanity your mother's blood has tainted you with."

"What taint? Has it something to do with why I've never heard anything about my maternal grandparents?" She spoke smoothly and slowly, the forbidden topic suddenly very permissible.

"You shall not speak of them, not ever. A fact you know very well. You see? I have always feared this day would come. Why do you think I have strived to remind you so often of the dangers of the Illuminists? Yet here you stand, defying my clear instructions to never ask about your mother's parents. The doctor is correct. You have been infected by that Illuminist."

"It was but a single dance," she countered in a smooth tone, despite the dread twisting her insides.

"It was more." Her father's voice cracked, and he pointed a damning finger at her. "I witnessed you returning from the garden myself. Did you really think I did not follow you outside when you had departed on the arm of such a creature? You have carnal knowledge of that…that Illuminist. Your innocence has been tainted. His nefarious actions have planted a seed inside your mind that will sprout into a weed if we do not sterilize it."

She covered her mouth with her hand. Her father spoke the truth. Darius had unleashed something inside her.

"You have defied me, Janette, and it led you to last night's catastrophe."

Her father marched across the parlor and pointed at a wooden box. "Dr. Nerval was wise enough to instruct me to have your room searched, and look at what was found."

He lifted a science circular from the box. "You see, madam? It is plain you have been reading the writings of those Illuminists, and it has unleashed a craving inside you that made you vulnerable to that man last night."

"But—"

"I will not hear your excuses. You are unwell, and it is my duty to see you are given proper medical treatment. Without treatment, you will be sneaking out in the dead of night to be with him. You will become a fallen woman and end up on the docks when he has had what he seeks from you. Giles!"

Her father's personal butler entered the parlor immediately.

"Giles, be kind enough to escort my daughter to her room and see she remains there until tomorrow morning. You will escort her to the clinic where this Illuminist infection can be sterilized."

"Yes, sir."

"Father, you cannot mean this."

Her sire turned on her, his expression solid and unrelenting. "I assure you, I do. You shall respect my word in this matter or never set foot in this house again. I tell you truthfully: fail to embrace the treatment Dr. Nerval prescribes, and I will disown you. You will be left to take your chances on the street corners with the rest of the unfortunates."

He might as well have slapped her. England no longer had whores or thieves, only a great many *unfortunates*. The men who had stood next to her father the night before in their white vests and had aimed condemning looks at her when she returned from the garden liked to discuss what treatments might cure the unfortunates of their impulses. Those ever-proud members of upper society firmly believed that common blood meant a person lacked the ability to control their emotions. They argued against the Illuminists because the Order offered their entrance exams to those willing to prove their worth. A family history wasn't required, and it didn't matter what station or race they were. Black, Asian, or otherwise, if they passed the entrance exam, they could wear the badge of the Illuminist Order. The Illuminists did it all without hiding their emotions behind stiff, judgmental expressions.

She'd enjoyed feeling her emotions running free. If that was a sin, so be it. She looked at the circulars, a desire kindling inside her to prove she was worthy of knowing more.

"Miss?"

Giles had moved closer. There was an unpleasant look in his eyes, but he remained firmly obedient to his master's will. Of course he did. If he didn't, Giles would find himself dismissed and on his way to becoming an unfortunate, for no good family would hire him without a reference from her father.

Janette bit her lip but tucked her right foot behind her left ankle and offered her father a curtsy. "As you say, Father."

The lie passed her lips more easily than she'd thought it would, but she realized she'd been lying most of her life. In fact, she'd learned it from her father—little comments that were untruthful but acceptable because they were polite. It had been the way she was raised by the man watching her offer a curtsy of respect, when the only feeling she had for him was pity.

"Yes, well, it seems you are not so far off the path if you can still behave in a civilized manner. Everyone in this house needs to understand I only mean the best for you."

Her father waved his hand, dismissing her.

Giles followed her up the grand staircase. She turned right instead of left and heard the butler clear his throat.

"I simply wish to have a word with my mother."

The butler offered her a short bow. "Mrs. Aston has left for the country at the command of the master."

She felt a chill tingling across her skin again. Now the entire house felt unfamiliar to her. Giles extended his arm toward her room. She could have sworn she heard the clattering of keys like a jailer would have on his belt, because she was very much a prisoner. The urge to flee began to clamor inside her. She looked toward the front door, realizing all she needed was the courage to walk away from her imprisonment.

The same courage that had seen her walking up the steps of the Solitary Chamber.

"Now, don't make me handle you," Giles grumbled. "I don't want to be telling the master you aren't in your room. The clinic won't be worse than the street."

"I'm not so sure about that."

The butler frowned and grabbed her wrist. He had an amazing amount of strength and sent her tumbling into her room with a hard tug.

"You're a lady; stay in there. I've no more liking for this bit of business than you do, but I can't lose my place any more than you want to give up the comfortable life you have."

Giles closed her door with a disgusted grunt. She was left staring at the things she considered hers. Today she had to face the fact that nothing in the room belonged to her. The law would support her father's right to manage her however he saw fit. The very clothes on her back belonged to him.

But a clinic?

She sat and covered her mouth with one hand. Those clinics were places of horror where pain was often used as therapy. Maybe she had heard the tales over tea, but women were most often sent to the places by men who wanted them to be obedient. Like her father wished of her.

Darius's face rose from her memory with all his insistence that she did not belong in his world. But maybe she did. At the moment, it seemed more welcoming than the society she'd been raised in, a society that would see her sent to a clinic because she enjoyed knowledge.

And kisses…

Even the memory of Darius's kiss wasn't enough to distract her from her dilemma. She paced until well after sundown, but Giles remained at his post until another man took his place.

It appeared she would be going to the clinic. Horror rose up so thick, it threatened to choke her. She swallowed, forcing herself to plan. She'd done a good job of being everything her father wanted her to be until now. She would have to try and convince him she was still docile.

It was the only way to get him to lower his guard.

And then she'd run—hurry as fast as she could to the only place where she might be respected. That place her friends looked down their noses at only because they had been trained to do so by their parents. Well, she wanted to know—wanted to know so much more than she did. She wanted to understand what she was.

The next morning, Janette climbed meekly into the carriage.

"I am relieved to see you calmly ready to follow my instructions, Janette," her father remarked.

She wasn't calm, but she offered her father a serene smile, one she'd perfected over countless tea services where the conversation had been dull enough to almost kill her.

The carriage came to a stop outside the clinic, and the footman let the steps down. Janette didn't wait for her father but left the vehicle, because like everything else in her life, it was closing in on her.

"Your demeanor gives me hope that Dr. Nerval will be able to cure you of this Illuminist nonsense," her father announced as the footman appeared with a satchel and placed it near her on the pavement. "The upstairs maid packed everything you shall need for your stay."

"My stay?"

"Yes," her father answered. "Dr. Nerval was quite clear. You will need to be completely removed from any sources of impure thinking while being purged."

She wouldn't be staying.

Two burly men started toward her from the clinic, making it plain her attempt couldn't begin immediately.

"Good-bye, Father."

It was a bittersweet moment, one she expected to hurt more. Instead, she felt a sense of strength growing inside her.

"Now, Janette, it is only for a little while."

She reached down and picked up the satchel herself. She didn't look back at her father. There was nothing behind her but a life spent in ignorance. Clarity dawned on her, a clear understanding of why she'd gone up those steps to the Solitary Chamber. Something had drawn her there, something inside of her.

Something she craved to know more about.

She wasn't even sure how long she'd battled the discontent that had prompted her to try to enter the Illuminists' building. At the moment, it felt as if she had been secretly yearning to escape her father's home for years. That wasn't very kind of her, for her mother loved her, but somehow, she had always sensed a distance between her father and herself.

The clinic attendants flanked her, their white jackets sending a chill down her spine. The sense of impending imprisonment made her mouth go dry. The urge to run needled her more and more the closer she came to the door of the clinic.

Janette clamped her control down on top of that impulse. The presence of the attendants told her they expected her to flee, so she would deny them the spectacle. She would employ every bit of intelligence and find a way to outwit Dr. Nerval's staff. If they believed her accepting, they would be less likely to watch her closely. That hope made it possible for her to step through the doors and conceal her cringe when they closed firmly behind her.

"Miss Janette, I am pleased to see you so calm."

The doctor stood with his stiff-faced matron one pace behind him. There was a look of anticipation in his eyes that doubled her resolve to escape.

"I cannot imagine being upset by anything my dear father has asked of me." She spoke in her sweetest voice, and the matron softened her expression. Janette widened her eyes. "The weather is lovely this morning," she offered sweetly.

"Yes…well, we have more important matters to discuss."

Janette smiled brightly at the matron as the doctor walked past her with a mild look of disgust on his face. Men of the upper class liked to preach about how they wanted their ladies docile, but most of them couldn't stomach the mindless conversation very well. More than one wife had encouraged her friends to prattle on about meaningless topics until their husbands all retired to the smoking room.

But Janette's anxiety increased as they made their way down the hallway. All the windows were covered with iron screens. There was the insistent jingle of keys, and she noticed that every door had a lock. A quick glance from beneath her lashes showed her that the matron had a ring of keys hanging from her belt like some sort of chamberlain or jailer from the Dark Ages.

Her hope began to diminish as they passed a door that rattled and she heard someone's desperate plea for release. Ahead of the doctor, one of the white-coated attendants opened a large door, his key ring clanking. The matron placed a hand in the center of Janette's back to guide her through.

"Now, Miss Janette, we will dispense with the charade and you shall show me your skills," Dr. Nerval stated victoriously.

The only windows in the room were up near the ceiling. Behind her, the door closed with a solid sound, and the key grated in the lock. Only the matron remained, and she reached out to pull the satchel from Janette's hands.

Janette didn't try to hold on to it. She was too distracted by the contents of the room. All around her she heard the rhythmic hum of Deep Earth Crystals. There were tables set up with different crystals on them. No table held more than one, and all of them were placed on copper plates. The look in the doctor's eyes had blossomed into full anticipation, and it sickened her because she could see that she was nothing more than another specimen for him to use in his quest for knowledge.

"You will show me exactly what sort of Pure Spirit you are."

❧

Sophia Stevenson covered her mouth and tried not to retch. Horror clogged her throat and threatened to make her lose her breakfast.

"Miss Sophia? We can't be staying here. Your father wouldn't approve. I shouldn't have allowed you to instruct me to follow your friend's carriage, for now we're in a poor section of town. We shouldn't be here."

Her driver sounded almost panicked, and she couldn't blame the man for losing his nerve. No one ventured into that section of town without good reason.

"Yes, let's go."

Her driver wasted no time in letting the horses have their freedom. He put the team into motion so quickly she fell back into the seat, but she didn't care.

How could she sniffle about being jostled inside her carriage when her dearest friend was being locked away inside an insane asylum?

The driver slowed his pace as they neared her father's shop. Sophia found the last few minutes in the carriage almost unbearable. She was twitching with the need to do something, anything to help Janette. But even when she stood in the back room of her father's shop where she and Janette had laughed so recently, she couldn't decide what action to take. What could she do?

Women had few rights, and Janette's father could insist on treatment if he had a doctor to testify that she needed attention. Sophia felt her temper spike. Janette had even fewer rights than a thief because she hadn't actually broken any law and wouldn't be given a trial before being locked away. Why hadn't Sophia noticed just how unfair the law was in regard to women? The suffragette cause suddenly took on a new appeal.

Well, she was going to help her friend. Sophia paced in a circle and then several more as she tried to concoct a plan of action.

"What is the matter, Sophia?" her sister demanded from the doorway.

"Nothing, Cora. Go and help Father."

Her sister stiffened. "Nothing, is it? You sound like an Irish jig dancer pacing about. Don't tell me nothing is bothering you. Why are you back so soon, anyway? I thought you were off to visit with Janette."

Sophia failed to hide the horror from her sister. Cora abandoned her harsh expression and hurried toward her so they might whisper. "What happened?"

"Janette's father sent her to…a clinic."

Cora paled. "We shall have to think of some way… to help her…" Cora's voice became softer as she fought back tears.

But it was the hopelessness in her tone that spurred Sophia into action.

"Don't you dare cry. We will not accept this… action from her father, do you understand? I refuse to weep for Janette because we cannot think of any way to help her."

Cora drew in a stiff breath. "I don't like it any more than you do, but I can't think of anyone who can help us. The law favors her father in every way. No constable will listen to us, and she doesn't have a fiancé to battle on her behalf."

"Oh, Cora, you are perfect to think of such a thing!"

Sophia hurried to the wardrobe and pulled it open. She had to force herself to move slowly so that her father wouldn't come to investigate the amount of noise she made. Sophia put on the cycling outfit without hesitation.

Cora frowned as she watched her sister button up the jacket. "What are you doing, Sophia?"

"Going to find someone who can help Janette."

Cora stepped into her path. "If you go looking for Darius Lawley, you'll only bring more trouble down on Janette. If she had refused to dance with him, he'd never have had the chance to take her into the garden and annoy her father so much."

Sophia stepped around her sister and pulled the leather top hat off the shelf, placing it firmly on her head. "You don't understand, Cora. Janette and Mr. Lawley had already met, and I do honestly believe they just might be fated to be together."

"You're mad, and if Janette is talking anything like you, I can begin to understand why her father believes her mentally ill."

"Don't ever say such a horrible thing like that to me again." Sophia yanked a kid glove onto her left hand. "Go out front and simper like a nitwit if you want to, but I will not listen to rubbish—curiosity and knowledge are not a disease. I will not leave Janette in that horrible place, not when I believe Darius Lawley can help her."

"But she won't be able to go home if he does."

Sophia picked up a pair of glasses and put them on. The lenses were round and darkened to keep the sunlight from hurting her eyes. She ran her hands down the peplum of the jacket and tightened her resolve.

"I believe Janette would rather live as an Illuminist than as a broken spirit."

Cora followed her, stopping at the back door. "I hope you're right."

So did Sophia. Doubt needled her, but she pressed on, leaving the yard and crossing the street. She hoped and prayed, but she never hesitated.

Three

WHEN JANETTE CONCENTRATED, SHE REALIZED THAT the crystals all had different tones. There was a clear division in the center of the room, the tables separated by several yards.

Male and female...

Professor Yulric's words rose from her memory.

"What do you mean when you call me a Pure Spirit?"

Dr. Nerval thumped his cane against the floor, but Janette didn't let the sound startle her.

"You shall have to decide what you wish, Doctor." She walked around the room, pausing to look at several of the crystals. "I can continue to act the simpleton my father placed me in your care to ensure I become, or I can dispense with pretenses and hold an intelligent conversation with you."

She stopped and faced him with a bright smile. Janette folded her hands perfectly at waist level, right on top of left, with fingers curled inward.

"A Pure Spirit has the ability to have the crystals interact kindly with the skin. It is hereditary and is only passed by bloodline. Just as a fish has scales to survive in the water, your skin has certain properties that Deep Earth Crystals share. Such properties insulate your skin from the power of the crystals. You are a human conductor of their power." His eyes glowed with eager anticipation. He lifted his cane and pointed at one table. "If my informants are trustworthy, you handled a level-four crystal, which makes you a Pure Spirit. Pick that one up. I want to know if it's true. You're worthless otherwise."

That uneasy feeling crept across her thoughts again, making her hesitate. She was only an object to the man directing her. Never had she felt like her actions might matter any great amount beyond the boundaries of her own life. Now she wasn't so sure. The crystals fascinated her, but she balked at performing obediently when she had no knowledge of why the doctor wanted her to handle the crystals. Or, more importantly, what were Dr. Nerval's plans for them?

"And if I do not?" She turned her back on the crystal to face the doctor. "My father wouldn't approve of this. He sent me here to be cured of any inclinations to explore Illuminist knowledge."

Dr. Nerval's lips curved up slowly, the folds of skin hanging around his mouth crinkling grotesquely. A chill went down her spine because she was quite certain she witnessed a flare of enjoyment in his eyes. A cruel sort of pleasure that promised no mercy.

The matron's keys jingled as she fitted one into the door and turned it. The burly attendants were still there.

"Take her," the doctor announced calmly.

Janette almost lost her resolve as panic rushed in along with the men. They grabbed her arms and hauled her out of the chamber. She wanted to resist, but the only true way she might defy the doctor was to deny him seeing her reduced to a screaming lunatic.

The matron hurried ahead of them, flipping through her keys with a skill that proved she performed this task often, then yanked a door open. The attendants pushed Janette through it, both men appearing somewhat confused as she continued to comply with them.

"Miss Janette is suffering from delusions caused by hysteria."

The doctor's voice was like an eerie chant coming from behind her as the attendants forced her into a hardwood chair with thick legs and arms. Wide straps of leather were secured to the underside of the armrests, and the men quickly lashed them around her wrists. Each one had a solid brass buckle, and the attendants knew how to use them expertly.

"Hysteria is a very dangerous condition. You should be grateful to your father for bringing you here for treatment," the doctor informed her gleefully.

"*Grateful* is not the word I would choose to—"

Her words were abruptly silenced when the matron slipped a thick cord of leather-wrapped rope through her open mouth. The woman yanked hard so it slid all the way between Janette's molars. She gagged twice before mastering the reflex. Meanwhile, the attendants secured her ankles to the chair, and a final strap went around her waist.

"The cure for hysteria is calmness. I do hope you will be more willing to participate in my prescribed treatments when you are released."

Enjoyment coated his words, but what sickened

Janette the most was the complete indifference of the attendants and matron. They performed their duties without even a shred of pity. Once she was unable to move, they left the room. Janette heard the key turning in the lock and tried to maintain her composure.

The silence was nearly deafening. Helplessness slammed into her so hard she fought back tears. She couldn't escape the horrible truth. She was at the mercy of whatever Dr. Nerval wanted to do to her.

Sweat beaded on her forehead as she battled to keep her grip on her emotions. Newspaper articles flashed through her mind with their blood-chilling accounts from those fortunate enough to escape from the care of the mental medical community. Every hour would be awful. Now she was in a chair, but there were cages and restraining jackets and...

No. Stop it.

She needed to focus on her resolve not to aid the doctor. Satisfaction began to burn away her panic, a true sense of pride for having questioned his motives. She wasn't the simpleton her father had hoped she'd become. No, by God, she had a mind, and she enjoyed using it. She drew in a deep breath and began to recite favorite songs inside her head. She closed her eyes and tried to envision herself near the pump organ in Sophia's house. She would not give in.

At least not without a damn good fight.

༺ঔ৹

The key turned in the lock, and Janette jerked awake. A soft moan was the only sound she could make, but she was powerless to contain it.

She ached—so badly it sent tears into her eyes. Her mouth was dry as a cotton ball. Her tongue felt swollen, and her hands were numb from how tight her bindings were.

She wanted to believe she wasn't willing to bend.

She forced herself to repeat that over and over as she waited for the door to open. The room was dark now, a thin sliver of moonlight coming in through the window to illuminate the doorknob.

She could endure if they were ready to remove her from the chair.

She heard the key grinding, but the knob never moved.

Tears slid down her cheeks as disappointment crashed into her so hard, she found it difficult to draw breath. She realized the matron wasn't unlocking her door but one nearby.

How long would they leave her? Until she soiled herself? Until she was so dehydrated she could no longer cry?

Until you bend…

She bit into the gag, and pain shot through her jaw. Even those muscles were strained. The foot-wide stripe of moonlight on the floor flickered. She blinked, wondering if dehydration was beginning to play tricks on her. She felt more tears slide down her cheeks.

"I warned you there were things in my world you were better off not knowing, Janette."

She jumped, every muscle snapping and straining against the leather securing her to the chair.

"Easy…" Darius said quietly.

She tried to turn her head, but the gag held her head in place.

Was he real or the cruel teasing of her desperation?

She struggled against the leather, needing to see him and confirm that he was truly there. That she was truly going to be freed.

"They've trussed you up well."

She felt his fingers seeking out the end of the leather strap on her right wrist, and she trembled. Relief flooded her as she felt him pull back on the leather to release the buckle. A tiny click announced her freedom, and she lifted her arm, impatient to move once more. But the muscles along her arm cramped, and she bit into the gag as pain slashed through her again.

"They left you in that damned chair too long," he said softly.

She'd heard Darius angry, but this time his harsh tone was on her behalf. She watched him in wonder as he worked to free her from the chair.

"You're going to hurt, but we can't linger here. Dr. Nerval is at supper. We have to escape before he checks in on you. I doubt the man will retire without trying to confirm if you are a Pure Spirit."

He pulled the gag out of her mouth.

"Thank—" Her tongue stuck to the roof of her mouth.

"No time," he whispered.

He lifted her up and gently placed her upright. Prickles of pain from returning circulation shot along her limbs. Her feet didn't perform as she expected, and she stumbled. Darius saved her from tumbling to the floor. He swept her off her feet, and she rose above his shoulders, gasping when his hand cupped her bottom to push her farther up.

"Darius…" This time her tongue worked, but his hand remained in place.

"You can berate me later for my ungentlemanly conduct, but we need to leave immediately," he muttered. "Grab my hands."

The voice came from the window. She looked up and saw another man leaning in from the outside. It suddenly made sense. The grating sound had been the iron grate being removed.

She lifted her arms and bit her lip to suffer the pain silently. Her hands were full of tingles as blood began flowing once more, but her grasp was weak. That didn't stop the man from dragging her up the wall and through the window. Darius aided him by pushing her up.

The night air had never felt so wonderful on her face. For one moment she was hanging half in the building and half out. The windowsill bit into her midsection. Janette welcomed the pain because she was escaping, and there was nothing she wouldn't suffer to be free of the clinic.

"Down here. I'll catch you," the second man assured her from where he stood in the alleyway behind the clinic.

In the moonlight, Darius's accomplice was only a specter, more ghost than man. But that didn't stop her from lowering her head so gravity would take her down to where he was. He kept his word, hooking her tumbling body with arms like steel. Her skirts flew up in a tangled mess, and dizziness assaulted her.

"Here now, don't faint on me."

"They had the straps too tight," Darius said. "Fix the iron grate. Let them wonder how she vanished."

Darius appeared next to her and swept her off her feet once more. This time he cradled her like a child as he walked away from the clinic wall. The street was mostly dark because they were on the back side of the clinic. She heard a set of carriage steps let down, and another unrecognizable man appeared to open the door for Darius.

"How…how did you know where to find me?" Her voice sounded gravelly.

"You can thank your friend Sophia. She marched up to the front doors of the Solitary Chamber and demanded to see me. I believe the doorman let her in because he was afraid she would in fact attack the next member who tried to get past her." Darius deposited her on a padded seat inside the vehicle. "She has your temperament. I see the reason for your friendship."

The carriage rocked as the second man climbed in. "They'll have a fine time deciding how she vanished now. Everything is back in order, not even our footprints left to betray us." He sat next to Darius, both of them only shadows in the darkness. The door closed quickly behind him, and the carriage steps were pulled up. One of them hit the wall with a fist, and the vehicle jolted forward.

But there was no sound of horses, only a strange hiss and gurgle. Once in motion, there was a smoothness to the ride she'd only felt once before, during winter on the lake in a sled pushed from behind by a boy.

"What…manner of…"

"If you're set on talking, you need something to ease your throat first." Darius reached inside his jacket and pulled out a flask. Moonlight came through the windows and flickered off the smooth metal of it.

"Could use a nip of that myself," his companion announced.

"I am...not..."

"Accustomed to strong spirits? Few ladies are." Darius cupped her head with a grip that reminded her too much of the way he'd held her while kissing her. Gentle, tender, but firm. Heat surfaced in her cheeks as he placed the flask against her mouth and tipped it up. She caught a whiff of the strong alcohol before it touched her tongue. It was potent enough to send tears to her eyes. It washed across her tongue and left her entire mouth on fire. Janette stiffened and tried to push him away.

"Swallow it, Janette. Your life has changed irreversibly, so toss your rules aside. You need to adjust to the current moment instead of worrying what anyone will think of your actions."

"Sweet Mary and Joseph!" she exclaimed when he released her. "What a vile concoction." But it was easing the dryness from her throat, spreading warmth through her chilled limbs and making her feel every ache.

"See? Should have let me have it. After all, I did help rescue her," his companion interjected.

Darius handed the flask over. "Enjoy."

The second man took the flask and offered her a salute before taking a swig of it. He seemed to enjoy the burn of the beverage and winked at her after taking a second swallow.

"This is Guardian Lykos Claxton, my counterpart from another Solitary Chamber."

The vehicle turned a corner, but there was still no sound of horses. "How are we moving?" She grasped the sides of the window and tried to see out.

"There's my thanks for risking my neck and my new waistcoat," Lykos muttered. "She isn't aware I'm alive."

"Oh." Janette turned her attention back to her company. "I'm terribly sorry. Thank you. I am deeply indebted to you both."

"What you are is completely tarnished now," Darius grumbled. "Return to your father, and he'll sign the papers to have you lobotomized."

"I refuse to go back to my father." Her hands twisted in the fabric of her skirt as the horror of the clinic replayed in her mind. "He gave me to that... *fiend* for treatment, and all Dr. Nerval wanted was for me to handle Deep Earth Crystals. Tell me, my ability to handle the crystals, why is it so important? Unique, perhaps, but nothing a good set of gloves cannot overcome—what is the reason behind all this?"

Her companions suddenly became deadly serious. She looked from Darius to Lykos and back again.

"What did I say?"

They glanced at each other, obviously weighing whether to respond to her.

"Are you claiming Dr. Nerval has knowledge of Deep Earth Crystals?"

Darius asked the question, his voice low and edged with suspicion. It sounded like a challenge, and she felt her strength returning with full force to face it.

"More than knowledge. He has a room full of them. When I refused to handle one he claimed was a level-four—like the one I caught in your Solitary

Chamber—he had me strapped to that chair to teach me obedience. How did you find me anyway?"

Lykos put the top back on the flask with a quick twist and dropped it onto the seat between them. Both men wore hard expressions.

"Did he tell you how he knew about the one you caught inside the lecture hall?"

"Answer my question first. I already responded to one of yours."

Darius frowned, but Lykos snorted with amusement. "I'm beginning to understand your irritation with her."

"I am not irritating, sir. How unkind of you to say so," Janette admonished.

Lykos grinned at her as his expression became one of contemplation. He studied her for a long moment. "Perhaps that is the wrong word, but you are certainly...an active element."

"Enough. We're straying off the topic," Darius said. "I bribed one of the bullyboys Dr. Nerval employs on his way back to the slums. The man was happy enough to spill a little information. Now answer my question."

She had to think for a moment to recall which question he meant. "Oh...well, Dr. Nerval claimed to know about the crystal I caught during the lecture from his sources. He pointed at one he said was similar and told me I was a...Pure Spirit. Which is the same thing the Professor giving the lecture said I was."

The two men glanced at each other again, confirming she was correct without a doubt.

A tingle of apprehension went across her skin as the carriage slowed down. There was suddenly much more light surrounding the carriage. Janette peered out the window to see some sort of gate. It rose on either side of them, apparently constructed of the same material as Darius's desk. The moment the carriage entered it, she felt the current go through her. The lapel pins on her Illuminist companions lit until they passed through the gate.

"So...this Pure Spirit business, it makes it possible for the current from the crystals to not harm me, but your pins protect you...by completing the circuit."

"Clever girl." Darius wasn't giving her a compliment. He was back to watching her suspiciously.

"Is it so wrong to want to understand what I seem to be? It's rather a relief to know there is a reason behind the melody I hear when I'm near those crystals. The only other explanation is I'm going insane."

"You aren't." Darius offered the pair of words with a hint of approval in his voice. "At least our community doesn't believe you are. I won't offer you the same assurance beyond our gates."

The carriage stopped, and the driver let down the stairs. Darius left his seat first, closing the space between them.

"But you're very lucky we were able to find you."

Tension renewed its grip on her along with the horror that had kept her company through the long hours of the day.

She might still be there.

"I believe Darius is offering that hand for you."

Janette jumped, startled by the comment. A quick glance toward the door showed Darius was waiting, his hand outstretched for her to steady her exit from the vehicle.

"Oh…yes." She took the offered hand, then stumbled on her way through the narrow doorway, stepping on her petticoat ruffle.

Darius's hand closed around hers, holding her steady when she would have lost her balance.

"You need to recover."

There was a hint of disgust in his voice, or maybe it was more like he'd been proven correct because she wasn't holding up better.

"I am right as rain now that I'm out of that horrible chair." She pulled her hand loose and smoothed her skirt while making sure her back was ramrod straight. For a moment she stared into Darius's unbelieving eyes, until the carriage captured her complete attention.

There truly were no horses.

"How does it work?"

Janette didn't wait for an answer but walked all the way around the vehicle in her quest to understand it. There were four wheels and a driver's box where she expected it to be. In the back there was a boiler with a steam pipe sticking up. When the driver released the brake, he also pulled on a second lever and steam hissed on its way up and out of the boiler.

Beneath the carriage there were gears connected by rods that moved them and then the wheels. The driver actually steered the carriage with a wheel that Janette could only compare to a ship's wheel, but it was much smaller and made of iron.

"You're in the Illuminist sector now, Janette. We don't depend on animals as much as the world you were raised in."

"Yes, I recall the gates."

Just like the Jewish communities, the Illuminists lived with their own kind. The main difference was that the Illuminists actually had gates to keep outsiders away. The air smelled different, and she realized it smelled like the country. Fresh and lacking the stink so often present in the city.

"Come inside, Janette. You need to keep out of sight. Now that others know of your abilities, someone will likely be looking for you."

A doorman held the door open, but he lacked the stiff formality of her father's servants. He offered them a jovial grin and was dressed in a shirt that was clean but not an unpractical color like white; instead, it was a deep blue. His vest had four pockets, two at the waist and a second set at the breast. An Illuminist pin reflected the light shining from inside the house.

"Glad to see you back, sir. Welcome, miss."

Janette found herself smiling back at him.

"Miss Janette will require a room and some supper, Hector."

The manservant closed the door before nodding. "I'll see to it, sir."

"I need you to answer some more questions, Janette." Darius held a door open to what looked like a study. Lykos stood behind her.

"You two act like constables."

"More like detectives, but your perception is accurate. Security and protection of the Order is our sworn duty. We are Guardians." Lykos offered the explanation as he extended his arm toward the open study door. He was still slightly behind her, reminding her of the burly attendants who had shadowed her every step at the clinic, ever ready to strong arm her. The difference was the ring of dedication in Lykos's voice. He and Darius had integrity, something the attendants had lacked. Besides, she wanted to be here.

She stepped through the door, and the room began to brighten. The level of light was only a glow at first but increased until the room was comfortably lit. She heard the slightest amount of crystal rhythm when she concentrated; otherwise, it didn't bother her.

"The reaction between the crystals—that's what powers everything." She walked closer to one of the lamps and laid her hand on it. She could feel the current and turned to see the badges on the two men's lapels lit.

"The stronger crystal is in your badges, which completes the current."

Lykos looked at Darius again, but Darius didn't notice because he was watching her. There was a gleam of appreciation in his eyes, which pleased her.

She felt her lips twitch up and turned to hide her smile.

"Do you know who told Dr. Nerval about your visit to the lecture?" Darius was back on his mission to discover what she knew. Janette turned to face him.

"No. But he knew the crystal I touched was a level-four, and I recall Professor Yulric saying the same thing. He also had a cane with a carved crystal on the top of it. He handed it to me at my father's house."

Both men weighed her words.

"What is a Pure Spirit? Please don't say I need to challenge your exam before you tell me. I believe we are past keeping me ignorant at this point."

"Possibly," Darius said. "But for the moment, we need to discover why and how information is leaking." He reached out and pulled on a thin tapestry sash hanging from the wall, ringing a bell somewhere in the kitchen.

Janette fingered her skirt, feeling alone. Darius was focused on his duty to protect his Order, and she was nothing but the incident that had brought this current dilemma to light. Like a piece of evidence. That awful feeling of being nothing more than an object was creeping through her again.

The world felt bigger, and her confidence, smaller. Things she had felt secure in that morning no longer gave her comfort. The door opened, and Hector appeared.

"Hector will take you to the kitchen, Janette," Darius said.

The desire to remain twisted her insides, but she refused to allow her emotions to rule her now that she had escaped the clinic. Things were certainly improved, and she'd hold on to that knowledge.

Clinging to Darius was bound to land her in a different sort of trouble altogether.

"Thank you, gentlemen. I am grateful for your assistance tonight."

Polished and polite, her exit was everything her father would have approved of—except she wasn't part of the world where such things mattered anymore. Still, part of her was humming with excitement because she'd managed to embark on an adventure, and this one didn't live between the pages of a book.

Of course, that meant the aches and pains would be real too. Along with the danger. But she was absorbed with the sense of anticipation warming her insides. In spite of the way the gag had bruised the corners of her mouth, she smiled.

❧

"I'd say Miss Janette just managed to make herself quite useful."

"Possibly, but at a great cost to herself." Darius discovered his attention wandering away from the task before him. He should have felt irritated, but as the moments passed, his ire didn't rise. No, only a desire to follow his guest into the kitchen to make sure she was seen to. *Comforted* was the more correct word, but it frustrated him to acknowledge the tender impulse.

"Hector won't appreciate your questioning his ability to run your house," Lykos offered drily. "Run out to check on your guest, and he'll likely overstarch your shirts."

Darius frowned. "The man works for me."

Lykos snorted. "You sound just like one of those society gentlemen. The servants work for you and all."

"Smart-arse."

His friend shrugged. "But you got my point."

"I did." It left him with a major infraction to deal with and Janette neatly taken out of his immediate care.

It shouldn't bother him, yet it did, because all he wanted to do was finish what had started between them last night. There were suddenly no barriers between them. The control he'd labored so diligently to perfect was threatening to crumble. Janette could pass the exam; he felt it in his gut, which meant she would no longer be forbidden to him. It was the worst sort of temptation because he was having the devil's time trying to think of another deterrent to seeking her out and kissing her.

But duty called, one necessary to keep Janette safe. That truth was strong enough to keep him in the study.

"Let's find out all we can about Dr. Nerval and his clinic."

Lykos abandoned his playful attitude, becoming the partner Darius knew so well.

For how late it was, Hector produced a meal that was quite pleasing. But once her belly was full, Janette was left with nothing to distract her from how rank she smelled. Terror and horror had sent perspiration to her skin and soaked her dress too many times. In spite of being dry now, she was as rumpled as a third-class passenger on a steamer.

The bathroom the manservant showed her to fascinated her. The tub had a round, eight-inch fixture held above it by a pair of pipes. There were tiny holes all over the underside of the fixture.

"Forgive me for being so forward, miss, but I believe you will find the washing tub quite nice. Use the knob to begin the water flowing. For hot water, raise the levers. The closer they come to the central pipe, the hotter the water. Be careful not to burn yourself."

The manservant closed the door, saving Janette from having him witness her astonishment.

No one had running hot water.

Some fortunate homes were becoming equipped with piped water—which was quite a nice convenience—but hot water was still added with a kettle.

She leaned into the tub and peered at the controls. There was a four-fingered knob she recognized, but there were also two-inch-wide levers that closed around the pipe the cold water ran through up to the fixture with the holes in it. They were both down and sticking straight out with the cold-water pipe in the center. They wouldn't move until she turned on the cold water. She heard it traveling up the pipe, and then it sprayed down into the tub like a rain shower, the water falling out of all the holes in the strange fixture.

She shivered because the water was icy cold, but even so, she was willing to suffer it to be clean. After struggling to get out of her dress, petticoat, and shoes, she approached the tub and stared at the twin levers. They moved easily enough, and as she pushed them up, they began to get closer to the pipe through which the cold water flowed.

She heard the crystals. They grew louder as the two levers drew closer to each other. Sticking her fingers between them, she felt the current. It went right through the pipe, and a moment later the water falling down from the fixture lost its chill.

So that was the secret. Some of the mystery lifted, allowing her to see the Illuminists for what they were—men of invention. The reaction between the crystals caused a current that might be used to heat water, which could then become steam. The carriage came to mind, and it was clear how the vehicle was powered. Even though she'd heard it discussed during the lecture, seeing it was far more impressive.

No fire. No coal. Only crystals, which were harmless until brought together to create a reaction.

Astounding.

Every ache in her body was suddenly worth it for the knowledge. She stepped into the tub and smiled as warm water flowed down her body. Her father could disown her, and she'd miss him, but she would never regret learning. Somehow she'd convinced herself that sneaking science circulars was enough. It wasn't. She needed more. There was a yearning inside her that was growing every day, and she wasn't going to ignore it any longer. She frowned when she looked down at her wet chemise. Her father had insisted she bathe in the undergarment to keep her innocence untarnished.

Keep her ignorant was more like it.

She pulled the wet fabric over her head. For just a moment she felt wicked, but she dropped the chemise over the far edge of the tub and stepped back under the flowing water. Illuminists had no need for foolishness, and she was going to embrace their ways. Cleaning her body would certainly be more efficient without clothing on. It was logical. Still, she felt exposed but reached for the soap bar to begin bathing.

Darius Lawley would just have to become accustomed to her being in his world, she decided, because she wasn't going back to her father's house.

You might be the one regretting that...

She tried to scoff at her thoughts but failed because

there was no way to hide how much the man affected her and how quickly she responded. Would she become brazen now? Her father had always warned her that would happen if she didn't fear his iron hand. He wasn't the only one preaching damnation for young women who weren't kept under close scrutiny.

But would it be such a terrible fate? Darius's face came to mind, and a tiny shiver rippled across her skin. Her memory produced a perfect recollection of the way he liked to cup her neck while kissing her, and her nipples hardened. Without corset or chemise to hide her breasts, she looked down and smiled at the way her body responded—to Darius.

Wanton. Brazen. Maybe she was, but somehow she couldn't accept that she'd fallen from grace. No shame nipped at her, only an urge to seek out the source of her fascination.

❦

There was no fire kindled in the bedroom she was shown to, but it was comfortably warm. In fact, there wasn't really a hearth but some unfamiliar machine. With the lack of fire, the entire house smelled so much nicer. There weren't smoke wisps lingering in the corners. She could definitely grow accustomed to the lack of coal dust.

On one wall was a large box with a pipe that ended in what looked like a sound funnel for a phonograph player with a brass tank beneath it. On either side of the box were two levers, sticking straight out. These levers were larger, and when she raised them, there was a hiss as water boiled inside the tank. Several rows of a dozen short pistons began to move, white puffs of steam escaping from the sides of the device. She heard air being sucked in through a grate at the base of the pipe, and then warm air began blowing out of the funnel end. She laughed with glee as it hit her face and warmed her chilled nose.

"You have an intelligent mind, Janette."

She turned to discover Darius watching her from the doorway. She was stunned but also noticed how breathless she felt. It was almost as if she'd stepped into a dream where it was perfectly permissible to be alone in a bedroom with a man who wasn't her husband.

"I knocked," he said, "but you were distracted. Not that I blame you. I forget how many conveniences my home has compared to the one you were raised in."

The tone of his voice was just as heated as the air, and it sent a tingle of awareness through her body.

"This is phenomenal. I could wash my hair every night without fear of catching a chill."

He watched her for a long moment. She could see regret shimmering there, and she raised her chin in defiance of his judgment.

"It's cost you a great deal to experience it. There isn't any way to confirm how many know you're a Pure Spirit now, Janette."

"Don't use my name if your intention is to placate me." She hugged her arms close, realizing she was holding a conversation with him in nothing but a chemise and dressing robe. "Or warn me."

"You're past the stage of warning," he admitted.

"I'm sure you believe I'm in shock and too frightened to think clearly, but I assure you, I am not." Her unbound hair was beginning to dry and float in a soft cloud, and she noticed his gaze on it.

Did he like what he saw?

Now she was thinking in an emotional way, one that promised to lead her into temptation.

"Am I to stay here tonight?"

The question was a desperate attempt to return to polite, safe conversation. She needed to forget she was alone with him and how many times she'd thought about his kiss since that moment in the garden.

"Yes, you're my responsibility for the time being. Unless you were going to demand I return you to your father."

Darius watched her with a measure of satisfaction. It was dark and touched off another ripple of sensation inside her. But there was also a clear challenge in his tone.

She squared her shoulders. "I am very appreciative of your hospitality."

He frowned. "I told you before; I have little interest in polite ladies of society, so kindly spare me your attempts to coddle me."

The reprimand in his voice stung, irritating her because she was fed up with being found lacking.

"So I should not be polite?" She shook her head slowly. "I don't believe that is the case among Illuminists. You are attempting to prod me into acting as you expect me to. Something you've done before, why?"

"What I think is you have arrived at a crossroads, and it is unsettling you. Rightfully so. But my world is one where you can be sure you'll have to back up everything you say you are. Females do not make their way simply because they are women. You'll be expected to make sense. Logical sense."

He abandoned his lazy stance in the doorway and closed the distance between them. There was such purpose in the way he moved that she retreated without thinking and ended up against the wall.

Darius didn't stop when she collided with the solid barrier but kept coming until he propped one of his hands on the smooth surface next to her face. She was fully aware of him, just as she had been the night before. Her senses felt keener, every detail impacting her more dramatically.

He cupped her chin, raising her face so their gazes met.

"You are a Pure Spirit, which means you could become one of us. But understand one thing: join my world, and I won't consider you off-limits any longer. Show me that stubborn determination, and be assured I will happily test your nerve. My polished manners are for business matters only."

"I see."

Something flickered in his eyes that sent a shaft of anticipation through her—some promise lurked there that was everything she'd ever wondered about but had been told was uncivilized.

"No, you don't, Janette. You understand nothing about my nature."

Her pride reared its head. "I understand you are more truthful than any gentleman caller my father approved of. They said pretty things while their eyes were full of the same things I see in yours." And he was using her first name easily now, something that should have bothered her, yet it felt very right. "I believe I prefer your approach, Darius."

He chuckled, but it was a dark, sinister sound. "Such a statement will have to be verified."

He slid his fingers along her cheek, moving his hand to cup the side of her face as he angled his head to press his lips against hers. The kiss was just as intoxicating as the first had been. Only now she wasn't so sure she wanted to resist. She craved his strength and the knowledge that he wasn't forbidden to have unleashed something wild inside her. He took command of her mouth, moving her face so their mouths fit together. She didn't let him do all the moving this time but tried to mimic his motions. She flattened her hands on his chest, spreading her fingers to feel more. There were ridges of muscle beneath his vest and shirt. She could feel the warmth of his skin and smell his scent as her breathing became rougher.

"Damn it, Janette." He pulled away from her, his breathing as unsteady as hers. "You shouldn't kiss me back."

Her eyes widened. "But you can test my nerve by kissing me? That isn't fair."

"Fair?" He laughed, low and full of warning. "What makes you think there is anything fair about the position you find yourself in?"

"You're making fun of me…again." She shoved hard at his chest, but his hand slid back into her hair. He threaded his fingers through the half-dried mass and gripped it to hold her head prisoner.

"I'm warning you, Janette."

"Which you have done every time we have met,

and I am weary of your dislike of me. Why do you keep trying to encourage me to reject you?"

His lips thinned, but his eyes still showed her desire. "Because it would keep me from falling victim to your siren song."

He kissed her again, his lips ensuring she didn't have the chance to argue with him. Instead, she found herself battling to recall anything he'd said. All that seemed to matter was the sensation flowing from their kiss. It was the sweetest delight, clouding her thinking and awakening a need to fan the flames so they burned brighter.

Darius kissed her harder now, pressing until she opened her mouth; when she did, his tongue teased the delicate skin of her lower lip. A ripple of delight went down her body, followed by another when he thrust his tongue into her mouth. It was shocking but immensely intimate. She'd never been so close to another human, and there was a sense of belonging she'd never anticipated.

Darius pulled away, the hand tangled in her hair holding her in place. Hunger danced in his eyes, and she recognized it even if she'd never seen such aimed at her before. It was as if she'd cast aside childhood and become woman enough to see all the things hidden from the eyes of the innocent.

"Go to bed, now, before I forget myself further."

He made a sound that struck her as disgusted before releasing her. She glared at his wide shoulders before dragging breath into her lungs.

"Well, if that happened, it would be because I decided I would, and not due to you strong-arming me."

He turned in a flash, displaying some of the raw strength she'd noticed he possessed.

"Don't challenge me. I'm having enough trouble resisting you." His tone was hard with warning.

She should have remained silent. It would have been the wise thing to do, but instead, she propped her hands on her hips and faced off with him.

"Don't threaten me, Darius Lawley. I've had quite enough of that today, thank you very much."

Surprise covered his face, but not for long. Savage enjoyment flared up in his eyes, and it sent a spear of anticipation through her. He lifted a hand and curled a single finger in her direction.

"If you have the courage, come here." His voice was almost hypnotic.

She shouldn't.

That bit of wisdom didn't stick; it slipped out of her mind as her feet began moving. Her confidence increased as she closed the gap and noticed the way his attention was focused so intently on her. She touched him, flattening her hands on top of his chest, and shivered because she was so aware of him, of their reaction to each other. Something was brewing between them, like a storm that threatened to either destroy them or take them on the journey of a lifetime.

"I am not afraid of you, Darius. But I believe you are of me."

He cupped the sides of her face, instantly taking control of their embrace. "Only because I know what happens when passion is spent."

He kissed her again, but this time it was hard, demanding, and rough. A tiny wave of fear rippled through her, but it didn't keep her from kissing him back. Hot need licked at her insides while his mouth demanded a response she was eager to provide. The kiss burned away every shred of thought, leaving her to enjoy the experience. But he lifted his head before she might sink further into the sensations, and it felt like they were being ripped apart.

"Consider why you trembled just then, Janette. The ride will be intense, but it will have to end eventually. Reality will be waiting, I assure you. The sun will rise, and consequences will be illuminated."

His words echoed in her mind long after he left the room.

She sat down on the bed, feeling too full of mental dilemmas to sleep, but her body was at its limit, and she slumped over onto the pillows.

❧

Darius poured himself a half glass of whiskey and tossed it back in one motion. The liquor burned a path down his throat, but it failed to chase the taste of Janette's kiss away.

Damn it. He was a monster. So why hadn't that frightened her?

He poured another measure but only stared at the amber fluid. He growled and turned his back on it. He wasn't ready for fate to toy with him again. Not when it came to women. He liked the way the last few years had been, filled with duty and dedication.

Janette was a huge distraction—in fact, she was a catastrophic one. It had proved almost impossible to keep from calling on her after their garden walk, and the arrival of her friend had been too welcome for the severity of the circumstances.

Only a beast would find delight in hearing she had been taken into one of society's clinics. But he had to admit he'd been excited by the prospect of rescuing Janette. The places were horror houses where sanity often slipped away as medical treatment drove the unfortunate victims mad.

Still, the rescue had been successful, and relief flowed through him. He sat down in a padded armchair, grateful to hear the soft steps above him that announced Janette was moving toward the bed.

Admittedly, he had been ungentlemanly and possibly even rough in his handling of her. But she was safe beneath his roof, and he was going to find a way to make sure she remained so.

Darius sat forward, dark thoughts drawing his attention away from his relief. Keeping Janette safe wasn't going to be easy. Dr. Nerval had avoided being detected as a Helikeian for years, in spite of suspicions surrounding his clinic. Janette was the first witness who could expose him, but even with that, being a Helikeian wasn't a crime in Britain.

Only the Illuminists knew the Helikeians for what they were—greedy men who would use the power of the Deep Earth Crystals to construct weapons, a habit repugnant to the Illuminists and everything the Order stood for. Theirs was a conflict that went back through thousands of years of Illuminist history, a conflict he'd devoted his life to ensuring the Helikeians didn't win.

If Janette fell into helping the Helikeians, it would

be his duty to kill her before she helped shift the balance of power in favor of the Helikeians.

He stood and took the whiskey. He swallowed it before moving toward his bed for the night. Duty had never disturbed his sleep so much.

Neither had a kiss.

❧

Morning light wasn't kind.

Janette rubbed her eyes, and memory rushed in to remind her of what she'd done over the last few days. Her life had altered drastically, yet she didn't feel exposed.

Or sullied…

She'd kissed Darius Lawley and enjoyed it. She refused to feel any shame—absolutely refused—and that was the end of it.

But that didn't keep her from lowering her eyes later when she discovered Darius at the kitchen table. The scent of coffee teased her nose, as did the smell of sweet rolls baking.

"Best eat while you can. The day will be long."

"Will it?" She slid into a chair and reached for the coffeepot, but Darius lifted it before she did and filled her cup.

"Dr. Nerval will no doubt be looking for you, and legally, your father is your guardian. He can have you returned to treatment if your presence here is discovered."

Horror shot through her like a bolt of lightning. She reached for the coffee too quickly, turning the delicate china cup over onto its side.

"Oh my…" Coffee went spilling across the table as she stood to avoid it running into her lap. "I'm sorry."

Hector appeared with a large length of towel to soak up the coffee. Janette turned to flee, her appetite gone. A hand landed on her shoulder before she made it very far.

"Did you think it was over?"

Darius wasn't gloating. He turned her to face him, but his expression was far from reassuring.

"I tried to warn you, Janette, because there are men who will kill to obtain you. Your natural talent is rarer than gold."

She peered out the front window, fearing the sight of blue-coated constables, which ignited her temper.

"I've had a bellyful of fear. That clinic reeked of it." She wished her voice sounded more confident, but she couldn't keep the desperation from ringing through.

"It's my duty to keep you out of the hands of the Helikeians, but they never would have learned of you if you hadn't trespassed."

"I can't lament that." She pointed at the road outside the window. A carriage went by, no horses pulling it. The rooftops weren't dusted with soot, and the air was clear. "For I never would have seen the wonders of this place. So I'll hide anywhere I can until I can take that exam—besides, apparently I belong among the Illuminists. Kindly stop warning me away. I intend to challenge the exam."

"Thank God for that." His voice was rough with relief. An odd little grin lifted his lips as he witnessed her confusion. "It's against the law for me to suggest or encourage any member of society to join our Order.

I believe Professor Yulric was as close to breaking that law as I've ever seen the man when I told him he had to let you walk out of our Solitary Chamber. But *you* have to ask."

"Well…" She shut her mouth, cutting off the tart retort she'd been about to make. The man was frustrating indeed, but she realized his dedication to upholding the law was something she admired. It made him noble, in spite of how much he vexed her. "That's why you were tapping your lapel pin before tossing me out."

He nodded, and she felt her cheeks burning because she'd failed so completely to take the hint.

"Becoming an Illuminist won't change the law. Your father is still considered your guardian unless he disowns you."

"He will. If I become an Illuminist, he will never speak my name again." Unlike the day before, she felt no pain over the parting. Maybe it was because her father had never been happy with her, and now she knew it was her very blood he detested.

"He can just as easily send you back to the clinic. I have no doubt Dr. Nerval is already at his door demanding to have you returned."

Janette looked at him. "Why did you rescue me if you are so sure I can't escape my father's authority?"

"Because Dr. Nerval told you the truth. You are a Pure Spirit, which means your bloodline allows you to handle and hear Deep Earth Crystals. Among Illuminists and Helikeians alike, you are a coveted thing."

"Helikeians…as in the fabled enemy of the Atlanteans?" she asked.

Approval shone in Darius's eyes. "You might have

a chance against that exam after all if you know where the Helikeians come from."

"But...Helikeians—"

"Have long wanted to use the crystals to power weapons that will make them invincible. It's something the Illuminists oppose them over."

"It's why your Order is so secretive." The knowledge stunned her. All the wonders about the house hadn't made her think about what other uses such a power source might have.

"You have a unique ability, one we can't afford to have used by the Helikeians."

His tone had turned hard, and a shiver went down her spine. "So...that's why you rescued me? In the hope I'll decide to work on your side? But that doesn't explain why you're trying to scare me now with the facts about the law."

His dark eyes narrowed. "I'm trying to make sure you understand how important it is for you to stay with me and not run off out of some worry your virtue is in danger."

It was in danger because she had no defense against him...

Heat churned in her belly, and her lips tingled. She just couldn't seem to separate the man in front of her from the one who had kissed her. The bright light of day should have made it simple, and still she felt excitement tightening all her muscles.

"Yes, I understand." But suspicion tingled along her nerves.

He made a low sound and reached out to cup her chin. He raised her face so their eyes locked.

"I believe you think you do, Janette. But I assure

you, you don't understand everything that is happening between us. Do the wise thing and reject it."

She stepped back so she could choose whether to keep her eyes locked with his.

"More warnings, Darius. You're being repetitive, and truthfully, you sound like the one most worried about virtue."

He tried to find fault with her comment, but he lost the battle and chuckled. His lips curved, and his expression softened. She glimpsed the boy he must have been once sparkling in his eyes.

"And you're too daring for the attraction between us." He stepped close once more and smoothed his fingers over her cheek. "Of course, we could simply plan to marry if you are discovered here." Hunger flashed in his eyes. "That would certainly solve more than one problem."

"Marry?" A woman came from the kitchen, her voice raised to gain their attention. Darius spun around, shielding Janette with his body.

"Now, see here. There will be no talk of marriage," she insisted.

The woman didn't seem concerned about the way Darius was glaring at her or the fact that Hector was wringing his hands behind her. She was dressed head to toe in a traveling suit and radiated confidence. Her tone wasn't hard, but that didn't seem to lessen the impact of her words.

"Who are you?" Darius demanded.

She flipped her lapel over, revealing the gold pin of the Illuminist Order. "I am Galene." Her voice was sultry and low. "I am Janette's grandmother."

Four

THERE WAS NO WAY TO DENY IT. JANETTE STARED AT the woman and saw her mother's face, but with less strain and unhappiness. Why had she never noticed how unhappy her mother was?

"What happened to my mother?" Janette demanded. Her throat had closed up, feeling as dry as a dirt road in summer.

"I would enjoy knowing the answer to that myself."

Galene sent a coquettish look toward Darius before walking right past him and presenting him with only her back. "In my day…"

She peered back at him while slowly drawing a hatpin out of her straw bonnet. "Even a rogue asked a lady to join him at the table before demanding personal details." She lifted the hat off her head and stuck the foot-long steel pin into it with a zeal that wasn't lost on her company. There was as much warning in her eyes as Darius was so fond of employing. Janette fought the urge to laugh.

Galene extended the hat, and Hector took it from her instantly. She rewarded him with a flutter of eyelashes and a soft smile. The butler left the kitchen with reddened cheeks.

"Did you also enter homes without invitation?" Darius inquired while extending his hand toward the forgotten breakfast service.

"I have done many things that shall remain none of your concern, Guardian Lawley." She looked at a chair, and Darius reached for the back of it with a short grunt. Janette lost her composure and laughed at the picture of frustration he presented.

"Delightful," Darius groused before pulling back a chair for Janette since she was still standing.

"Oh, but it is very delightful to hear my grand-daughter discarding some of the stiff nonsense her father insisted on feeding her during her childhood."

Darius sat down hard. "Why wasn't she raised within the Order?"

Galene traced the delicate handle of a china coffee cup, her expression darkening. "I suppose you shall discover the truth soon enough."

She slowly took a sip of coffee, which felt like it took an hour as Janette waited to hear the reason behind her mother's last instruction to her.

The coffee cup was placed back onto its saucer before Galene spoke again. "My daughter passed the exam early." Unmistakable pride lit her eyes. "But alas, she was not a Pure Spirit. That blood comes from my mother."

"Four generations back?" Janette interrupted, anxiety shredding her composure.

"Yes," Galene answered quickly to cut off Darius.

"But you still haven't explained how your daughter came to be wed outside the Order," Darius asked.

Galene abandoned her charming demeanor. The woman transformed into a formidable person instantly. She faced off with Darius as though she believed herself his equal—which, as far as the Illuminists were concerned, she was; her gender was no longer a deciding factor when it came to judging her.

"She was accused of treason," Galene delivered softly.

A muscle on the side of Darius's cheek twitched.

"The charges were never decided upon," she quickly added.

"Which would have happened only if you had no way of proving her innocence," he snapped back. His expression was unbendable. There was a core of nobility in him that she couldn't help but admire, even if it was frustrating.

Galene drew in a deep breath. "True, but the important matter now is my granddaughter's future." A shadow of pain passed through her eyes, but she shook it off quickly. "I am here to take Janette in hand, and gladly so."

Galene stood. Now she was all business and intent on having her way without charming it from Darius. It was fascinating. Janette felt her yearning to join the Illuminist Order growing stronger with each passing second. Equality—she craved it.

"What manner of protection can you offer her?" Darius demanded. He was on his feet the moment her grandmother rose. "If the Helikeians find her, I doubt they will be so careless in allowing us the opportunity to steal her away again."

"Which is an excellent reason for her to be removed from this area," Galene countered.

"Not to a blood relative's care. How did you know where to find her?"

Hector was suddenly behind Janette, grasping her arm to pull her away from Galene.

"My daughter told me Howard had sent her to the country and of the events that led to his decision to send Janette to the clinic," Galene answered without hesitation, proving once again that she considered herself on equal footing with Darius. "I slept in my carriage to make sure I arrived as soon as possible because I knew in my heart it had to have something to do with the Order. I've often hoped Janette would prove to be a Pure Spirit."

"But you didn't advise your local Guardians of the peril your granddaughter was in."

Galene hesitated for the first time, and Darius flattened his hands on the tabletop. "You ignored procedure, one you took an Oath to follow in spite of tender feelings."

"Enough, Darius—" Janette interjected as she shrugged out of Hector's hold.

"I don't think I've said even close to enough." Darius straightened and aimed his smoldering glare at her. The man was furious. She could see him battling to control his temper.

What made her clamp her mouth closed was the way he seemed intent on protecting her. That noble quality was fully aroused on her behalf.

"The aches you suffer would not be a burden this morning had your grandmother gone directly to the Guardians of her Solitary Chamber. I would have been notified in time to keep you from being taken to that clinic."

"Then you wouldn't know about Dr. Nerval. If he is the monster you claim he is, I'd say my suffering was little compared to the good it has served."

"Janette, she has allowed you to be raised in complete ignorance."

"I did not allow any such thing. The choice was taken from me when my daughter was falsely accused," Galene declared. "I will not overlook this opportunity to know my granddaughter at long last."

"If you believe I will allow you to take her away from the protection I can provide for her, you are sadly mistaken, madam," Darius snarled and snapped his fingers at Hector. The man reached for her once more, this time pulling her away from Galene despite resistance.

"Stop bickering over me," Janette demanded. "I am challenging the exam, and I will be making my own decisions on where I go."

"Don't be a fool, Janette. You don't understand the lengths the Helikeians will go to to control a Pure Spirit. Being anywhere near your grandmother will only tell them where to look."

Darius's tone had changed. She stiffened at the command. "And you are a fool if you believe I will tolerate being spoken down to like some senseless, spoiled child."

Surprise flickered in his dark eyes. "You're naïve. Such a lack of knowledge could get you killed."

Janette bristled at the condemning look he gave her, but what grated on her nerves was the way her muscles tightened with dread. Part of her believed him, trusted him. There was a sincerity in his gaze she couldn't argue against. Yet it frightened her also because it was just too tempting to lean on.

After yesterday, she never wanted to be dependent on others again.

"Nonsense," she insisted. "Since I am such a rare commodity, no one is going to kill me, even if the methods employed to bend me might be extreme."

Darius's expression hardened, but he remained silent, something that made her belly twist with dread.

"What are not telling me?"

"Mr. Lawley is hesitating to tell you that a Guardian's duty includes ensuring our enemies do not acquire Pure Spirits, even if the only way to do that is to destroy them," Galene provided in a soft tone.

The blood drained from Janette's face. For the first time in her life, she felt like collapsing into a faint to escape the horror.

"Well, now, I see the morning milk is gone sour," Lykos said as he strode into the room. He looked at Galene. "It would be kind of you to recall the lengths we went to, to recover your granddaughter before you make us out as villains."

Janette's hands had gone cold; she only noticed when Darius shifted his attention to the way she was rubbing them. For a moment, regret flickered in his eyes.

"Janette has the right to know," Galene insisted.

"Agreed," Darius said. "Just as she has the right to know leaving with you would be exactly what Dr. Nerval would expect."

"Which is why I told the lot of you that I intend to challenge that exam. Today."

Everyone turned to stare at her.

"Don't be foolish, Janette. You will need time to prepare," Darius said.

"You do not know everything about me, Mr. Lawley." Janette enjoyed the way her formal address made him draw in a stiff breath. "The fact is, my mother may never have told me of my heritage because she promised my father she wouldn't, but that didn't stop her from directing my education. She snuck in more than one tutor under the disguise of scripture teacher."

Surprise appeared on Darius's face.

"Yes. You see, Sophia is one of my only friends because she is the only one who can hold a decent conversation."

And suddenly everything made sense. The insistence of her mother that she could master higher mathematics when all the girls she met at parties were told it was for men. The special tutors arriving to teach her about the cosmos when only Sophia had any notion who Galileo was. In her secretive way, her mother had taught her everything.

"I am ready."

Galene beamed, but it was the way Darius's eyes darkened that fascinated her. She'd only glimpsed fragments of passion before. Now it was there, in full blaze while he did nothing to hide his interest. It would seem she had finally impressed the man.

At least so long as she didn't give him a reason to kill her.

❧

"Fate has a twisted sense of humor, my boys," Professor Yulric declared jubilantly. He rubbed his hands again, but Darius wasn't sure if the man had ever stopped. It was a good thing he was wearing leather gloves, or he'd be risking blisters.

"Look how intent she is…"

On the other side of the window, Janette sat in his office with the pages of the entrance exam in front of her. She dipped her quill again and again as she worked her way through the questions. Color didn't brighten her cheeks to betray uncertainty, which left him with a growing sense of satisfaction coupled with dread because his gut told him she was going to pass, and then what? A hard hand landed on his shoulder.

"It does appear our little adventurer is going to be placed under your stewardship," Lykos said. "How splendid."

"It is indeed!" the Professor answered, proving that the only frailty the man had was in his aging flesh. He might be balding and his face spouting white whiskers, but his wits remained sharp. "A Pure Spirit…at last."

"But the daughter of a traitor," Darius muttered.

The Professor's joy faded, but only for a moment. "Her mother was never convicted."

"Only because she fled. Janette will have to shoulder the burden of being the offspring of a coward."

"Yes, yes…well, we all must make our way through the more difficult tasks in our lives," the Professor replied. "Besides, the woman has clearly had her daughter educated well. Just look at the way she is moving through the exam! I dare say she belongs here and her mother has done her duty in making sure it would happen."

Darius caught himself grinning. She had spirit, and

he admired it. He smoothed out his expression when
Lykos looked his way. It was an opinion he needed
to keep to himself. Janette was going to be in his
charge, which meant anything personal would be out
of the question.

Duty before preference. Always.

❧

"You passed!" Galene beamed and kissed her on both
cheeks. Tears shimmered in her eyes as Janette felt her
muscles easing for the first time in hours.

Had she truly only been playing with Sophia's
scandalous fashions a few days ago?

"Just as you said you would," Galene continued.
"My daughter did well." The old lady faltered, her
voice cracking with emotion.

"Your daughter would have done better to
return and face the accusations leveled against her,"
Darius stated.

Janette wanted to snap at him—he was ruining
her moment of triumph. But there was a warning in
his eyes that made her hesitate. Alienating the man
when she intended to live among his brethren wasn't
the wisest course of action, even if it was tempting.
She would just wait to speak her mind when they
were alone.

Eager to be alone with him, are you?

Her impulses were going to be the death of her.
She shook off the thoughts that tried to take control of
her attention—hushed rumors of the Illuminist ways,
which included being allowed lovers. Intimacies were
not considered a duty but a pleasure members might

indulge in as their right, something she'd been raised to believe was wrong.

Or maybe not. For certain her mother had warned her what their neighbors thought of the Illuminist ways, but that wasn't the same as being told her body was sinful. More than one young lady she'd known during her childhood had been reared to believe any enjoyment of intimacies was low-bred and dirty. A lady only endured such things to conceive. A true gentleman took his baser needs to a mistress once his wife was expecting.

Her gaze focused on Darius. His kisses were definitely an indulgence—a wicked one.

"I will be pinning that on her, Mr. Lawley, if you please."

Galene held one gloved hand out for something Darius held. It was a lapel pin, cast with the symbols of the Illuminist Order but made of silver instead of gold.

"This is your novice pin." Galene gently pinned it to the collar of her dress. "Before you may be awarded a gold one, you shall have to memorize our laws and take the Oath of Allegiance to uphold them. You shall be a novice for an entire year."

Galene patted the pin once it was secured, and tears trickled down her cheeks. She hugged her tightly before Darius cleared his throat, and she sighed.

"Yes, I understand. You are correct, Mr. Lawley." Galene stepped back and drew herself up stiffly. "You shall begin your novitiate here, and I must leave or risk drawing the Helikeians to you. Promise me you shall telephone often."

"Telephone?"

Galene nodded. "You'll be allowed to use one if you ask. I will call you often, though not too often, for you will have a full schedule on your way to your first degree."

"I see…" Actually she didn't, but Janette maintained her composure while she battled to keep her uncertainty from showing. Of course there were levels inside the Illuminist Order. She was a fool to believe a new member wouldn't have to work to achieve respect. Earning it would be a pleasure, because for the first time in a very long time she would be judged on things that mattered instead of social niceties. Knowledge and learning—all of it was now at her fingertips.

"I am looking forward to the challenge," she declared, much to Professor Yulric's delight.

The door opened, and Lykos stood there wearing his overcoat. Behind him, another Illuminist Guardian held Galene's cloak, his message clear. Her grandmother lifted a hand and waved.

"Study well…"

The doors closed behind her grandmother, and Janette felt a pinch of loneliness. It surprised her because Galene was almost a stranger to her, but at the moment, the old lady was the only family she still had contact with.

"Since you have joined us, I will escort you to your quarters in the women's section." Darius pressed on his ear device and extended his arm toward the door, which opened. She heard the tiny hum of the crystals. "All new members—"

"Stay in the dormitory for their first year. Yes, I know." She was interrupting but needed to feel as though she knew what to expect from her life, or maybe what she needed was to make sure Darius didn't see her as a lost child in need of comforting. A sense of uncertainty was threatening to eat through her fragile confidence and leave her vulnerable to despair. Well, she would just have to muster up some courage. The year of living inside the dormitory was yet another reason many people suspected the Illuminist Order of strange and grotesque dealings. Why else would new members need to be separated from their families?

"I used to come to Sophia's to buy a circular outside." She followed Darius from the room. "My father was very displeased when he found them, but I am glad I have some knowledge of life inside your Order."

"Our Order."

"Yes...of course..."

His eyes narrowed slightly in response to the hesitation in her tone. Janette diverted her attention to the décor of the hallways they were passing through.

She was simply overstimulated.

You certainly were this morning...

She shook her head and felt another look from Darius as heat suffused her cheeks.

The man read her emotions too well. She reached up to finger the Illuminist pin, seeking proof she wasn't dreaming. It was cool beneath her fingertips

Darius didn't stop to comment but took her farther into the secret world she'd only read about. The Solitary Chamber was much larger than it had appeared from the street. They went down wide corridors before going through a gate. She heard the hum of the crystals but her pin didn't have any secured in it.

"Novices need permission to leave their dormitory wing because our secrets could leak out with them before they take their Oaths," Darius informed her. He turned to face two large doors and pressed his earpiece. "The first gate is enough deterrent for other novices."

The doors opened to reveal another long corridor, and two men standing guard on the other side of the doors.

"But I'm a Pure Spirit and can cross the gate without a gold pin." Knowing the facts didn't stop her heart from accelerating when Darius pulled her to a stop and the two guards studied her face.

He raised an eyebrow. "Misgivings already, Miss Aston?"

"Your arrogance is ugly, Mr. Lawley." She stepped away from him. "Is it so hard for you to understand that my tolerance for being placed under lock and key might be strained today? Well, I do assure you, I shall weather the conditions necessary for me to make my place here."

He reached out to capture her arm. To be sure, her pride didn't care to know she liked the way he imposed his will on her, but there was a part of her that enjoyed feeling his strength and recognizing that it was greater than her own. He was arrogant, but that fact seemed to give her satisfaction. Part of her found it attractive. *Foolish…*

She needed to focus on beginning a life for herself, not on the way Darius Lawley made her feel. Her father was correct about one thing: emotions would lead her astray.

"Your door to your rooms will not be locked,

unless you do it yourself." He guided her down the hallway to the very end and reached for his earpiece.

"But you have the power to open any door here, don't you?" she asked, distracting herself from the guards. It was becoming jumbled inside her mind, and she needed to keep yesterday's experience at the clinic far away from the adventure she was on today.

Yes, that was it. Adventure. Such a marvelous opportunity.

He glanced down at her as the door opened. "I am a Guardian and the head one here. Don't mistake our Order, Janette. There are laws that are ironclad, and we will protect our knowledge. Treason is punishable by death. I escort every new novice to their chamber when they arrive."

He pointed into the open chamber. There was a small entry room, with a table in the center of it. A lamp cast white light down onto an open book placed neatly on the table's surface. "Read the laws first, Janette. You can still walk away. The Guardians at the gate will allow you to leave today if you decide you do not want to follow our ways. You've proven you have a fine mind and can grasp more knowledge but we share our learning only with those willing to protect our secrets. You will not be allowed into our most important classes until you complete your Novice year and take the Oath of Allegiance. Only then will you be a full member of this Order."

She lifted her chin and quashed the urge to shrug off his grasp. Let the man see how little he frightened her.

"I will read the laws, but do not waste your time waiting about for me to bolt like some frightened rabbit." She turned and walked away from him. He released her, but she felt his gaze on her. Her father would have been proud of her poise; it lacked not a bit of formality as she covered the distance to the table. She picked up the book and turned to look back at him.

"I know you are not a rabbit, Janette." His voice was edged with frustration, and it touched a similar feeling inside her. "But I do wonder if you aren't wearing that badge because you believe you have nowhere else to go."

"Maybe I wonder if you're bringing up such a thing because it will remind me that you offered me marriage this morning as an alternative."

An alternative she needed to ignore…or risk thinking about his kisses again. She blushed, as both options left her the possibility of taking him for her lover. That knowledge was too much; she wasn't even sure how to think about it. The topic had been so forbidden until an hour ago.

Now it wasn't…

"But I am wearing it," she continued. "So there is no reason to discuss the matter further."

Her pride came to her rescue, insisting she not begin her life among the Illuminists with rumors she'd gained entrance by becoming the head Guardian's lover. Maybe among the Order it wasn't as frowned upon as in high society, but she still wanted to be seen standing on her own. She drew a deep breath.

"Since you claim my privacy will be respected here, kindly leave me to begin my life as a member of the Illuminist Order, Mr. Lawley. We should avoid being overly familiar with each other while I am a novice. Since you claim to escort all newcomers to their chambers, it's best I do not appear unique. Such would undermine your position."

"You make an interesting point, Janette."

She turned back to face him and regretted giving into temptation. His expression was dark, but not with anger. The man was battling the same urges as she. She didn't need to see him contemplating her lips, couldn't stop herself from licking them because they were suddenly dry. His eyes narrowed instantly.

"I believe addressing me so familiarly is unwise," she sputtered, searching her mind for all the lessons her mother had given her on keeping men at arm's length—something she'd failed to do with Darius. What foul luck she had with this man. There was something about him that unraveled her composure.

"At least, it's wiser. Surely you can see that," she implored him. Every bit of poise she had seemed misplaced between them. What chafed was the way she noticed how dishonest she was being. She did not want him at arm's length.

"Because of my position?" He chuckled, but the sound was far from pleasant.

She heard only a faint sound of his feet hitting the floor before the man was looming over her. He left only a scant inch between them, grasping her arms to pull her close.

"Yes...you're—"

"I know who I am, Janette." His breath teased her lips. "I do not need you to protect my good name."

"Well, you needn't be so cross."

He shook his head. "And you needn't be so mesmerizing."

His eyes darkened, hypnotizing her. He growled softly before his lips claimed hers. It wasn't a kind kiss; it was an assault, one designed to break through her defenses. What surprised her was the way she curled her fingers into his vest to pull him against her. Delight speared through her, hard and sweet. Need pulsed inside her, and she turned her head so their kiss might be even harder. She wanted to know everything about him—his taste, his scent, and the feel of his demands.

"Enough, Janette. I should have listened to you and left."

He put her away from him, but she felt his hands shaking. Just the hint of a tremor, one his eyes never betrayed. Instead, she witnessed the flare of lust in those dark orbs and understood exactly what it was... because it was the same thing gnawing at her insides.

"Then leave me. But don't you forget that I am not a frightened child anymore."

His lips rose into a mocking grin.

"Yet neither are you completely a woman." The door began to open in response to a press on his ear device. Heat rose to her cheeks at his comment. How dare the man call her immature after kissing her so passionately!

"If I am not up to your standards, Mr. Lawley, kindly stop kissing me."

He stopped and offered her a half bow. "But my dear Miss Aston, you are the one who was so determined to enter my world. How could I fail to welcome you to it...personally?" His eyes flashed a promise at her before the door closed.

Welcome, indeed. More like a warning. *Or a promise...*

She felt the need inside her twisting and biting now that he was gone. Her skin was too sensitive, both her nipples drawn into hard points behind her corset, and hidden between the folds of her sex there was a point that throbbed bitterly with frustration.

Janette laughed. She forced the sound out of her body, denying the urge to sink into longing. Smoothing her fingers over the Illuminist pin, she laughed again, this time lower and rich with satisfaction. She turned and picked up the book, placing a soft kiss against its binding. Her life, her future was in her hands. Something she'd only dared to fantasize about in the darkest hours of the night. It had seemed such a far-fetched idea, one she'd doubted she had the courage to pursue. Maybe she'd always hoped her father would find her science circulars. If so, she was a bit of a coward for not being able to step past the threshold of her comfortable home and seek out what she wanted.

You weren't afraid to kiss Darius back...

Well, she admitted to being unsure. He was no virgin, nor was he the type of gentleman she'd practiced flirting with. For all the warnings she'd heard from matrons about the unsavory realities of what nongentlemen did, she couldn't say she believed them. His kiss had excited her, and she liked the feeling. It was wild and unpredictable, but she discovered herself pleased to know he'd be watching her.

She lamented nothing.

❧

"Perhaps you are too old for such an important task."

Dr. Nerval drew in a sharp breath, but the man sitting in front of him only smiled at his outrage.

"Do not forget, Compatriot Silas, I am the one who discovered the girl."

"And allowed her to slip through your fingers."

The doctor stood, refusing to remain in the chair that sat alone in the middle of the room while Silas and two of his fellow Helikeians viewed him from a raised dais.

"A temporary situation. Her father still believes I am her salvation, and I will utilize his faith in me to bring the girl back into my custody."

"See that you do," Silas informed him. "Nothing else will satisfy us."

Silas picked up a gavel and pounded it on the desk in front of him. The sound was like a pistol discharging in the room. The other Helikeian compatriots hid their faces in the shadows, never uttering a single word to help him identify them. The two doors opened, and he had no choice but to leave.

"Do you think he can do it?" one of the other men asked solemnly.

Silas laced his fingers together and sighed. "You should never have lost track of the mother, Compatriot Peyton. Your failing has now resulted in the Illuminists gaining yet another Pure Spirit who was supposed to be ours." Silas turned to look at the man on his left. "The only reason we still tolerate you living is because you somehow manage to maintain your post among the Illuminists."

"The girl would have been born inside their Order if I hadn't succeeded in having her mother accused of treason. It wasn't a simple task to plant enough evidence on her to convince them to proceed with charges. The grandmother has a great many friends. The end result was a victory. Mary Aston left the Order, thereby providing us with the opportunity to claim her children. Such was my mission. It is Dr. Nerval's failing that allowed the girl to be discovered by the Illuminists."

Silas flattened his hands on the tabletop. "You make excuses like a child. Your mission was to marry Galene Talbot so her bloodline would become Helikeian, and it would not have been necessary to claim her grand-daughter." He looked at the other man. "Things ran more precisely within our ranks when the weaklings were disposed of regularly."

"Now they survive long enough to spawn, so we may watch our proud race become less perfect with each passing year," Compatriot Heron agreed. "You have a mission to complete, Compatriot Peyton. Bring honor to your name, or expect every member of your line to suffer for your failing."

~☙~

"I can see your new novice is keeping you awake at night," Lykos muttered the moment he arrived in Darius's office.

"How is the little lady settling in after four weeks as a member of our Order?" he continued while shrugging out of his overcoat. He hung it on a coatrack along with his top hat. "Happy, is she?"

"Happiness isn't a requirement."

Lykos raised an eyebrow before sitting down in one of the chairs in front of Darius's desk. "But sleep is."

Darius handed over the report Lykos had come for, but his friend left it on the desk after one disinterested look. "I wonder if her eyes will be as darkly ringed as yours."

"My lack of sleep has nothing to do with Miss Aston."

"I should have come sooner. You've been stewing too long in your own musings and are beginning to believe them."

Darius pushed the report closer to Lykos, but Lykos leaned toward him. "You've all the makings of a jilted bride, my friend. Do us both a favor and enjoy Miss Aston's fascination with you."

Lykos picked up the report and stood.

"Considering her past, it could well end in disaster," Darius remarked.

Lykos shrugged into his overcoat and tucked the report into an inside pocket.

"Has she shown any signs of disloyalty?"

"No." Darius stood. "She's inquisitive, insatiable for more knowledge, and curious about the sections of the chambers off-limits to her.

"Hmmm…inquisitive, insatiable, and curious," Lykos repeated with a smirk. "Some of my favorite qualities in females." He reached for his top hat and settled it on his head with a smooth motion. "Stew too long, and I believe I will be happy to help her leave Puritan society behind completely."

"The hell you will," Darius growled.

Lykos abandoned his teasing demeanor. "She's

been here for four weeks. Keep locking yourself away in this office, and you'll never notice when she finds someone else to befriend."

Darius chuckled. "I notice everything about her."

Lykos pressed his ear device. "Why do you think I came to fetch this report myself? Someone needed to make sure you heard reason."

"I am doing the logical thing by ignoring her."

The door was fully open now. "Perhaps as a Guardian you are, but I rather hoped I was talking to the man you've hidden beneath the duty."

Lykos turned and left, the hem of his overcoat swaying slightly.

Darius didn't allow the door to close but strode out into the hallway. He knew where Janette would be, had a full accounting of her every movement. But he stayed away from her, watching her when he knew she couldn't see him. There were corridors that ran parallel with the ones the novices used, giving him the chance to observe her without her knowledge. He found her with ease, spotting her among the other novices. She'd abandoned her dress and moved easily in a pair of cycling pantaloons. There was no blush teasing her cheeks for how much of her legs were on display, only a sparkle in her eyes that told him she was enchanted with her studies.

He stared at her and cursed himself for a coward. Here, he could feast on the sight of her, all the while knowing he couldn't lose the battle to reach out for her because the wall would stop him.

He'd lose the battle otherwise. That knowledge was hard and smoldering deep inside him. For the moment, his determination was strong enough to keep his feelings under control.

But it was a battle. One being fought between time and the strength of his fascination with Janette. His discipline wouldn't last forever.

❧

Janette collapsed into the plush chair in her chamber. She sighed as her feet rejoiced, but the rest of her body still throbbed and ached.

"It didn't take you long for you to insist on joining an advanced class."

Janette jumped. She landed on her feet with her arms up in a fighting position, but Darius only considered her with a slightly amused expression.

"These are my chambers."

"Privacy is not the right of a novice," he reminded her. "Ten weeks should have been long enough for you to read through the laws of our Order."

"I've read them several times, Mr. Lawley." She lowered her arms and resisted the urge to smooth back the hair glued to her forehead from class. Her Asian fighting uniform was rumpled and soaked with perspiration. No man had ever seen her in such a state, or at least not until she had become an Illuminist. But truthfully, she was more annoyed that it was Darius catching her so disheveled. The class itself she adored because it was teaching her to defend herself, an idea that gave her a great deal of satisfaction.

Besides, she didn't need to be thinking about pleasing the man with her appearance. "I should have expected you to choose such an inappropriate time to exercise your right to inspect my chambers."

He took a long step closer, looking far too comfortable for her. His emotions were neatly concealed behind an expression she couldn't read, while she battled to keep her feelings from erupting.

"The entire point of novices being told they can expect inspections at any time is so that you understand any misconduct will be uncovered."

Janette swallowed a sharp retort. "Do not despair, Mr. Lawley. I have noticed your bullyboys watching me with complete devotion."

"Good."

He walked past her, inspecting her chambers. The laws gave him the right, and she had seen the logic in such an action, but having the man in her personal space agitated her.

Liar…you've been pining for him…looking for him as often as he's been watching you.

She walked into the small room that served as a kitchen. It was only a space of four feet but had everything she might need since she took all her meals in the hall like inhabitants of a castle had done centuries in the past. At least she had a private bedroom and wasn't expected to sleep in the kitchen as her ancestors had.

She opened the water line and watched cool, clean water flow from the spout into a cup. Ten weeks still wasn't enough time for her not to marvel at the clearness of the water. As crisp and clean as country water, and it smelled good too.

"It was best for me to avoid you, Janette."

She jumped, not expecting him to follow her into

the kitchen. The water sloshed onto the front of her Asian top before she turned to face him. Darius appeared pleased with his effect on her.

"I agree. Please let us continue to ignore each other."

His expression darkened. "You understand my position now. A relationship between us would only complicate the action of performing my duty."

She set the cup down. "Your assumption that I will turn traitor is quite insulting. My mother was not convicted."

"Yet my suspicions are justified, considering your mother never faced the charges levied against her." He moved closer. "Only a guilty person would run to avoid punishment."

"Or one who felt trapped and helpless," Janette offered. "I know a thing or two about seeing those around me who I considered family turning into my worst enemies."

His expression softened. For a moment, he appeared caring and even tender. "Your mother had rights, Janette. We expect every member to answer accusations without turning cowardly."

He believed her mother's actions confirmed her guilt. His gaze was hard and unyielding on the point, but Janette couldn't accept it. Her mother had educated her with a purpose in mind; she honestly felt it was so she could join the Order her very blood was a part of.

"All the more reason for us to continue to ignore each other." Disappointment went through her, digging its claws in deep enough to make her ache.

Darius didn't miss it either, but what surprised her

was the similar look flickering in his dark eyes. It lasted only a brief moment before he masked it.

"It isn't a sin I believe you carry simply because of your association with her," he offered, but the note of kindness in his voice only pressed on the wound she'd felt since being ripped away from her mother by circumstances.

"Association? She is my mother. I love her."

Darius shook his head and tapped the pin on his lapel. "To wear one of these, you will have to take an Oath of Allegiance."

"I am aware of that."

One of his dark eyebrows rose before he shook his head.

"I know you haven't read the Oath yet, because you aren't allowed to see it until you've studied for nine months. Believe me, Janette, this isn't a time to assume you know more than you do. The Oath of Allegiance will force you to be firmly on one side or the other. Your mother is not a member. For the moment, she is on the other side of where you stand."

She wanted to insist that he was wrong but knew otherwise. What was it about the man that needled her pride so much? All she wanted to do was stand up to him, no matter what. It wasn't logical, but it was almost too much to control.

"Part of the Oath will entail your promising to stay away from members banished from the Order. Your grandmother received a reprimand for taking a message from your mother."

He held up a hand when she opened her mouth to argue. "Your mother failed to present herself in front of a Marshal when she was summoned. The only contact she is allowed with any Illuminist member now is to face those charges." His tone had softened, but it was deeply serious. "You will be expected to maintain a silent distance until she proves herself innocent. She must honor our laws or be cast out. The Helikeians would have sent an assassin after her if she were a member of their Order. We believe she has the right to be heard before being judged."

He was warning her again. This time it cut deeply. Janette struggled to maintain her poise. Her father had always been fond of telling her that nothing in life was free, no clean bed nor bowl of morning porridge. Everyone earned their way by some means or other.

If she wanted to remain safely behind the solid doors of the Solitary Chamber, protected from her father and Dr. Nerval, she would have to earn the right.

"Then by all means, finish your duty and be gone before I am tempted to be friendly toward you." She walked back into the main parlor room so he could pass her on his way to the door. Reaching forward, she tapped the section of wall where the Deep Earth Crystals were held and completed the circuit so the door opened. "I wouldn't want you to hesitate when you come to kill me because we had engaged in pleasantries."

He shut the door with a press on his ear device and stopped in front of her. "This is not a game, Janette. Turn against us, and I will have to silence you." His expression remained deadly serious, sending a chill down her spine. She was certain of one thing: he was not a man given to flights of fantasy. He would judge the world around him on fact alone.

"Five other young women your age were taken into that clinic and lobotomized."

She raised a hand to cover her mouth, but he wasn't finished.

"You were raised in a secluded portion of town, Janette. I assure you, the guards at my doors knew very well they might have to defend their posts with their lives. A newly acquired Pure Spirit such as yourself would be worth killing for. Dr. Nerval has already destroyed the minds of five other women to find a Pure Spirit, and he'd have sent you to surgery if you'd failed his test."

She'd be sitting in a cell, a ward of the state, if it had happened. She forced the horror down her throat.

"Make no mistake. Dr. Nerval is a Helikeian and a prime example of just how savage his kind are. If he fails to recover you, he will be executed, along with his entire bloodline."

"That is barbaric," she sputtered. "Just because the knowledge that this Order is founded on goes back to the ancient world doesn't mean we should act like them."

"Yet clinging to that knowledge when the rest of the world was collapsing into the Dark Ages is what formed us. Inside our Order, learning continued without the interference of the rise of religions or the sanction of monarchs. Honor is still the core of who we are."

"Yes, and that is what I admire about you." She spoke without thinking.

For a moment, she was caught in the grip of renewed desire. He was so close, the scent of his skin teased her senses. She found his features too attractive, his dark hair gaining her attention. His jawline was always perfectly clean, no hint of stubble, only the slim sideburns he kept to a minimum. A ripple of sensation moved across her skin, awakening longing. She wanted to touch him, to allow her fingers to glide along the border between smooth skin and whiskers.

"Go. Now that you've performed your duty."

Before she said anything else foolish, before she responded to him again.

His eyes narrowed, making frustration nip at her. It wasn't easy. She wanted him to stay, to kiss her again. She forced her desire down and made herself recall her rights.

"According to the laws, I have the right—"

"To send me on my way once I have made my inspection," Darius finished for her. His voice had lowered, becoming husky. "You also have the right to ask me to stay."

And become her lover.

Of all the things she had learned in the last month, discovering the Illuminist attitude toward sexual activity had been the only thing that shocked her.

"I won't be taking a man who doubts my integrity as my intimate companion, Mr. Lawley."

She expected him to be frustrated by her rejection; instead, admiration appeared in his eyes. He reached out and stroked the surface of one cheek with the tips of two fingers.

Sensation shot through her, stunning her with just how intense it was. Despite his having touched her before, it was as if being apart had heightened her senses. Or maybe it was because she knew how much she'd enjoy his touch that her heart accelerated.

"Which is exactly why I wouldn't have accepted the invitation. I am not just a Guardian. I am the head one here."

So the man was testing her. Her temper threatened to boil over. "So your decisions concerning me must remain above reproach?"

He nodded, but she could see in his eyes that he didn't care for her words.

Good, at least she wasn't alone in her frustration.

"Kindly vacate my chambers, Guardian. If you're satisfied, that is."

At least she was becoming quite used to being tested. It made it easier to push her emotions down and lock them beneath the resolve she harbored for achieving her goals. She stared straight into his eyes now, able to aim steady confidence at him. Now frustration made its appearance in his eyes, but there was also something that looked very much like satisfaction.

"I am not satisfied, and neither are you, but I will leave."

She closed the door behind the man, but the gears running the automatic workings of it didn't allow her to slam it shut like she wanted to. The soft sound it made when at last it finished closing was far from satisfying.

Testing her.

That knowledge should have soothed her. Or at the very least given her more resolve to dismiss the man. Instead, she battled to keep her longing for him locked behind the logical reasons she'd spent too many nighttime hours assuring herself were valid.

Still, she felt the heat of desire licking across her skin. The damned need had remained persistent through her first month as an Illuminist. If her classes hadn't already confirmed that infection came from bacteria, she'd be tempted to say her father had been correct in saying lust was a disease.

But it wasn't. It was worse than that; it was part of her nature, something no amount of self-control might destroy completely. Oh, she might resist temptation, but the need would always be there to test her resolve.

At least, when it came to Darius that was proving so.

She moved into the bathroom and discarded her Asian clothing. Every other part of her training was beyond satisfying. There weren't enough hours in the day to soak up all the new experiences at her disposal. Including taking a lover.

She stepped into the shower, as it was called, and let the cool water fall down on her. So much better than a bath, the continuous running water prevented dirt from lingering on her skin.

Healthy and logical. Such words formed the foundation of her life now, which should have allowed her to easily dismiss her longing for Darius. Her mother had never discussed with her the frank details of married life, but her Illuminist sisters had no blushes staining their cheeks when they teased her about the dark Guardian caught so often watching her.

In a way, it had been a relief to have him speak to her at last.

She sighed and finished washing her hair. Moving

over to the heated air vent, she turned it on and raised the levers until it was warm enough to begin evaporating the water left in her hair.

She and Darius had been facing off like duelists, and plenty of members had noticed it. Which only made her angry; because the man was in charge of the entire complex, he could easily leave her to his men.

"His eyes follow you," they teased her.

She knew that without being told. More times than she cared to admit, she'd felt his gaze on her and looked around to discover Darius watching her. Part of her wanted to rail against his distrust, but the other half found contentment in knowing he was near. Many would tell her she was being childish to cling to him. After all, she was her own woman now, one training to earn her way without the need to marry.

Illuminist women wed only for love.

Her father would call it *low-class*, and she finally understood just why she'd been raised to never stand next to Illuminist girls her age. Their ideas were vastly different, but Janette admitted she liked them. They had a confidence she envied and was working hard to gain. There was no topic forbidden, no information denied her because of some belief it would lead her down a path of damnation. Honesty was more important to the Illuminists—and being open to the hard facts as they appeared. That didn't mean she was going to take Darius for a lover.

Her nipples drew into hard points in spite of the warm air flowing across her skin. She muttered something grumpy before moving off to find a chemise. She hurried because the air was chilly once she left the heated air unit behind. Yet her hair was dry, and she did adore being able to wash it regularly. Her skin felt smoother and cleaner too. The chemise floated down into place, but she still felt exposed. Even after several weeks of not having a matron dictating how many layers were necessary to preserve her morality, the feeling of her breasts being unbound was still very noticeable. But she slept so much better without the stiff stays.

The spring was giving way to summer now, and the air was warm enough that she enjoyed having her feet bare at night and not hidden beneath the ruffle of a nightgown. Her first night had been a shock when she'd opened her wardrobe to discover not a single full-length gown to smother her while she slept, only chemises that ended at her calves and hung off her shoulders by soft cotton yokes.

She was at ease and yet more aware of her body. Darius watched her from her dreams as well, tempting her with memories of his kisses and the longings they unleashed. She was a fool, but at least not so great a fool as to not have sent the man away without taking his bait. She wouldn't invite him into her bed; she didn't want him in her bed.

Liar…

&c&

"Where's Decima?" Darius asked Lykos as he entered his office. The most common reason for his fellow Guardian to be in his Solitary Lodge was because Decima was hunting in the area. In spite of Decima's full standing as a Guardian, Lykos rarely allowed her to perform her duty alone. A fact that frustrated her greatly. "Don't tell me she evaded you."

Lykos eyed him from the chair in front of his deck with a laziness Darius knew was false. Normally he was amused by his friend's ability to appear so disinterested in his orders; today he wasn't.

"Your dark visage sent her scurrying away for fear you'd use those teeth your growling displays so prominently on her soft neck."

"I swear, Lykos—" Darius warned.

"Yes, I heard you quite clearly, as did the men in the outer room, because you let loose before the door was completely closed. You used three languages too, no doubt to ensure you made your point to any and all listening."

Darius sat down. "Your point is well taken."

"Good. I'd rather not give you Decima's message. The important issue is whether you recognized just how deeply Miss Aston is digging into you." Lykos grinned, offering Darius a view of the devilish good looks the man was blessed with: even teeth that were creamy white to complement his fair hair. "Decima put it ever so much more bluntly, and you know I don't care to smear a lady's name, even when she did charge me with delivering the message."

Darius opened his mouth but shut it before demanding to know what his fellow Guardian had said. Decima was a female, but she could cut to the bone with her words as well as any man.

"Miss Aston is my responsibility, nothing more."

"In that case, Decima suggested you visit a brothel before she's tempted to geld you for the sake of mercy." Lykos offered him a slip of paper with an address on it. "Decima does know a fine establishment from a poor one."

Darius took the paper and crumbled it. "All Decima knows is how to follow you, my friend, and take down the name of the tart you run to anytime she sends you away unsatisfied."

Lykos stiffened, but it was only a momentary crack in his polished exterior. "You seem to be misinformed, my friend. Decima has never satisfied me, nor have I asked for the pleasure of her rather notable skills."

"And you dare to accuse me of being the fool," Darius countered. "At least I haven't known Janette as long as you have been hiding your interest in Decima."

Neither man was comfortable with the topic. Tension filled the office as they faced off. Lykos never took unmasking well, and when it came to Decima, he was even less amused by having his emotions noticed. He shrugged at last.

"It is easier to judge than critique one's own actions," Lykos admitted.

Darius drew in a deep breath before turning the conversation toward business.

"Any word on Janette's mother's whereabouts?"

"None," Lykos said. "She's disappeared as cleanly as she did the first time, proving she's a better Illuminist than we gave her credit for."

"Raising a daughter among high society who could pass the entrance exam the first time while her husband opposes our ideals was clever," Darius remarked. "We need to find her."

Lykos contemplated him for a long moment. "To

prove her innocence, or to confirm your choice to ignore how badly you want to be in Janette's bed?"

"Finding her will force my hand one way or the other."

There wasn't another man alive Darius would have admitted it to either. Mary Aston needed to be found—alive. Watching Janette was his duty, one he felt tightening around his neck with each passing day because the situation was simply too settled for his liking; they couldn't stay that way. His suspicions were aroused as he toyed with the idea that Janette was every bit as clever as her mother.

Had her illegal entrance into his Solitary Chamber been innocent? Or a carefully crafted test to see if she was a Pure Spirit? Was Mary continuing her treason through her daughter? It was a possibility he'd be a fool to overlook. It was also possible that every flutter of her eyelashes was carefully employed to snare his attention and redirect it away from the facts.

She'd kissed him back.

Why?

The question was burning a hole in his mind. Tonight's visit to her chamber was a slip he couldn't afford. He'd given into the urge to see what she was doing in her private space with his own eyes, distrusting his men and their reports on her activities.

Would he have declined her offer to share her bed?

He wanted to believe so but honestly wasn't sure. Desire nipped at him constantly. It wasn't fading as the days slipped by, and he ensured they had no chance to be alone. Instead, he'd allowed himself to be drawn to her tonight and found himself being grateful she hadn't risen to his barbed invitation.

Was she innocent, or had she been groomed to dupe him?

"You have more than your fair share of suspicions," Lykos muttered.

Darius drew in a stiff breath, cursing his mental wanderings. "They keep me alive as well as they serve you, or shall we discuss just what the root of the barrier is that keeps you from taking Decima to your bed?"

Lykos surprised him by laughing. "The root of the issue is while your so-charming distraction has only begun to study Asian fighting, Decima is a full master of the arts. Allowing her anywhere near my cock could be very costly if I misjudged her mood."

"I'm sorry to hear you doubt your Asian fighting skills."

Lykos stood and offered him a bow. "I'd say it's been a pleasure, but you'd know I was lying. I believe I am going to try to shake Mary Aston out of the shadows now, because I do miss the congenial man you used to be."

"Do convey my gratitude to Decima for her note," Darius offered, his voice polished with gentlemanly grace.

Lykos grinned at him. "You'll see her before I will. She's decided to assist in your Asian fighting classes in an effort to befriend Miss Aston. No need to thank me. I'm sure you would have thought of a similar course of action…eventually. After all, women will seek out other women for confidence before a man."

Lykos sounded playful, but he was studying Darius's response. Tension returned to needle him with just how deadly the game might turn. But the fact of the matter was they needed to trust Janette. Deep Earth Crystals powered their world. Only a Pure Spirit could hear them, and such individuals were born so rarely.

The ruling council was no doubt counting the days until Janette took her Oath and they might put her into service. Mining was pitifully slow without a Pure Spirit. The dirt had to be lifted away with blasts of air because any trauma to the crystal would kill it.

They needed to trust Janette, and yet her mother's actions had made it almost impossible. Darius waited until the door closed securely behind Lykos before cursing again.

❧

"It's nice to see another woman in class."

Janette looked up from her stretching to see the woman from the Brimmers' party watching her.

"I am Decima. I don't believe we were introduced."

"No, but I remember you," Janette said, trying to hide a grimace as she reached for her toes.

A soft laugh came from Decima before she sat down next to her and assumed an identical position. The woman could lie all the way down, hooking her hands around the arches of her feet.

"That just isn't fair," Janette muttered.

Decima turned her head to look at her over the top of her kneecap. "I'm surprised your mother didn't have Asian fighting arts included in your education. I hear she did a very good job preparing you, in spite of your father's disdain for our Order."

"I see Darius has given you the details of my family."

Decima never blinked. "I am a Guardian."

Janette was stunned but smiled because it was wonderful to see another example of how woman weren't kept out of any part of Illuminist life. "I'd

never even heard of Asian fighting until I came here."
But she was going to learn. It was another amazing
thing the Illuminist lifestyle offered, a type of fighting
that allowed a smaller person to have just as much
impact as a large, muscular man.

Of course such a skill didn't come for free. She
drew in a deep breath and forced herself to stretch.
The muscles along the back of her leg hurt, but she
succeeded in grabbing her toe. Flexibility was a key
factor in some of the kicks, and she had a long way
to go.

Janette stood as the instructor walked toward the
front of the classroom. The floor was polished wood
and might have been used for a dance studio or sword
instruction, but hidden in the back of the Solitary
Chamber, this room was used to teach a type of
fighting that made boxing look like child's play. The
pugilists competing in gentlemen's clubs were amateurs
when compared to the skills she was beginning to
learn: graceful kicks that were brutally effective, hand
techniques that could shatter wood, or even concrete.

Not that it was going to be easy to learn the art.
There were very few women in the class, and by the
second day, Janette knew why. When she'd awakened,
she hurt in places she hadn't known could hurt. By the
end of the first week, she was sure she might never walk
again because her thighs hurt so much. Sunday was the
only day of the week the class didn't meet, and it had
given her enough of a break to restore her determination
not to allow anything to intimidate her into quitting. Or
admitting she just didn't have the will to continue.

But a moment of inattention almost made her

rethink her position. Decima ended up as her partner during kicking practice. The woman was obviously more advanced in the study of Asian fighting. Janette never saw the kick coming. One moment Decima was facing her, and the next all Janette heard was a snap of fabric from Decima's pants as her leg hooked around and connected with the side of Janette's head. Pain shot through her and sent her stumbling. At some point her ankle twisted beneath her falling body, but she was fighting too hard to maintain consciousness to notice all the details of how she ended up sprawled on the floor.

"Janette, I'm so sorry. I didn't realize you didn't know how to drill with a more advanced student."

There was a buzzing in her ears, but a few deep breaths ended it. "Um…what was that kick called?" Janette took the hand Decima offered her and stood up. Her knees wobbled a little, but she shook it off. "And when can I begin learning it?"

Decima stopped contemplating her and smiled. "You've already begun. All kicks begin with the basics. It will take you time to build the proper strength."

"I see." She didn't, but she intended to find a book somewhere in the vast library that would shed light on the matter. "So, show me how to avoid getting kicked in the head."

Decima's lips twitched up again, and this time there was a flare of enjoyment in her green eyes as well.

"Like this…"

❧

"You hit her too hard."

Decima stiffened but didn't turn around to look

at him. "It was necessary. No one can control their instincts. If her mother had trained her, she'd have blocked or landed with skill."

Lykos made a small sound of agreement. "So now that you know she is truly a novice, at least when it comes to Asian fighting, maybe you should get back to tracking her mother down."

Decima turned. Every line of her body was visible in the Asian clothing. Even Illuminist women found the lack of corset a bit exposing, but she wasn't among them. Let them look at her natural shape; she wasn't going to hide who she was to please any man.

"Ruthlessness isn't a commodity you and Darius hold exclusive rights on. I will use my skills to form a relationship with her. If her mother has inserted her daughter into our midst to use her as a source of information, all I need to do is be close enough to catch them when they believe it is safe to meet."

"So now you have the perfect reason to talk to her again. Well played, but ruthless."

Decima turned her back on him. Lykos was a distraction she didn't need. His gaze traced her curves too often, and she didn't care for the heat that rose into her checks when she noticed him looking at her. Becoming a Guardian hadn't been easy; even in the Illuminist community, the security posting was still widely considered more suited to a man.

Well, she was a Guardian and she intended to be the best one possible. Such a goal did not allow time for personal relationships. Besides, it wasn't as though Lykos had tender feelings for her. The man only harbored lust for her, and he satisfied it often enough at the high-end brothel he liked to believe she didn't know he visited. There was one thing all men, from all classes of society, had in common—they didn't like going without physical comforts and had no trouble lying about it.

She did know, and the knowledge stung. So she walked away from him, intent on ensuring he never noticed the weakness.

A Guardian could never be vulnerable. She had learned that lesson well from Darius.

❦

"Dr. Nerval to see you, sir."

Howard Aston looked up at his butler in surprise. "Show him in immediately."

His butler nodded, which Howard felt was wasting precious time. The house had felt empty for the last month. Too quiet by far and he was eager to hear that his daughter was ready to return home. Such an event would allow him to bring his wife back from the country, and they could return to being a happy family.

"Dr. Nerval, I am delighted to see you."

"Hmm, yes. Unfortunately, I do not come under pleasant circumstances."

Howard's blood chilled as he watched the doctor settle into one of the armchairs in front of his desk. He discovered it was an effort to maintain his dignity as he waited for the man to explain himself.

"Your daughter's condition is quite advanced."

Howard forced himself to sit down and appear civilized. "How so?"

The doctor peered over the rim of his spectacles.

"She is not responding to treatment, at least not in the manner that I had hoped."

"I see." Howard flattened his hands on the desktop. "Will you be sending her home now?"

"Absolutely not." The doctor punctuated his comment with a tap from his cane. "It would be irresponsible of me. She is quite ill."

"I am not following you," Howard said.

The doctor held up a finger. "The infection stems from her mother. To sterilize it, I shall need to treat both of them. By neglecting to tell me of your wife's familiarity with the Illuminists, you made this process much longer than necessary."

"Now see here, sir, my wife is well-balanced."

"Is that so?" The doctor leaned forward. "I find your faith in me lacking. Everything I told you about your daughter proved to be true."

"Well…yes," Howard admitted. "But I have never seen any symptoms from my wife."

"You mean she has concealed her Illuminist weakness since your marriage."

Howard stiffened. "Of course she has. It was the only condition under which I would wed her."

The doctor shook his head. "And who was responsible for directing your daughter's education?" He leaned forward as Howard settled back in his chair. "Did you give her freedom to instruct your child? Abovestairs? Behind closed doors?"

"Children belong in the nursery. It is the only civilized way for them to be raised," Howard defended himself.

The doctor stamped his cane against the floor.

"Your wife was a member of that foul collective. She reared your daughter to respect them while you remained confident that she was performing her motherly duties. Yet there is the difficulty. Your wife was raised on the milk of the Illuminists, and she passed it on to her daughter."

Howard leaned forward. "So you cannot cure her?"

"Of course I can, but there would be little point in returning her here to be infected again. Your wife needs to join her daughter in treatment."

Howard drew in a deep breath. "I sent her to the country."

"Recall her."

Howard nodded before really thinking the matter through. The doctor stood the moment he did and bid him good day. The empty house felt strange, the sound of his heartbeats growing louder as the silence became nearly deafening.

He slapped the desktop again and once more until the stinging of his palm distracted him from his emotions.

Logic was the way for civilized men to run their lives. Order produced contentment, while emotions only yielded chaos.

He reached for a sheet of paper and began to pen a letter. A very precise, logical message.

❦

Her head ached.

It was the only reason Janette woke barely an hour after going to bed. At least, it was the only reason she'd admit. She hadn't felt Darius in the room with her—no, she would not allow him to invade her dreams.

Even if she was lying to herself. The man had been in her dreams.

Her bedchamber was dark and silent, but as sleep cleared from her mind, she looked about, searching for what had awakened her. She could feel the man near her, as if another sense had appeared with her introduction to him. It irritated her, making her restless because she always seemed to be thinking of him.

Tonight, it was worse than usual. She couldn't seem to banish the feeling that he was watching her. His men were at their post most certainly, but the feeling of being watched was much stronger. She was tired but fully awake, and closing her eyes felt wrong— dangerous, actually.

Passing her fingers over the base of the bedside table lamp, she pushed the operating crystals closer together until soft light illuminated the room. Only the bare essentials furnished it, but she still wasn't satisfied just by seeing that she was alone. The dark outer room teased her with possibilities.

She felt like she was being studied. A tingle of awareness went down her spine, but it wasn't frightening. She owed that to Darius. She felt secure in the building because it was under his charge, and yet the feeling that she wasn't alone persisted.

She pushed the bedding aside and stood.

"Who's there?" She strained to see through the shadows of the entry room, searching for the owner of the gaze she could feel on her. "I know you are there…"

"But you cannot see me. Still, your instincts are good, Janette."

She jumped. Darius materialized from the shadows with a look of satisfaction on his face.

"You certainly needn't appear so pleased by the fact that you…" She hesitated over admitting just how upset she felt.

"Frightened you?" He closed the distance between them, and she realized he'd left his overjacket somewhere. He was clad in only a vest, his shirt-sleeves bare. Heat teased her cheeks as she noticed, the knowledge oddly intimate. It was the first time he had looked at ease. The man had always been so frustratingly formal in her presence.

Except for when he kisses you…

"You simply startled me." She lifted her chin and forced her lips into a smooth line. "It isn't very kind of you, Mr. Lawley."

"Then why did you jump?"

His tone was full of arrogance, and perhaps if he'd been in his overcoat and cravat, she might have swallowed the urge to argue with him.

"Why? Because you appeared in my bedchamber in the dark of night when I am not accustomed to receiving company. You are quite mistaken to insinuate otherwise, Mr. Lawley." She drew out his last name and watched his eyes narrow. Good. The man deserved to be set down, even if she didn't believe he'd remain there for long.

His ear device was still in place, but his hat was missing, granting her a rare, unobstructed view of his dark hair. It didn't lay smooth but curled slightly, increasing the feeling of intimacy. Heat stung her cheeks, and his gaze settled on the telltale stain.

He bent slightly, offering her a bow that was just as informal as his clothing. Yet somehow it felt more sincere than any courtesy he'd ever offered her. For the moment, he wasn't a Guardian and she wasn't a novice. It made her tremble. The need they tried to cover up with their formalities was more than happy to be allowed free.

"My purpose was to uphold my duty by ensuring you did not overlook seeing a doctor after your accident today. Yet you are correct. My approach is less than appropriate."

He was studying the side of her head. She reached up, feeling only a slight tenderness now.

"I am fine and old enough to decide if I need medical attention." She had to temper the urge to snap at him again. She looked away, worrying her lower lip as she tried to still the tempest brewing inside her. The storm of emotions defied her comprehension. She should have been alarmed to be standing there in naught but a chemise; instead, her thoughts dwelled on just how much she liked his lack of formality.

Her father was correct about one thing: becoming an Illuminist was certainly causing her to behave wantonly...or at least to think that way.

But for now, they were only two people, their allegiances discarded. Relief traveled through her like an evening breeze on a summer day, leaving her to simply enjoy the moment. His dark gaze studied her, and for a long moment, it looked like he was enjoying himself as well.

"You are unaccustomed to just how deadly Asian fighting arts are. A single kick can kill, Janette."

His tone was firm and edged with authority. It crushed the mood, allowing her to look back at him and see only the Guardian he'd been for the last few months. She was suddenly sick of the battle between them. "I don't want to quarrel; it's been a long day. Don't you trust your night Guardians to be as dedicated as you? They saw me as I entered and asked after my welfare."

His lips twitched, granting her a flash of teeth. "I don't trust you not to speak up out of some sense of invasion of privacy or hesitate because your recent encounter with a so-called doctor was less than pleasant."

The heat burning her cheeks doubled. His attention shifted to it, but there was no real way he could see her blushing in the darkened room. "I understand the risks of the class. Besides, I am not so foolish as to ignore my own health."

Even if he'd uncovered something she'd liked to avoid thinking about. A tiny shiver traveled across her skin as she recalled the matron and orderlies at the clinic.

"I would have gone for help if I needed it," she insisted to dispel the memory. There would be no lingering trauma from the clinic. She refused to allow Dr. Nerval such a hold over her.

"You may see for yourself."

She turned her head so the light bathed the spot Decima had hit. But he reached out to trail his fingers across the hot surface of her cheek instead of the place he claimed to be concerned about. Such a simple touch, but it sent her heart beating faster.

"But something else is affecting you, Janette. Something you're fighting to ignore."

"You're being inappropriate again," she scolded softly. "I didn't invite you here."

He chuckled and stroked her cheek once more. This time he stepped closer and she retreated, only to have the wall stop her. His hand slid upward into her unbound hair.

"You have, with every flutter of your eyelashes when you pass me in the hallway. Every time I see you, your cheeks turn scarlet, and that is without a doubt an invitation of the most personal kind."

"You're only seeing what you want to see. Looking for justification for your forwardness."

His lips thinned. "I'm being truthful. You wanted to be an Illuminist. Truthfulness is part of our nature."

"What you are being is bold, Darius, and it has nothing to do with the Order you serve."

He combed his fingers through her hair, and the sensation silenced her. It was overwhelming, so many points of awareness being triggered by so gentle a touch. He returned to her nape, cupping it in a solid grip she recalled very well. The memory had appeared often in her dreams.

"Which is your fault for appearing like a siren."

"I was in bed. Besides, I am not so irresistible." But she was breathless. Her lungs were working double time to keep pace with her racing heart, and she could smell his skin now with each quick-drawn breath. It was dark and hard, and when combined with the way he held her neck, rational thought threatened to escape her completely. She didn't want to think; she wanted to fall back into the swirling storm of emotions and experience them fully.

One dark eyebrow rose. "I beg to differ," he whispered. "Your effect on my defenses is devastating."

He moved close enough that she could feel his breath against her lips. He pressed closer to her and placed a gentle kiss against the burning warmth of her cheek.

"The light in your bedroom illuminates every curve through the ever-so-delicate fabric of your chemise. Even the hard points of your nipples were illuminated to draw me to you."

She gasped and tried to push him away, but he had her pinned to the wall.

"Either you are a calculating female or ignorant." Another kiss landed on her temple before he raised her face to look into her eyes.

"I am not ignorant." The retort came from her pride before her common sense intruded enough to warn her.

"Then I happily accept your invitation."

"It wasn't—"

He silenced her with a kiss. It was harder and more demanding than the ones she recalled, but something inside her approved wholeheartedly, that wild, primitive need that had bothered her every night since the last time he touched her. It consumed her like a fever, rising to engulf every inch of her while he pressed her mouth to open. It wasn't a request, not a gentle teasing, but raw demand. A hand landed on her hip, smoothing over the curve and up the indentation of her waist until he brushed the side of her breast.

She shivered, but he didn't stop. He cupped her breast and brushed his thumb across the puckered nipple.

"Exactly as I witnessed." His fingers teasing the hard nub.

He was nearly growling, but that pleased her; the sure evidence that she had pushed him beyond his polite persona fed the wildness swirling around inside her.

"Exactly what I cannot resist…"

He trailed a line of kisses down her neck, hungry, needy ones that set off a yearning deep inside her belly. She found herself straining toward him, offering herself to him as he moved lower to where he was still cupping the mound of her breast.

"Oh sweet Christ…" She moaned when his mouth closed around her nipple, the thin cotton nothing between them as he sucked the entire tip inside his mouth. He toyed with the sensitive peak, circling it with the tip of his tongue while he cupped the entire mound to hold it in place. His other hand found the curve of her hip and slid around until he was urging her forward and bending her back to allow him better access to her breast.

It was insanity, yet she didn't fear the surge of emotions boiling over the top of her self-control. It felt natural, as though she'd known exactly what she wanted, despite not really understanding how her desires might be satisfied.

But she did have one fear. It pushed its way past the delight wrapping around her.

"Go away if all you are going to do is tease me, Darius."

He lifted his head, the light behind him making it impossible to read his expression. He was part of the night and yet solid beneath her fingertips. More than solid, he was hot, and she could feel the beat of his heart.

But she resisted being drawn down into the web of sensations before making her own demand.

"I mean it." She curled her hands into fists and pushed against him. "I've spent enough dark hours longing for what you start but never finish."

"You don't understand what you're asking."

But he did. She could hear it in his tone—hard and edged with a promise that sent a shaft of need tearing through her belly. She felt empty, the walls of her passage transmitting how much they wanted to be stretched around his male organ. Oh yes, she understood the carnal nature of her yearnings, and with the darkness surrounding them, ignoring her desires didn't seem so important. Being truthful did.

"I understand that you make me want you in my bed."

She slid along the wall until she could move away from him. Her chemise billowed as she moved, allowing the crisp night air to tease her overheated skin. "You know what you are doing, which makes it the worst sort of unkindness to tease me with kisses before you rip yourself away, glowering at me as though I've tried to sully your virtue. Well, Darius Lawley, you entered my private chambers tonight, so don't you dare attempt to pin the guilt on me. Take responsibility for your actions. You're an Illuminist, after all."

He growled softly and followed her, stalking her slowly. "You're justified in that accusation, Janette."

She bumped into the opposite wall, and he braced his

arm across the space to keep her pinned in the corner. Raw emotion blazed from his eyes, fascinating her.

"I'm drawn to you, in spite of every logical argument." He moved closer. "In spite of every suspicion I harbor about you, I still came here tonight, still lost the battle to stay away from you."

"And you are still angry with me for it," she said, his words hurting her pride. "A high-society girl isn't good enough for you? Just wait. I'll make something of myself. Your world is not too much for me to handle, and neither is anything you can tempt me with."

She stepped up to him and slid her hands over his jaw. A shiver shot down her spine instantly. She savored the sensation, moving her hands slowly before lifting them away. A tiny sound of regret escaped her lips.

"I can shoulder responsibility for my actions, but I refuse to allow you to accuse me of causing your fall from grace."

She ducked beneath his arm, full of longing but satisfied with herself. She'd faced him like an equal, like an Illuminist.

But he caught her about the waist, binding her to his length as he placed a kiss against the side of her neck. So quickly she was at his mercy; he controlled her completely while she felt the unmistakable tremor of him fighting to hold on to his control.

"I fell from grace long ago…" He cupped her chin and raised it to expose the full expanse of her throat to his lips. "I'm drawn to you by the promise of regaining what I lost."

He silenced her reply beneath a kiss that threatened to burn her. She'd never known another human might be so warm or that she could enjoy a kiss so much. He grasped her hair, maintaining control of her head while she turned to face him. His mouth slipped along the delicate surface of her lips before pressing her to open her mouth for something deeper.

When she yielded, his tongue swept across her lower lip before thrusting down to tangle with her own. She jerked, twisting away from him because there were too many points of sensation; it was impossible to understand what she wanted to do. But he kept her steady, stroking his tongue across hers until she mimicked the motion.

She thought they'd kissed before, but she had been naïve. Now she truly understood what passion tasted like. It was consuming and intoxicating, blinding her to everything but the next touch. Darius didn't make her wait for it. He released her hair and slid his hands down the sides of her body, slowly, too slowly for the need pulsing in time with her racing heart. She reached for him, cupping the sides of his head, but froze when her fingers encountered the cold metal gears of his earpiece.

He was still on duty.

And yet he continued to kiss her, fanning the flames licking at her insides. All of it was threatening to send her emotions boiling over, and she couldn't bear to have him turn his back on her. She feared she'd abandon every scrap of pride she had just to stand up to him if he left her now.

She pulled on the earpiece, trying to disconnect him from the duty he was so dedicated to.

He lifted his head, interrupting their kiss. The light

shone off his eyes as his hand stopped hers from lifting the bit of technology away. She could see the protest flickering in his eyes.

"I have only myself, Darius, so if you want to be my lover, I am only interested in the man beneath the Guardian."

His lips twitched, but only for a moment. The grin never reached his eyes; instead, she witnessed him battling to understand her. Or maybe just the effect they had on each other. It felt like a living, breathing conflict surrounding both of them.

"It's been a long time since I have been myself..."

It was an admission, one that caused her breath to catch in her throat. Tenderness filled her for the first time when he lifted his hand off hers and allowed her to remove the emblem of his office. He watched her set it aside before a gleam of wickedness brightened his eyes.

"This clothing is part of the job too..."

He had the vest open in a flash, the sound of several buttons hitting the floor making her smile.

"So you were a boy once." She marveled at the playfulness appearing in his eyes.

"A very long time ago." The shirt followed the vest but floated more slowly until it disappeared into a dark shadow.

She hadn't realized she'd been retreating until her legs hit the bed. She would have tumbled onto it if he hadn't wrapped an arm around her waist to steady her. She still ended up on it, but he controlled her descent and scooped his opposite hand beneath her knees so her legs joined her. The bed rocked as he sat down beside her.

She only had a moment to realize he was in bed with her, bare-chested, before he extinguished the light. Her belly twisted with something that was a mixture of excitement and trepidation—she refused to acknowledge fear. She was an Illuminist woman, or at least on her way to being one and taking a lover was her choice.

His shoes hit the floor before his hands cupped her hips once more. He eased her up onto her knees while his mouth found hers again. There was something intensely enjoyable about the way his hands gripped her hips. A spike of need tore through her thoughts, rendering her mind useless again. Darius seemed to feel the same way. He kissed her but slid his hands down her thighs before grasping the delicate fabric of her chemise and pulling the garment upward.

She gasped, unable to control the sound. Even firm in her choice, she still felt the bite of vulnerability as the night air became the only thing touching her skin.

"Siren...luring me close with your song..."

His voice was husky and almost unintelligible, but he pressed her back while laying a trail of kisses along her body. It was so much simpler to close her eyes and allow herself to be immersed in sensation.

Delight...really.

And she wanted more than to have it given to her. She reached for him, running her fingers along the ridges of muscle his clothing had hidden. It was suddenly clear why men dressed in so many layers; their bodies were lust-inspiring.

She wanted to touch and kiss every inch of him, but Darius was intent on the same course. They moved around each other, taking the opportunity to touch the skin available. The bed rocked as they rolled, and the bedding ended up on the floor.

He captured a nipple, and she arched up, twisting her hands in the remaining sheet beneath her.

"So…damned sweet…" He moved to its twin, capturing it with a soft growl.

"Flesh is not…sweet…" she panted. Logic had not completely escaped her yet.

He chuckled, the sound full of promise. "Yours is. I could dine for hours upon it."

One hand had left her hip and smoothed a path onto her belly. Why had she never noticed how soft and sensitive the skin there was? Her passage was aching with need, sending tremors along her limbs.

"I'm ashamed to say I can't wait that long."

She sighed with relief and reached for him, craving more contact. His hand traveled lower, until he was teasing the soft curls covering her mons.

"It is a shame truly to not taste all of you…"

His fingers parted the folds of flesh protecting her clitoris. Her breath froze in her throat but went shooting out when he touched the little bud at the top of her sex. Pleasure so acute, it shared commonalities with pain tore through her. There was no time to think, only to respond. Her cry echoed around the room, sending a scarlet blush to her cheeks with just how out of control she was.

"But I'm as needy as you are…" Darius confessed.

He didn't grant her the opportunity to argue. His mouth claimed hers once more as he freed his length. Curiosity urged her to look at it, but Darius never stopped kissing her long enough for her to see. Instead, he lifted her leg and pushed it up to allow his hips to nestle between her thighs. She felt the hard nudge of his cock burrowing its way between the folds of her sex. She was far wetter than normal, the fluid easing his way. It was hard, harder than she'd ever believed a man's organ might be, but her passage ached for it. Even as he began pushing into her body and her flesh protested, she was arching to take him deeper out of instinct.

But the pain became white-hot. She gasped and tried to twist away. Darius didn't allow her even a tiny bit of freedom, his larger body pinning hers to the surface of the bed.

"I can't—"

"You can," he whispered against her neck, his tone rich with confidence. Her pride swelled in response, and her body suddenly stopped protesting his entry. With a final moment of resistance, his cock slid completely inside her.

There was nothing but burning pain; it raced up from where his hard flesh pierced her. No sound escaped her throat because her lungs had frozen as the agony held her tight in its grasp.

He withdrew, granting her relief, and she sucked in a deep breath before he sent it racing out of her lungs when he thrust back into her. She moaned, the sound low and primitive. The pain wasn't as intense. Her cry faded, and so did the overwhelming hurt.

"I should have realized you were a virgin…"

His body shook as he tried to rise. With a soft curse, he lowered himself again and began thrusting slowly.

She wanted to know why he'd thought she wasn't a virgin, but it suddenly didn't matter. Nothing mattered except the growing sense of satisfaction building beneath the friction his thrusting produced. She moaned again, but for a different reason. This time, the cry was forced out because there was too much pleasure to contain. She lifted her hips, meeting the next plunge, and gasped when the pleasure tightened.

"That's the way. Meet me, Janette. Take a hand in your own pleasure…"

His voice was dark and dangerous. Each word was spoken through clenched teeth, and she found his tone suited her perfectly. She wanted to arch and take his length. There was nothing controlled about the moment; it was a storm of yearning that saw her straining upward for each thrust while she grabbed his shoulders and held him in place. Her fingernails cut into his skin, and he growled with satisfaction. Deep inside her passage, every muscle clenched tighter and tighter until the passion burst like a bubble, sending shards of white-hot delight out in every direction. She was swept away by the shock wave, held in place by the hard motions of Darius driving his length into her a few final times. He tensed, snarling something unintelligible before his cock delivered a hot spurt of seed.

They were locked together for a moment, currents of pleasure hitting them from within until they both collapsed into a warm puddle of satisfaction. Janette sank straight into it, never protesting when it took her away into oblivion.

∽

The room was dark.

Janette opened her eyes, confusion sweeping through her.

Had she been dreaming of Darius again?

The certainty that she hadn't imagined him was hot against her back. One hard arm was draped across her waist while he gently cupped a breast. A dull ache made itself known between her thighs, driving away any remnants of confusion. Her mind cleared completely, bringing details back with a rush. Her cheeks burned with a blush while her temper flickered to life.

"Why didn't you trust I was a virgin?" She moved, gently trying to dislodge his arm, but he only pulled her closer until he was curved around her back and his feet caught hers.

"We are not holding a discussion tonight, Janette." His voice was full of authority, and it chafed.

"I didn't invite Guardian Lawley into my bed, so stop issuing orders," she insisted while trying to squirm out of his hold.

He held her tight. "As you like, *sweetheart*. I'd suggest discussing this topic in the morning."

She wiggled, but he kept her secure. "Why? Oh yes, you like to be the one handing out the accusations. Well, Darius Lawley, I have as much right to be suspicious of your Order's plans for me as you do of my desire to be here."

He sighed, sounding exasperated. "A well-founded point, which we can debate in the morning."

"Because that is when you shall withdraw behind your duty? Put your suit back on like armor?"

She meant to sound stronger; instead, hints of insecurity edged her words. Doubts began to undermine the confidence that had seen her so boldly losing her virginity to a man who was not her husband.

Who would never be her husband.

"Because lovers only allow pleasure between them in bed."

He kissed her head, gently stroking her body and lulling her back toward slumber. She wanted to ask him questions, but it was far more satisfying to heed his words.

"I'd much rather be only your lover for the moment, Janette. The harder edges of life will be waiting for us at dawn. There is no need to rush into contact with them. Indulge me, at least for as long as the sun is down. Neither of us can change the fact that life is hard, but we can enjoy the moments when it decides to leave us alone."

Now his tone was soft and tender, tempting her to just follow his lead. He was her lover. By her choice. A desire that was natural, supported by scientific fact, and nothing to be labeled immoral. At least among the Illuminists, it was. She smiled and surrendered to sleep.

She was an Illuminist, even if Darius didn't trust her.

But do you trust him?

She realized she wasn't sure.

Five

"Janette?"

She sighed. "Why are you always in my dreams, Darius?"

The pillow was warm and comfortable beneath her cheek. She snuggled against it but frowned when the bedding slid off her shoulders to allow the morning air to nip her.

"As much as I find your confession charming, I cannot remain to enjoy it. I must return to my post."

He was real.

She rubbed her eyes and stared at the undeniable evidence that the night had not been some elaborate dream. Darius was dressed and sitting on the edge of her bed. In the morning light, the man looked too large for the modest room. She must have slept half on top of him because the bed wasn't wide enough for them both. But his hair lacked formality, the dark strands curling just a bit around his temples. The top button of his shirt was still open, betraying the fact that he didn't care for being confined. Little hints of who he truly was, and she wasn't the only one noticing them. His eyes narrowed in a lazy manner while he studied her and stroked the side of her face gently. His gaze settled on her lips for a long moment as enjoyment flickered in his eyes.

"I did not want to leave without saying good-bye."

There was a tenderness in his tone she didn't know how to deal with. He stroked her cheek once more, and she wiggled away, uncertain of everything in that moment. His expression became guarded.

"And Decima hit you too hard." His attention had shifted to the side of her head.

"It is only a bruise, and not the worst one I have ever had." She sat up and had to grab the sheet before it slithered down to expose her bare breasts. "I was quite the energetic child. Much to my father's disdain. Yet my mother encouraged me. I suppose I understand why now."

"Sitting about in a nursery is unhealthy." He stood, and his vest gaped open where three of the buttons were missing. He pulled the edges wide in response to her attention on it. "The motivation for my early departure. I would rather not give the rumormongers a feast. They'll have enough to discuss as it is, since the Guardians at the gate will log my exit time."

The earpiece was back in place. "We'll talk tonight."

"That isn't necessary," she insisted. "I understand the way it is here. You made no promises to me last night."

One dark eyebrow rose in response. He came back toward the bed and planted one hand on either side of her. She was trapped, unless she wanted to release the sheet to push him away. It wasn't the first time he'd insisted on making her see his point, but this time it felt intensely personal. This wasn't the Guardian imposing his will on her; it was Darius, even if it was impossible to separate the two completely.

"I disagree, Janette. You don't understand me as well as you think you do." He pressed a hard kiss against her mouth. "Which is my fault. We will talk, and I will be back. That is a promise."

He was on his way out of the door before she sputtered a retort.

"You certainly do enjoy telling me what to do."

His gaze slipped over her, and his lips curved roguishly. "That is not the thing I enjoy doing most with you."

She blushed scarlet and heard him chuckle on his way out of the entry room.

"Knave…" she said as she rose from the bed.

"Rogue…"

Her next thought got stuck in her throat when she looked at the bed. It was marked with her blood.

Had he used her?

Guilt chewed on her as she began to dress for the day. If the man had only been interested in satisfying his lust, there would have been no reason for him to wake her and promise to return.

Had she used him?

Was she just trying to prove she was no longer her father's obedient child? If so, she should be ashamed. Darius might be an arrogant rogue, but he deserved better than to be used.

✦

"Why hasn't she been put into service?"

Darius fought to maintain his control. His office was full of Illuminists from different branches of the Order. Grainger was a Guardian of the highest rank like himself, but there was also a Marshal and a Cultivator. Lykos had ushered them all in with a frown darkening his face.

"Miss Aston is installed the same as any novice. She has taken well to her regimen of classes," Darius answered.

"Yes, yes, indeed she has," Professor Yulric agreed. "Quite the bright and very inquisitive young student."

"She should be in the field," the Cultivator insisted.

Darius felt his temper straining. "Without proper training? Are we so desperate we would forget the foundation of our Order and leave her ignorant while utilizing her natural abilities like a beast of burden?"

"I think of it as more of an acceleration of her training," Grainger said, "and a recognition of just how important it is to be ahead of the Helikeians in the hunt for Deep Earth Crystals. The recent eruptions in the Hawaiian Islands have produced perfect conditions for crystal growth. Now is the time to ensure we harvest the new crystals."

Darius directed his next comment to the Marshal standing by silently. "What about her Oath? She isn't bound to the Order. Showing her the Crystal Fields might well see us handing our critical information over to the Helikeians."

Everyone turned to see what Marshal Agapitos would decide. As a Marshal, he could adjust the time frame of a novice's training, but Darius had never witnessed it in his lifetime. It was one of those laws put down for the direst of circumstances.

"I am willing to hear her Oath now. Captain Kyros is ready to depart for the islands as soon as we transport the girl to the airship port."

"How did you know about the girl?" Darius demanded, losing control of his composure for a moment. It was suddenly very personal, their desire to rip Janette away from his authority. Lykos eyed him curiously but held his tongue for a change.

"Yes, an excellent question," Professor Yulric said. "Rushing leads to mistakes. The girl should observe our laws. A fact made more important by her unfortunate upbringing outside the Order. She has a great deal to learn about Illuminist life, facts she needs to accept and understand fully before taking the Oath of Allegiance."

"She is not a normal member," Grainger insisted. "As a Pure Spirit, her posting will be in the field. Since she knows nothing of life at a Solitary Chamber, better not to risk her forming any attachments here."

Grainger sent him a pointed look, one that made Darius suspicious. It was early afternoon, just enough time for a spy to have reported where he had been last night.

"Since the Marshal has made his decision, I will have Guardian Decima assigned to Miss Aston on the journey," Lykos announced.

Grainger frowned and cut a look toward Agapitos. The Marshal waved his hand. "That will not be necessary."

Darius raised an eyebrow. "It is the law and the right of any female novice Pure Spirit to have a Guardian of the same gender. Since I do not have one under my command, I am grateful to Guardian Lykos for sharing Decima."

"Yet—"

"I am not finished," Darius interrupted Grainger. "I am also resigning. Effective immediately."

"You are what?" Professor Yulric demanded.

Darius grinned at him. "My apologies for the abruptness of my announcement, Professor. I hope you will forgive me, but I intend to accompany my fiancée on her journey to the Crystal Fields."

"Your what?" Marshal Agapitos demanded.

"Miss Aston and I have discovered a strong draw to each other."

Marshal Agapitos stepped forward. "Spending the night in her bed does not mean you have the right to accompany her. She is a Pure Spirit. It is in the best interest of the Order for her to be put to work in the Crystal Fields. As a Marshal, this is my decision, and you are out of line to dispute my dictate, Guardian Lawley."

"Her field assignment clearly falls under your authority," Darius countered. "Which is why I have resigned my posting. A spouse or soon-to-be spouse of a Pure Spirit has the right to accompany them to their posting. Only a Helikeian would be savage enough to deprive her of her happiness."

The Marshal was turning red. "One visit to her bed does not make you her fiancé."

"I beg to differ with you, Marshal," Darius cut through the man's sputtering. "Miss Aston was raised among high society. She never would have shared her bed with any man she did not believe would do the honorable thing. Besides, I'm curious as to where you are gaining your information about my personal relationship with Miss Aston."

"I'm quite curious myself," Lykos added, the tone of his voice menacing. "None of this was revealed to me when I brought you here."

Marshal Agapitos glared at him. "Your duties as Guardian do not include being present for decisions about where Pure Spirits are deployed."

"But it is our duty to understand just where your information on private matters is flowing from," Darius interrupted. "Miss Aston was in the hands of the Helikeians before we rescued her. Information on her has been held secret, and yet you appear here with full knowledge of who she spent the night with. If we serve the same Order, why are you gaining information about my Solitary Chamber through any other channel than myself? I have approved no information transferred on Miss Aston."

"Members talk, Mr. Lawley, especially when a man in your position is getting involved with a novice," Agapitos said. "You are jumping to conclusions. We have been wrestling with this decision for some time now, ever since her membership was recorded— which is common information, I would like to remind you. The news that she was forming a relationship with you only urged us to take her in hand before there were any complications. Explain to the girl that she needs to go and think over such a serious matter as marriage. It is only an emotional response to her unfortunate incident at the clinic."

"That would be futile," Lykos insisted smoothly. "They are quite taken with each other."

"Nonsense," Agapitos insisted.

Darius leaned forward. "I assure you, Marshal, I will be accompanying Miss Aston." His tone had become deadly.

"Only if she supports your claim of an engagement," Agapitos shot back. "Something I wish to hear from her lips before you have the opportunity to inform her of my decision. You will remain here while two of your men find her."

⚓

She had a lover.

Janette found the knowledge distracting. By mid-afternoon, it was bordering on being irritating. She attended her classes, but her thoughts shifted to Darius more and more often.

That sinful thing matrons whispered about and preachers warned all good souls to avoid. Lust was the instrument of the devil, an occupation of the low-bred. In short, the path to damnation.

Or was it simply the truth of human nature? Many of her classes had opened up her thinking on the matter of right versus wrong. Among the Illuminists, honesty was more important, which made taking a lover acceptable…so long as both partners were honest, and a man never forgot to ensure his partner didn't conceive without her consent.

Having a lover was such a foreign idea, and then again, she realized her mother had always answered her questions about intimacy. It was an oddity she hadn't questioned but should have when she considered the other girls in her age group hadn't been raised with such openness. Most of them eagerly awaited enlightenment on just what their wedding night would consist of, and they whispered during balls.

Well, she wasn't wed, but she'd lost her virginity. Obviously her father was correct about the Illuminist teachings taking her away from the path of straight and narrow because she didn't feel any shame. In fact, she was relieved to have finished what Darius had walked away from before.

Maybe she was wanton, but at least she was honest—an Illuminist trait. She smiled as she walked back toward her quarters, but the men stationed at the gate made her pause. They recorded her comings and goings, and today, it chafed to know she was scrutinized so closely. Yes, she was a Pure Spirit, but there were moments when she felt branded by it instead of unique.

Was that the reason Darius resisted her so strongly?

Was she a pariah? Destined to be set apart simply because of her ability? She fingered her badge, marking the lack of Deep Earth Crystals. She was different. Uncertainty chewed on her, and she turned her back on the gate. The Guardians watched her curiously, but she left them wondering where she was going.

She found herself in the library. It wasn't the first time she'd wandered among the aisles of literature. Housed in the back of the complex, it was filled with books on every subject, not just the society-approved ones.

She often ignored her fatigue because of some engrossing book she'd discovered here, but now, she found her thoughts returning to Darius. He'd always held the superior position, always looked at her like he knew more than she did. When it came to being lovers, she wanted to change that, which sent her searching out books she wasn't even sure the library would have—erotic books.

There had been rumors of young boys being caught with such books and in high-priced brothels that promised patrons delights found among the pages of some Eastern manuscript.

Would Darius enjoy such things?

Heat stung her cheeks. She was assuming the man would be interested in another night in her bed. In spite of his promise to return, she really needed to prepare for the night to pass without him making an appearance.

Illuminists did not place the same moral importance upon coupling.

She cringed at her own harshness. Perhaps she was not as converted as she wished because she could not label her night with Darius as coupling. It had been vexing, irritating, frustrating, and satisfying like nothing she'd ever experienced or even suspected she might. A storm of sensation she discovered herself longing for now that she had sampled it. Ignorance truly could be bliss.

She frowned, rejecting that logic. She had known there was something she craved from the moment she met Darius. Something she felt only he would be able to satisfy. It had always been between them, the urge to needle him or stand firm in the face of his arrogance to prove...to prove...well, to prove that she was worthy of his attention. Many would label her primitive, and she had to agree that their encounter had indeed been primal. A combination of urges and responses she didn't contemplate. She had merely responded.

"What you're looking for is farther down."

Janette jumped, startled by Decima's voice. "Excuse me?"

Decima smiled, a small, knowing curving of her lips. She lifted one hand and pointed to the back of the aisle.

"Down there. You're correct to be searching under 'erotic arts.'"

"I…umm…"

Decima shook her head and walked past her until she reached up to pull a book from the shelf. When she looked back at Janette, there was a wicked gleam in her green eyes.

"All the female novices make their way here." She looked up at the row of books in front of her. "And why shouldn't they? Men do not hold the exclusive right to enjoyment when it comes to intimacy."

Janette moved closer, excitement sending her heart beating faster. Decima offered her the book, and she reached for it while fighting off the urge to look over her shoulder.

"This social trend of insisting women be ignorant of sexual pleasure is relatively new," Decima added before pointing at some of the books. "Many of these are translations. The pleasures of the flesh have long been recorded so the next generation can learn and enjoy producing the following generation. Many cultures believed sexual gratification kept one's life energies in alignment." Decima looked back at her. "That's a pillow book. They used to be given to brides to enhance their wedding nights. Be careful. Once you look at those illustrations, you won't be able to stop thinking about them until you try them."

There was a promise lurking in her tone, but what interested Janette the most was the hint of challenge shimmering in her eyes, a sort of test from one confident female to one who wanted to be on even footing with her.

"Not that I wouldn't mind you employing some of those tactics on Darius."

The book nearly slipped from her fingers. Her cheeks burned, but she bit back the stupid question that tried to pass her lips. Of course people knew where their head of security had spent the night.

"Why would you say that?" Her second question was more thought-out. Decima nodded with approval.

"He's too arrogant," Decima announced. "Forgive me for being so forward, but it would delight me to think of him being at your mercy with his ever-so-solid control shattered for once."

Janette covered her mouth before her laughter traveled through the maze of bookshelves to others nearby. She actually had to run her fingers over the small silver pin on her lapel to remind herself that the topic wasn't scandalous. At least, not for an Illuminist.

Decima reached up and pulled another book free. "Mind you, that's just the woman in me talking. Darius is a fine Guardian, one of the best. I respect him. Highly." She opened the book and smiled when she viewed the illustration. "And still, the woman in me would like to know that he is just as capable of being reduced to a quivering mass of cravings like everyone else."

She snapped the book closed and returned it to the shelf. "Under the cover of privacy, of course. I'd never wish him to be undermined where others might see. He has honor, something too rare to be tarnished."

There was a hard warning in her eyes that fascinated Janette because Decima looked so feminine and fragile. But the spot on the side of her head throbbed, reminding her just how capable the Illuminist woman was. Janette's gaze moved to the Guardian symbol on Decima's lapel pin. Even among Illuminists, a female Guardian was rare.

"I'll leave you to your studying."

The Pillow Book felt heavy in her hands once she was alone.

A quivering mass?

She opened the book, curious to know how a man such as Darius might be made to quiver. Her cheeks never cooled, but heated up until she was sure they were likely to catch fire, but she didn't stop turning the pages. The book was illustrated with bold colors. The first pages were innocent enough, with the couple meeting each other. But then they appeared without their clothing, and her nipples tingled before drawing into hard points when a turn of the page offered her a view of the male suckling at the breasts of his female consort.

Darius had done that to her…

Her hand shook, and she did look over her shoulder before turning the page again. Now the male was unclothed, his cock standing swollen and hard. His consort was taking the head of the engorged member between her lips while he leaned back in ecstasy.

Could she really do that to Darius?

The whispers of the good wives and matrons filled her ears until she forced herself to turn the page.

Now her jaw dropped because the male was returning the favor his companion had just done for him. Clearly depicted, the female had her thighs spread while her lover lapped at her open slit.

Her heart was beating faster, and between the folds of her sex, her clitoris began to throb. She had enjoyed Darius fingering the sensitive nub, which made Decima's words echo in her thoughts.

Be careful. Once you look at those illustrations, you won't be able to stop thinking about them until you try them.

At least that way, she'd get a look at the man's cock. She smothered another round of giggles. Cock indeed. Well, she knew what it was called and not just the scientific term.

You know what it feels like too…

But she hadn't seen it—Darius had made sure to control the pace of their encounter. She returned her attention to the pages of the book, determination cutting through her astonishment. She would look and learn, and if Darius returned to her bed, she would do her best to make sure the man spent as many hours thinking about her as she was about him.

Decima felt the tension in the air. It prickled along her nape as she entered the security offices. There were too many hats on the stand, announcing visitors. She ducked into the closet and discovered three overcoats. She reached for one and turned back the lapel without hesitation. In the business of being a Guardian, there was never a time when unusual circumstances shouldn't be investigated—especially when they had a newly discovered Pure Spirit installed as a novice. There would be more than one Solitary Chamber that would like to take her under their wing, and there were also the field councilors, who would enjoy getting their authority on the table before Janette completed her training and understood fully what she would face as a full member of the Order.

Men and their ambition. They always tried to take advantage of women.

A hard hand wrapped around her face as she was pulled back into the coats. She reached for the fingers clamping down on her mouth, but he had her trapped against his body in a second.

"Easy…"

She sent her elbow back into her captor's ribs anyway. Lykos stiffened and muttered a curse.

"There's the thanks I get for trying to warn you."

He had her bound to his body, and she cried out softly as a tremor traveled down her length. "Warning doesn't include touching."

She expected him to release her, but instead, she felt his breath against her temple and along her cheek, as though the man was smelling her.

"I need you out of sight," he whispered softly against her ear. "But you already noticed we have visitors and considered it worthy of investigation."

"Which does not involve touching."

He chuckled, his chest rumbling against her back. "Kindly refrain from removing the single element of enjoyment from this moment."

"Release me, Guardian Claxton."

He sighed, sounding frustrated. She tried to ignore the sound, tried to remain irritated by his manhandling, but the tremor moving down her body was eroding her resolve. Her flesh was responding to him in spite of every reason she had to resist. Solid, logical reasons that didn't seem to be fending off the sensations flooding her.

"Such animosity, when I was preventing you from being discovered."

Decima heard the steps outside the closet and the door closing behind a pair of men. She wanted to refuse to thank him but needed to deny the impulse to be childish. Lykos Claxton would not strip her of her control.

"Your point is well-founded and passed now." She pushed against him, but he held her still. "And another begins. Perhaps we shouldn't be so quick to discard it."

His voice was husky and thick with promise. It should have repulsed her, but her response was more horrifying than that. Her nipples contracted, proving without a doubt that she was tempted by his touch.

She could not tolerate such weakness.

"I believe we should."

She made to move away from him, and his arms loosened. Relief speared through her for a brief moment before he turned her around and bound her in his embrace yet again.

"Damn you, Lykos."

He chuckled at her again. "In a manner of speaking, yes, you have cursed me, Decima. Is it so wrong of me to want to test just how much I affect you?" He cupped her nape, teasing her with his strength.

"Yes. It is unprofessional, Guardian."

"But you are trembling, Decima."

Somehow, she'd managed to blind herself to just how much larger he was than herself. He loomed over her, leaning down until his breath teased her lips.

"And we are in a coat closet." He flouted her attempts to remain proper. "What better location to dispense with formality?"

"I was seeking evidence." She pressed her thumb straight up into the soft, unprotected flesh behind his jaw. "What better time to recall my dedication to duty?"

He stoked her nape a final few times as she increased the pressure against his throat. She was hurting him; she knew her skill well, but she could see him enduring the pain, challenging her to see how far she would go. Sweat popped out on her forehead before she stopped pressing deeper into his flesh. Her cheeks brightened with shame.

"I should kiss you anyway…" he muttered. But he released her with a short grunt. "You're a woman, Decima. There is nothing wrong with remembering it from time to time."

There was everything wrong with it. At least so far as it went with Lykos. No Guardian would respect her if she took any of them into her bed. She had to be only another Guardian among them, her gender irrelevant.

"I am glad you didn't."

The words threatened to stick in her throat, but she

forced them past the longing biting at her. It would pass. She ordered it to do so.

"I'm not," Lykos groused. "However, we have work to do."

Decima should have been relieved to have him turn the topic toward duty. Yet she was torn between what she wanted to feel and the desire to have him make good on his promise.

It had been a very long time since she'd been kissed.

But Lykos's expression was sober now, telling her she would not be changing that fact anytime soon.

"She is not in her quarters."

Marshal Agapitos frowned. "At this hour? I find that highly suspicious."

"You needn't."

Decima moved into his office on silent steps. Today she was wearing a tweed coat with a pair of cycling pantaloons that made her look very much like a member of the Illuminist community, but she still gained narrow-eyed glances from their guests.

Decima measured up expertly, arching one delicate eyebrow in response to the chilly welcome. "She is in the library. Rather predictably so, I might add. I deduced where she'd gone when the gate personnel told me she'd turned around instead of going into her chambers after classes."

"Just how is it predictable?" Grainger demanded.

Decima offered him an innocent look. "She was raised outside the Order, but as it has been noted, she is happy to adopt our ways."

"You are telling me nothing, Decima Talaska," Marshal Agapitos complained. "Make your point. You are after all a Hunter; as such, you should be able to tell me precisely where Miss Aston is."

Decima offered them all a knowing look. "I perform my duty well. One large disadvantage Miss Aston has suffered due to her mother's decision to leave the Order is being raised amid Puritan teachings. Since she and Guardian Lawley have an understanding, it's logical to realize she went to the library to expand her knowledge of intimacies."

Grainger flushed, but Decima was more interested in Darius's reaction. A flare of heat appeared in his eyes. For a brief moment, his perfect control vanished. She discovered herself envious of Janette.

Marshal Agapitos snapped his fingers at the two men clearing their throats near the door. They hurried to press their ear devices and escape the harsh demands of their superior.

Decima discovered herself fighting the urge to glance toward Lykos. She won but suffered the sharp sting of regret.

❦

She really needed to stop.

Janette replaced the book and tried to force herself to leave before opening another volume. There were already dozens of ideas swirling around inside her mind, teasing her possibilities if she were bold enough to try them.

If Darius ever returned to her chambers was a more prudent question. The man might well rethink his position on making good on his promise, after all. She had not been a very accomplished lover. Not in the least.

But he would honor his word. She felt that fact burning like a candle inside her heart. Beyond the need that flared up between them, she realized there was a deeper emotion allowing her to be drawn to the man.

Trust.

The man was arrogant, and it irritated her, but he was also honorable. She'd heard the word her entire life, had had it wielded over her like a whip, and yet Darius was the first man to actually embody it.

So was the real reason she'd allowed him into her bed because she needed someone to cling to?

Her memory offered up a vivid recollection of the way his kiss had sent her flesh to tingling.

No…it wasn't the only reason.

She reached for another book; this one, in Japanese. She couldn't read the text, but the drawings seemed to be about erotic games—to be specific, challenges to see how well a man might control himself while his cock was being sucked. She stared at the images of females hiding beneath a banquet table and nearly turned purple as she contemplated such things happening in the formal dining room at her father's house. Her sire would die.

Or maybe it was just what he needed.

You're being wicked.

She smiled, unrepentant.

"Miss Aston?"

The book went tumbling to the floor as her cheeks

flamed scarlet. Two burly men stood at the end of the aisle, watching her intently.

"Yes?"

"Please come with us."

They both wore lapel pins with the Guardian seal set above the crystal, but she had never seen them before. She was bound to cooperate with them, but they reminded her far too much of Dr. Nerval and his orderlies. Tension knotted her belly instantly. It was so acute, she felt nauseated. The months of security she'd enjoyed suddenly disintegrated, dropping her back to that time when she had been prey to everyone around her.

But she wasn't that girl any longer.

She lifted her chin. "Where are we going?"

One of the men shook his head, but Janette stopped and shot him a stern look. "Every member has the right to know where they are being summoned," she quoted from the law book. They were in the middle of the library now, and her voice carried to several other members. An older woman stood and stepped forward.

"You have been summoned by Marshal Agapitos; that is all you need to understand, Novice."

Her insides remained twisted when the older woman frowned and moved closer. "We have no Marshal here," the older woman remarked.

The pair of Guardians exchanged a look. "He has arrived to deliver this Pure Spirit to her field posting. You need not be concerned."

"I am still a Novice for the better part of a year," Janette informed them.

Two more members drew near. They brought a

sense of family to her that made her realize how alone she'd felt.

"You are a Pure Spirit, and your Novice year is being cut short."

"How illogical," the older woman remarked. "The value of solid training should never be underestimated."

"You are not involved in this matter," one Guardian snapped, but the woman refused to be intimidated.

"I disagree. You have failed to uphold the law. Because she is a Pure Spirit does not absolve you of answering her when Miss Aston asks where she is going. Someone please summon our Guardians."

Janette felt the sweetness of relief for only a moment before one of the men grabbed her upper arm and tugged her toward the entrance of the library. The older woman gasped, and chairs skidded against the floor as other members tried to intervene, but they were too far away. The Guardian pulled her into the hallway before anyone reached them.

"Meddling old bat," he muttered while pulling her down the corridor. He and his partner looked rapidly around them, betraying their intention not to be caught again.

Janette lifted her arm and dropped it neatly over the hand clamped onto her arm. She struggled to use the Asian fighting technique exactly as she'd been taught, but she lacked the skill only practice would have given her.

She ended up scuffling with the man but broke his grip long enough to sweep his leg out with a low kick. He went tumbling, but she didn't have time to watch her success. She turned to confront his partner.

There was a muffled curse as two of the members from the library grabbed him from behind. Their actions granted her a moment of freedom, and she turned to run. She had no idea where she was going, only that she needed to flee.

She ran headlong into a solid body. Her control was slipping, and she fought against her newest threat with rising panic.

"Easy, sweetheart."

She went still in an instant, shock freezing her.

Sweetheart? Since when did Darius call her sweetheart?

His tone had been low, but when she looked up, she was hypnotized by the flicker of rage in his eyes. It wasn't aimed at her but flared up bright in response to the men trying to force their will on her. He gave her only a moment to absorb such a change in demeanor before he shoved her behind himself.

"Now, what are you two doing to my fiancée?"

❧

She would have liked to believe she was dreaming—ascribing everything that was happening to the illogical actions of her subconscious would have made sense.

But Darius was still sitting beside her, and the tension inside the carriage was thick enough to slice with a butter knife. The two burly Guardians were perched on the outside of the carriage while Marshal Agapitos and Guardian Grainger sat across from them.

It was a good thing she'd cast off wearing petticoats, else her dress would have been draped over all their knees. Illuminist carriages were smaller, most likely a result of their women wearing more practical clothing.

Her simple skirt fit easily in the space available, but Darius was pressing close to her. The hissing of steam kept them all silent, but they came to their destination soon enough. Lykos was waiting to offer her a hand down from the carriage, and he held on to her hand until handing her off to Darius. The two men flanked her, actually pushing her slightly behind them as the carriage released the last of its steam and went quiet.

"Miss Aston, I need to make it clear to you how important it is for you to take this next step in your life among the Order. I will hear your Oath."

Marshal Agapitos was smiling at her and moving closer in spite of Darius and Lykos. Janette stepped forward, but her belly twisted because the Marshal reminded her so much of Dr. Nerval. He was a well-fed man—his vest was tight across his belly where he was trying to hide his overindulgence. He had a thin nose on which a pair of double-lens spectacles perched. Professor Yulric often wore a similar pair, but the Marshal reminded her of a weasel instead of a man of learning. In his eyes, she could see him looking at her like some treasured possession.

"I have a year to consider such a commitment."

No one liked her answer. Frustration appeared in the Marshal's eyes, but it was the suspicion in Darius's dark gaze that needled her the most.

"If that is your position on such promises, I find it easy to question this so-called engagement."

"I am going with you, Marshal," Darius remarked, but underlining his normally perfectly control was a clear warning.

"Only if Miss Aston says you are," Agapitos argued.

"Why do you care if he comes or not?" Janette demanded. She tugged her hand free and stepped several paces away from them all. "Are you not all members of the same Order? Why are you fighting over me like a pack of hounds?"

"As a Pure Spirit, you must accept that you will be deployed for the good of the Order. A fact you should know at this point in your training, Novice."

"Except you have the intention of taking me away from my studies while they are still incomplete," Janette countered. "What are you worried I'll learn before pledging myself and ending up subject to your authority?"

Marshal Agapitos smiled at her. The sort of smile one would aim at a child. "No place in life is free. It was members of this Order who rescued you from what your father had decided would be your lot. Don't be naïve in believing enjoying those fine chambers is free. Deep Earth Crystals power our world, and the demand is great."

That much rang true, making her pause before arguing again.

"Why are you resisting pledging yourself to the Illuminist Order?" Guardian Grainger joined the attack.

"Because I don't know where I'm going, and you seem to be in a hurry to separate me from anyone I know."

Maybe she was being foolish to voice her thoughts so completely, but she did enjoy being able to speak her mind. The pin on her lapel grew more precious every day as she wasn't made to simper because of her gender.

"You don't know Guardian Lawley, my dear girl," Agapitos said. "He's only employing a different method of cajoling you into being his to command. He's seducing you to keep you docile."

The Marshal was closing in on her, but Darius stepped into the man's path. Almost in the same moment, Lykos moved her farther back and Decima took up a position near her.

"Enough," Janette snapped. "Get out of my path, Darius. The lot of you may say a great many things about me, but you shall not label me a coward."

Darius shot her a hard look. "You are not the only one the Marshal is insulting, Janette, and I'll be damned if I stand by while he tars and feathers us."

There was a hint of something in his eyes that tugged at her heart. Something she couldn't quite name but recognized nonetheless. Quite by surprise, she discovered herself on the same team with him, and it filled her with pride.

She pushed her way between Lykos and Darius until she was facing Agapitos. She folded her hands in the prim fashion she'd been taught to perfect by the time she was five.

"It does sound rather un-Illuminist to be so concerned about our personal dealings."

"You need to understand what your future will be. By taking the Oath, I will be able to trust you."

"I see, and you, sir, are interrupting," Janette continued in a soft tone. "The issue of trust really is the root of this conversation."

"Exactly," the Marshal agreed.

"The lack of it, actually."

Darius frowned at her, but he held his thoughts behind a stern expression.

"Now you have pointed out that I shouldn't trust Guardian Lawley or his compatriots, and I discover myself unwilling to trust you when you seem insistent on my taking an Oath I am not completely ready to take."

She held her hand up when the Marshal began to sputter. "And kindly refrain from telling me that because I am a Pure Spirit, I must do as you say. Perhaps I am naïve; my view of the Illuminist Order never included my being shackled by your authority like a slave simply because of my blood. So it would seem, if I am going anywhere, we are all going together."

❧

Janette intended to turn her back on the Marshal. But she made it only two steps before she stopped— *froze*—because she hadn't really looked about until just then. The boardwalk beneath her feet was the same as at any train station, but the transportation waiting for passengers was nothing like a train.

Airships.

She stared in wonder, her amazement with the Illuminists renewed. What were a few sputtering, arrogant men compared to the wonder before her eyes? The ships were moored on long towers with escalators carrying up passengers. Constructed of three main balloons, the center being the largest, each airship had a passenger bay strapped to the underside.

If she were a child, she'd think they'd harnessed the clouds.

On either side of the center balloon, there were large propellers with what appeared to be steam engines beneath them. A steady stream of white vapor escaped out the back as they turned gently. The station was a masterpiece, with large windows and a raised ceiling. Everywhere she looked there was art—delicate sculpting running between the panes of glass or the benches in the waiting area adorned with carvings. The young queen's new palace could not be finer.

"At least this part of the journey will please you."

Darius placed a hand on her back. It was a personal touch, one that sent enjoyment through her.

She wanted so much to forget her suspicions and simply enjoy the wonder of the airships. But a glance at Darius, and she knew it couldn't be so. His expression was hard, and for the first time, she could see in his eyes just how deadly he might be. A chill raced down her spine. She'd read more of the laws than she'd confessed. A Pure Spirit could never be allowed to fall into Helikeian hands. It was a Guardian's duty to prevent it at all costs.

Even if it meant taking her life.

❦

"Damn Agapitos and his authority."

Lykos took the opportunity to speak his mind when Marshal Agapitos went to meet the captain. The officers were lined up at the base of one of the escalators, proving that the Marshal had seen to his details before coming to take Janette. The Marshal's Guardians flanked Janette while Decima ensured she remained at her side. They had a moment to step far enough away to speak their minds while the passengers hurried by on their way to the waiting airships.

"This entire situation stinks of Helikeians," Darius stated while looking around, searching for an escape route.

"Especially the part about not allowing either of us to converse with anyone before our oh-so-hurried departure," Lykos said. "Or Grainger's attempt to have Janette taken away while he was in your office, so nicely distracting us."

"Exactly," Darius agreed. "I do believe you and I had better learn to sleep light or risk suffering a very fatal accident."

Lykos nodded. "At least Janette had the foresight to refuse to take the Oath."

"Which will only make it simpler for Agapitos to hide her by saying she ran away once in the Crystal Fields. He's pushed her hard enough to detest her future inside the Order."

Lykos smiled slowly. "I noticed that tactic myself."

Agapitos lifted one hand and gestured his men forward. They made to grip Janette's arm but discovered just how adept Decima was at Asian fighting arts. She intercepted the first hand to touch Janette and twisted it until the man's knees buckled.

Janette gasped, half with shock and half with envy. She watched Decima reduce the larger man to a crumpled heap in seconds. The second Guardian reached for her, but she moved out of the way and felt herself bump against Darius. He pushed her behind his body with one smooth motion. But he stopped in a stance she recognized.

"So you've taken Asian fighting too," she said softly. The second Guardian held his hands up and extended one hand toward Agapitos.

"Of course, I am a Guardian."

But he was hesitating. She could see it in the way he looked around, judging his chances of escape.

"And I will protect you."

He spoke too softly for anyone else to hear her, stepping up next to her and whispering as he pulled her hand up and placed it on his forearm.

Who was he trying to convince? Her or himself?

They were surrounded, so the only path seemed to be toward the escalators.

∼∞∽

"Zenais."

Mary Aston stiffened. How long had it been since she'd heard her birth name? Her Illuminist name? She was trembling in another moment and stumbled when she turned around to look behind her. Tears stung her eyes, rising too quickly to control.

"Mother."

Galene was crying too, wet tracks of tears shimmering on her cheeks.

"You mustn't be here," Mary declared. "You should go, immediately." Pain replaced the joy that had flooded her. How long had it been since she had seen her mother or heard her birth name? She shook her head, reminding herself why she'd turned her back on everything she loved.

"You will end up before a Marshal. Please go, Mother." Mary looked out the garden window, fearing Guardians would arrive before her mother could escape. "I couldn't bear it."

"I entered under the cloak of darkness," Galene insisted. "Remember who taught you how to disappear, my daughter. Age hasn't stolen my wits."

Mary smiled and hugged her mother tightly. "You taught me well. I survived because of your mentoring. But why would you take such a chance? You'll be brought up on charges, even now, after all this time, if anyone sees you with me. You'll be convicted of consorting with a traitor."

"I know the law," Galene said grimly. "The only way a case of treason is decided is by a Marshal. I couldn't allow you to face him. There was too much evidence against you."

"I didn't betray the Order, Mother."

"I know, else I would have made you face the consequences of your actions." Galene drew in a stiff breath. "It would have torn my heart from my chest, but I would have." She nodded. "But only if you were guilty, which you were not. Now I am more certain of it than ever."

"Have you found new evidence?" Mary had to press her fingers against her lips to silence herself as hope flared up inside her. How long had it been since she had felt such elation? She couldn't recall.

Galene offered her a suspicious look. "Marshal Agapitos has had Janette's Novice tenure cut short."

"My daughter passed the entrance exam?"

Galene smiled. "Yes, she insisted on challenging it

immediately. Not that I blame her—Howard had her admitted to a clinic that was a front for the Helikeians. Thank goodness her friend saw her being locked away and went to Darius Lawley."

Mary went pale; one hand covered her mouth as horror widened her eyes. "Howard wouldn't have done such a thing…"

"He did."

Mary flushed with anger. "He banished me here and then sent my daughter to a clinic? How dare he!"

"Very easily," Galene said. "After all, he believes himself master of his house and all who live there. You and Janette are his chattel. He is not an Illuminist."

Mary shook her head. "I had nowhere to go, Mother—and before you say it, I was not going to stay and watch you lose everything by sheltering me. I love you as much as you love me. I couldn't stand the idea of you tarnishing your name by standing up for me at a trail.

"I would have," Galene said.

"I know that and I couldn't let you, not when there was no chance of my name being cleared."

"They did do a good job of making it look impossible for you to be innocent," Galene spat. "Damn them. But did you have to wed such a narrow minded man?"

"Howard fancied himself in love with me; it was better than living in the slums. He thought his sons would be men of intelligence if he wed himself an Illuminist." She laughed softly. "I don't suppose he ever considered what might happen if we had a daughter. Besides, he was my only option. I used him as much as he used me. It was fitting, in it's way. Logical…cold."

"Oh…you always did have a sharp, logical wit."

Mary suddenly frowned. "Did you say Agapitos?"

Her mother smiled with pride. "Yes, I did. The man is a Marshal now and arrived without any warning to take custody of Janette. He even cut her novitiate short with that authority. He went so far as to attempt to have her secreted out without her Chamber Guardians knowing. I am happy to tell you your daughter is not so easy to dupe."

"How did he know about her?"

Galene grew serious. "I want to know the answer to that myself—so does Guardian Darius Lawley."

"But…where is he taking her?" A hundred questions flooded her mind, but so did memories. "Guardian Agapitos was my accuser," she said softly.

"Yes," Galene agreed in a menacing tone. "And his father, Photios, was the Marshal who listened to him and placed charges against you. But what you do not know is that he also wanted to wed me. I refused him, a slight Photios never forgave me for."

Mary frowned. "Why not? Did he love you so deeply?"

Galene shook her head. "He lusted after our bloodline. His mother was a Pure Spirit, but he didn't inherit the gift."

"That's how you kept faith in me."

"Yes," Galene admitted. "It is also how I made sure no one ever tracked you down. I changed my duty after you left and changed Solitary Chambers. Oh… many believed it was to hide from the shame, but I was making sure no one could track you, since I had already done so."

"You knew?"

Galene smiled. "I am your mother, but I was also a Guardian Hunter. Alas, I only had my suspicions and nothing to prove your innocence with. Until now. Photios has exposed his hand now."

"But not enough so to clear my name."

Galene's joy faded, but her eyes still flickered with hope. "It is a beginning. The first crack in their camouflage, and it is a large one, my child. They have underestimated Janette, and Darius Lawley is a formidable man."

"He is still a Guardian and bound to obey a Marshal."

"True," Galene confessed. "However, he resigned his post to travel with Janette. That man knows the scent of trouble."

Mary frowned. "How could he go with her? Surely Agapitos wouldn't want anyone along who might expose him?"

"Darius Lawley is Janette's lover. He claimed they were engaged."

Mary stiffened, and her mother laughed.

"Oh, do relax, Zenais. I never raised you to be such a prude. There is quite the flame between them. I witnessed it myself. It comes as no surprise to me to see them together. Janette is young. It is summer…"

"Mother, the Regency has long passed. Your granddaughter's reputation will be shredded."

Galene drew herself up straight. "I am more interested in restoring your reputation so that we might all enjoy having our family name cleared. Darius Lawley is the man to assist us with that goal. I don't believe for one moment that Janette truly agreed to wed him. She wouldn't throw her newfound independence away so quickly, but she is wise enough to not trust Agapitos."

"Even if Darius breaks her heart?"

"I am spending my effort on worrying about whether the man can save her life," Galene insisted. "A heart can heal."

Six

HER EMOTIONS WERE THREATENING TO DROWN HER.

Excitement ruled her as she stepped closer to the escalator that would carry her up to the airship. It was like stepping into a fantasy, only better, because she could hear the gears making contact as they were driven by steam engines. She felt the wooden step beneath her foot when she stepped on it and didn't need the soft push Darius gave her to move fully onto the escalator.

His hand remained on her back, cutting through some of her elation. The man was guarding her. She could feel it, actually sense his heightened awareness. Lykos and Decima were in a similar state. The three of them never allowed the Marshal's Guardians near her. They functioned like a team, one stepping in when another was forced to move away from her. The hand on her back almost burned. In a way, Darius was branding her. It was a familiar touch, one uncommon in public, but she felt sure he was doing it to uphold his claim that they were engaged.

She could have disputed his announcement. Part of

her delivered a large dose of guilt for not correcting him because it was dishonest to continue such a charade.

But her arm tingled where the Marshal's Guardians had bruised her in their attempt to drag her away from Darius's stewardship. The handrails on the escalator were high, obviously to keep passengers from tumbling off.

"The airship travels faster than a train and is far more versatile on the path it may take," Darius offered as the airship grew larger and larger.

"I would say so."

The hand on her back rubbed gently, reassuringly. She took her attention away from the airship and locked gazes with him. He appeared surprised for a moment before his lips twitched into a grin.

"I suppose I shouldn't be surprised to see you enjoying the moment." His lips returned to a smooth line, while his eyes flickered with a heat she recalled very well. An answering flame licked along her insides.

"Your spirit is truly amazing, Janette."

His fingers curled slightly against her back, sending a ripple of awareness down her body. She looked away, heat teasing her cheeks. All around them, other passengers were in the process of boarding, and still she responded to Darius so strongly.

She truly was a wanton.

They reached the top and stepped into the cabin of the ship. Large windows were set around its exterior. The design reminded her of a basket set beneath a hot-air balloon—only on a massive scale. The lobby was the size of a hotel's, and people hurried about.

"Welcome aboard."

The man greeting them wore a dark maroon coat that ended at his hips. An ear device similar to Darius's sat comfortably in his right ear, and his Illuminist badge had a small compass on the top of it.

"I am the First Officer, Bion Donkova."

He was also a huge man. His shoulder span was impressive, and Darius didn't have to look down to make eye contact with him. There was a sharpness to the way he inspected her, and his dark eyes didn't appear any friendlier. His brown hair was cut extremely short, and his square-cut jaw was shaved clean.

"Captain Kyros instructed me to welcome you aboard."

Two more men in maroon coats flanked him, their stares hard. *Welcoming* wasn't a word she would have used to describe them. Darius and Lykos seemed to agree. They remained close to her, keeping her between them, while Bion gestured one of the men forward.

"We will be under way shortly. Until then, my man will show you to where you may be comfortable."

"Somehow, I doubt it."

She hadn't realized she'd muttered aloud until Bion raised an eyebrow at her. Darius's eyes narrowed as Lykos shook his head, but her nerves were ready to snap.

"For heaven's sake, look at the way the lot of you are pressing in on me." Janette surveyed the group before settling on Bion. "I feel like the only meat pie being set down at the orphanage supper table."

"Janette—"

"Honestly, Darius, don't try to warn me to be silent." She stepped away from him, and Lykos earned a deadly look from both of them. For a brief moment she admired their dedication to their duty, but it gave way to her pride. She was sick unto death of being labeled and having a value placed upon her like a sack of dry goods. They were clustered around her, pressing in on her. Marshal Agapitos came up the escalator with his men behind him.

"You are a Pure—" Marshal Agapitos began, but Janette interrupted him.

"I am a person. A woman. A student, and perhaps a shrew at the moment, but I am sick of the lot of you fighting over me."

She began walking, desperate to escape, but they moved with her, Darius and Lykos pushing their way to be at her side. The Marshals' men responded by blocking her path. "Move aside. This is my first journey by airship, and I intend to watch us clear the station."

"Allow me to escort you," Bion offered. The First Officer inserted himself into the group surrounding her and offered her his arm, and she took it while feeling Darius's glare burning into her back. Let him be angry.

At least they would be fine company for each other, a true match indeed.

❧

"Are you quite certain, Doctor?"

Dr. Nerval nodded, a rare gleam of enjoyment in his eyes. His wrinkled cheeks rose with a smile as he lifted a withered hand to point.

"I have been waiting for this moment…anticipating it for many years. Carry out my instructions. We need to be aboard the airship soon, or we shall fall short of our time schedule."

The orderlies inclined their heads before hurrying off. Neither of them wanted to be responsible for a botched time schedule. They didn't look at each other. Guilt might gain more of a hold over their consciences if they knew their partner was harboring reservations about their task. Better to see it done quickly. At least that way, they could hand off their burden with the sure knowledge that the doctor was gone and their positions secure.

A man did what he had to to survive.

That was nothing to feel guilty about.

೭೪೦

"She's got a point, you know. We are a bit fixated on her bloodline."

Darius tossed back the contents of a brandy snifter. The alcohol burned a path to his stomach and added to the inferno raging inside him. He shot a look at Bion that was a clear challenge. The First Officer watched Janette lean over a nearby railing to peer out the window before he offered Darius a smirk.

Darius felt the need to hit the man grow.

In spite of the airship leaving the station, the First Officer was still with them, and the man looked completely ill-placed as supper was served to them in a windowside table section.

"Forget her point." Darius cut a sidelong look at Lykos. "Don't think about her beyond keeping Agapitos and his men away from her."

Lykos studied him intently. "Fair enough, my good

man. It does look like you are doing enough mental deliberation over Miss Aston's attributes for the pair of us."

Decima tilted her head. "She is his fiancée."

"So I heard," Lykos said loud enough for Janette to overhear. A blush stained her cheeks scarlet when she locked stares with Decima. "It's my understanding they are very devoted to each other's pleasure."

Janette drew in a harsh breath before clamping her lips together to keep from sputtering. She turned on her heel and headed away from the public areas with Darius on her heels before Lykos had stopped chuckling. "You're very welcome…"

"I don't believe he heard you," Decima muttered as she reached for a china teacup.

"He heard me."

Decima smiled before drawing off a long sip of tea. "He did, and he owes you a debt of gratitude for ensuring he and Janette share some private time tonight." She fell silent as she took another sip of tea, but this one she didn't savor. Her eyes remained hard.

"Once we reach the Crystal Fields, there will be little time for pleasantries."

Lykos nodded. He reached for a plate of sweet breads because Decima was right. Tomorrow, the tension would double.

But for tonight, he was sharing a fine meal with a beautiful woman. It was as good as it got for Guardians such as themselves.

⤫

Along the interior of the passenger area were passenger

berths. Doors were set at even intervals like any steamer ship. Darius caught up to Janette quickly, and with a few turns, he guided her to a cabin for which he produced a key. She was grateful for the privacy, but it seemed to be her undoing as well.

"I'm just sick unto death of it."

The words bubbled up the moment she heard the door close. Her control was slipping out of her grasp. The cabin was tiny, but the four walls gave her relief from the constant surveillance.

"Janette, you must listen to me. It is imperative that you…"

Darius was using his authoritarian voice again. The same one she recalled vividly from their first meeting, when he'd invested so much effort in attempting to frighten her into submission. She turned on him, her skirt whipping around with her quick motion. "Oh, I've listened to you, Darius Lawley. I've listened very well to you declaring I agreed to marry you when you never asked me such a question."

Her temper was rising, and she welcomed it because it cut through the fear twisting her insides. She propped her hands onto her hips and faced off with him.

"I've heard everything you've said, but I wonder if you've listened to me at all. If I desired a life full of being submissive to a man's will, I could have stayed with my father."

His visage suddenly changed. The somber, alert expression cracked as a grin appeared, only it wasn't a pleasant expression. It was menacing, and his eyes flickered with a challenge.

"I listened when you demanded I finish what I start,

and I'm in just the right mood to answer the challenge you are flinging in my face," he said. "Dare me to try you and I will, siren."

"Only an arrogant knave would view my words as a challenge." There was too much energy coursing through her. She had to move; maintaining her poise became impossible. "I am no siren, sir. I am—"

"A bitch," he finished with a smirk.

She gasped, but he smothered the sound with a kiss. It was a hard one, designed to silence her protests. But she wasn't ready to surrender, wasn't nearly ready to bend at all. She balled up her fists, just as she'd learned in Asian fighting class, and tried to drive them into the soft portion of his chest below where his ribs ended.

He captured both hands.

"How dare you call me such a thing?"

And how dare her body respond so quickly to his kiss?

"With complete pleasure, I assure you." He twisted her arms behind her back. She ended up trapped against his chest, unable to do anything more than wiggle.

"You wanted to make me jealous, Janette, admit it." He released her hands but gripped her bottom and pulled her into contact with his lower body before she might step back. "I've been hard since you pranced away ever so saucily on Bion's arm. But the sight of your hips swaying held my attention, have no doubt."

The truth of his words was hard against her belly. "You're being vulgar, Darius."

He didn't release her. Instead, his hands smoothed over the cheeks of her bottom, squeezing and rubbing as he grinned. Desire speared through her, awakening her clitoris with a vengeance. All the swirling emotion inside her began to transform. Instead of being furious with him, she was desperate to have him once more.

"And you're being provocative."

She should have taken his words as an accusation, but instead, they landed on her like a compliment. "That doesn't grant you leave to call me such a thing."

"As a bitch?" His voice dipped low and mocking. His eyes darkened, making him appear sinister, and damn her for a fool if it didn't make her want to scratch him. Just for the release of energy it would provide her.

"But I prefer to see you sticking your chin out in the face of this situation instead of cringing." Something flared in his eyes that made her belly twist with lust so tightly, she ground herself against his erection. He lowered his head until his breath was against her neck, denying her the sight of his face and any hint as to his emotions.

"You have strength in you, Janette. I could ignore anything else, but your spirit is indomitable, and it draws me to you."

He bit her gently, sending an electric urge through her. Thoughts refused to form as she was consumed once more by raging need. His erection teased her, and she craved it, twisting against him while he ran a trail of kisses against the sensitive skin of her neck. It stole her breath.

"I'm happy to see you fighting mad, and very happy to meet you in the middle of the ring."

He scooped her up and dropped her on the narrow bed. Her simple skirt went flying with a sweep of his hand, allowing the cool night air to brush the insides of her thighs where her knickers were split.

"And I shall be very happy to show you I can tame you." He'd never seemed so attractive before, so completely irresistible. She stared at the glittering depths but fought the urge to be hypnotized. Submission was the last thing on her mind; in fact, it felt absolutely necessary to refuse him, even as she felt the need licking at the walls of her passage.

"You will do no such thing," she insisted. "And you can go find someplace else to sleep. This is my cabin."

He laughed at her, sounding like some demon described in the pages of a horror story. He tore his vest off before opening his trousers. Beneath the vest was a leather harness that held a pistol against his side.

"Neither of us is going to be sleeping." His cock appeared, swollen and hard. "I thought you spent the afternoon learning how many opportunities to increase our pleasure we wasted last night."

He knelt and pushed her thighs wide, her split-crotch knickers giving him full view of her sex. She placed her hands behind her on the bed to keep from flopping onto her back. A cry rose from all the emotion swirling around inside her as she struggled to remain upright. Darius took the opportunity to spread her sex open completely and gently stroke it with his fingertips.

"*Oh my Lord…*" A hoarse cry escaped her lips without any consent from her mind. The sensation was too intense, too acute, and her body wanted nothing more than to respond. She had never suspected any part of her body could be so sensitive.

Darius snickered, still too arrogant, but she was too busy trying to pull air into her lungs to protest.

"I wonder how you taste, sweet siren."

"You can't—"

He chuckled and grazed her open slit once more as she fought to draw in her next breath. Pleasure pulsed through her in a wave so thick, she couldn't fight her way free of it to remember why she was arguing with him. The pictures of the erotic texts flashed through her mind in the same moment that she felt his breath against her folds. Her clitoris throbbed so hard, it felt like she might climax the moment he touched her. But he seemed to sense it and offered her only the softest of strokes from his fingers.

"Can't what, sweet siren?" His fingers grazed her slit back and forth, producing pleasure so intense her eyes closed because she only wanted to feel. "Can't... stop?" He targeted the little nub at the top of her cleft and rubbed it. "At last we are in agreement. I don't believe I can stop either. The idea of tasting you is driving me mad."

Anticipation nearly twisted her in half. It felt like her insides were being wrung, and breathing took every bit of strength she had.

The only thing she could do was moan and twist as he replaced his fingers with his lips. She'd never thought a man's lips might feel so hot. Darius's tongue lapped along the inside of her slit before toying with her clit. Her muscles tightened and felt like they might snap, sweat rising on her skin as her heart raced. Every thought was centered on the soft strokes being applied to her clitoris. Time slowed down, and it seemed a small eternity between each lap. She was suspended between need and pleasure, yearning for it the moment his tongue moved away. She strained toward him when pressure returned, desperate for just a tiny bit more to send her over the edge into climax.

Darius didn't give her release. Instead, he sucked on her before teasing the entrance to her passage with one fingertip.

"More, Darius! I need more."

He thrust his finger deep, drawing a moan from her. The sound bounced around the tiny cabin, but she hardly recognized it. All that mattered was lifting her hips, straining upward to be filled. The walls of her passage were slick with desire and ultrasensitive, but his finger wasn't enough to make the pleasure crest either. Instead, she remained poised on the edge of the abyss, longing threatening to destroy her sanity.

"More!" she demanded. Forcing her eyes open, she curled up. "Give me more, damn you!"

The sight of him between her thighs was too erotic, too forbidden. He looked up her body, his dark eyes glittering with determination as he sucked harder on her clit.

She cried out, sure the sound was ripped from her belly because it felt like she was being torn open by the surge of pleasure moving through her. It traveled up her body, forcing the air out of her lungs as she twisted beneath him. By the time she drew in breath again, her vision had gone dark and her body collapsed onto the bed.

"Damn you, Darius…" She panted. "I'm an Illuminist now…You will not…dominate me."

He sat back on his haunches, satisfaction gleaming

in his eyes. "I was proving my worth. A siren would be satisfied by nothing less."

Janette sat up, the muscles of her belly feeling strained, but her desire was still only partially sated. Yet it was enough for her pride to rise above her yearnings. Her gaze centered on his cock, which stuck up swollen between the edges of his open trousers.

"Well, if you insist upon calling me by the name of a mythical Greek creature"—she slid off the narrow bed and cupped both sides of his face—"perhaps I should act like it."

"You are mesmerizing, Janette. I fell victim to your song the moment you refused to cower in my office."

His voice was husky and needy. She slid her thighs over his until she felt the head of his erection pressing between her slick folds. His hands found her hips, gripping them firmly, but she remained poised above his length while she leaned down to kiss him.

His hand trembled, and she heard him groan.

"And you reduce me to being willing to beg at your feet because I'm so besotted by you." His face had drawn tight. "Because I can't think beyond my need to be inside you."

"A feeling I share."

She slid her hands down his firm jawline and along his neck until she gripped his wide shoulders. He thrust up into her, sending delight through her belly.

"No," she admonished him. "I am taking you. I saw it in a drawing…"

"You are taking too long to gain the saddle, sweetheart, and your stallion is ready to ride."

He lifted her, proving that his strength was merely

controlled. Beneath the thin fabric of his shirt, his shoulders were packed with hard muscle. It pleased her in some dark corner of her mind.

He released her and thrust up at the same time. She gasped as his cock penetrated her deeply and immediately rose off it. This time he used his hold on her hips to push her down.

"That's the way, siren. Prove you're my match, and I promise to make you work for the privilege of saying you kept pace with me."

He was challenging her, but she liked the sound of his words. Pleasure began to build inside her once again, their position placing more pressure against her clitoris. The light was still on, granting her a clear view of his face. Savageness lit his eyes as she ground herself down. His grip had become tighter, bordering on pain, but somehow it enhanced the flames burning inside her. Her heart was racing, but she felt more alive than she ever had.

"Come now. Where's the spirited ride you've been promising me, Darius?" She leaned forward and bit the skin on the side of his neck. He growled and thrust up into her with a powerful motion.

"You'd have to accept letting me off the bit…"

His tone was edged with warning, but instead of making her hesitate, it sent excitement through her. His hand was on her nape, holding her head steady, and their gazes locked. She watched something flare up in his eyes in response to her lack of hesitation.

For a moment, he stopped moving. One arm bound her against his body, stilling her efforts to continue their ride. She felt fragile against him, completely engulfed by his greater strength. But she wasn't alone in her emotions; beneath the savage enjoyment of the moment, she witnessed the first uncertainty she could recall seeing in his eyes. She cupped his cheeks once more, slipping her fingers along his smooth skin until she encountered the short sideburns.

"Do your worst." She sounded husky and confident in a way that surprised her. But it thrilled Darius.

He pressed a hard kiss against her mouth before lifting her off his length. The man handled her body like she weighed nothing, turning her and depositing her on her knees so she was facing away from him. She only had a moment to feel vulnerable before he flipped her skirt up, removing the fabric from covering her knickers. He grasped her hips and thrust into her with enough force that she fell forward and braced herself on all fours.

She should have been offended or maybe…something else; instead, all she knew was that she was caught up in the intensity of the moment. He rode her hard, driving his cock in and out with enough force to make her body jerk.

"Some men prefer their women do the riding, but I admit I enjoy proving my worth to you, Janette."

He was half snarling while increasing his pace. She discovered an urge to move back and meet him. It increased with every solid thrust. Need was threatening to rip her in half again, her desire insisting she move faster, harder, and somehow press his length deeper.

She cried out with the need. It was all-consuming, and she heard an answering cry from her partner.

Their skin smacked when it met because they were moving so fast, but her clitoris was left begging for enough pressure to send her into climax again.

"Now finish with me."

He reached around her body, sliding one hand across her belly until he found the opening of her drawers. Her palms hurt because she was pushing them against the hard floor to maintain her position as he worked in and out of her from behind.

Nothing mattered but the progress of his hand. Her clitoris throbbed unbearably when she felt his fingertips parting her curls.

"I want to feel you milk me."

He groaned, but she was more fixated on the decreasing distance between his fingers and her clitoris. She felt suspended between seconds, every hard thrust forcing her breath from her lungs, and then she frantically gulped it back in so she wouldn't miss the first stroke.

It was soft. When he reached her tender flesh, he pressed down and rubbed. She cried out, her need snapping like a thread pulled too tight. Pleasure went sailing through her at an incredible speed; it cut through everything and continued until even her scalp tingled.

"Ah…yes, milk me dry."

Her passage was tightening, and his cock began to jerk as his seed erupted. She didn't control it, merely experienced it as her body contorted with satisfaction. Her lungs refused to work, but she didn't care because she was too busy smiling as she heard Darius crying out.

It was harsh and male, but satisfying beyond even the pleasure pulsing through her nerve endings. He collapsed onto the floor and pulled her down onto his chest. Somehow she ended up in his embrace, his hands smoothing the hair back from her face as their hearts slowed.

She let her eyes close and ordered her mind to remain fuzzy. Clear thinking was for the morning. For now, all she wanted to concentrate on was the steady beating of her lover's heart.

          ✑

"I hear you are a good man to have about, Bion."

Bion watched Grainger as the man slipped into the chair across the table from him. The dining area was nearly deserted, the passengers all preferring their cabins and a good night's sleep.

"You shouldn't listen to rumors. There are a lot of men who covet my position here, and they say the worst things about me."

Grainger lifted his hand, signaling the barkeep for another glass. Bion pulled the cork out of the brandy bottle sitting in front of him and filled the glass. Grainger took a healthy swig of the dark brown liquid before sitting back in his chair.

"You aren't drinking, First Officer?"

Bion folded his arms over his chest. "Never while this vessel is under way. I might be called to the bridge at any time."

Grainger looked at the brandy suspiciously. Bion offered him a dry laugh.

"The staff is dedicated to their duty of making sure

anyone who sits here is well supplied, but they forget I am still in uniform."

Grainger nodded. "It's that dedication that I wish to inquire about."

"How so?" Bion asked softly.

Grainger tilted his head slightly while studying him. Silence stretched out between them for a long moment.

"Pure Spirits are very rare."

Bion nodded but denied Grainger any further comment.

"Keeping her focused is in the interest of the Order."

Bion slowly grinned. "If you are asking me if I believe emotional entanglements to be distracting, the answer is yes."

Grainger smiled, a cold, satisfied twisting of his lips. "Excellent. I see my information is correct. You are a man to be trusted in difficult circumstances."

Bion nodded. Grainger tossed back the rest of his brandy before standing. He offered the First Officer a stiff bow before walking away.

But Bion watched. He kept his attention sharp because without a doubt, someone was keeping sights on him.

❧

She was tired but uncomfortable. Even in slumber she twisted, trying to relieve the pinching disturbing her. Her pillow moved in response to her restlessness.

"We'll likely find the bed more comfortable now that we're both more relaxed."

Her eyes opened wide as Darius sat up and took her with him. He sat her on the bed, but she stood. She picked up her peplum jacket and hung it on a

wall hook. Her skirt followed, along with her shoes
and stockings, which she placed neatly on the floor
beneath the hook.

"Decima brought some more practical clothing
along for you, since you weren't given any time to
procure your own."

"How do you mean? My clothing is already far
more practical than any I've ever owned."

Darius hung up his jacket and vest too, but he
kept his leather pistol harness in place. The sight of
the polished handle of a weapon resting in the holster
chased the last of sleep from her mind.

"If the situation weren't so questionable, I'd
encourage you to try sleeping as the Islanders do." He
propped the pillows up where the wall and bed met.
"In your skin."

He didn't really lie down but reclined against the
pillows and propped himself up against the wall. He'd
even left his shoes on.

"For the moment, I believe you've got the right
idea to leave that corset on, even if it will be uncomfortable to sleep in."

He patted the surface of the bed, raising an eyebrow
when she smiled with amusement.

"Don't you know, Darius?" She settled herself next
to him with her back toward him; in the narrow bunk,
being on her side was more comfortable. "Young
ladies always sleep in their foundation garments."

He ran his hand along her side. "Sleeping in a steel-
boned cage—it's bloody ridiculous ."

"It makes as much sense as this journey." She
should have kept her mouth shut, but the memory of

the pistol resting so near to her head refused to allow her any peace.

"Oh, it makes sense, Janette. I only wish it didn't."

His voice had gone hard. She raised her head, but he pulled her close and gently pressed her face back onto the sheet.

"Rest. I fear you're going to need it when we reach the Crystal Fields tomorrow."

"So soon?"

"The Navigator will take us through a dimension gate in another hour."

He smoothed his hand over her hair, almost as though he was trying to savor the moment. Her heart wanted to believe it was so, and her mind only helped out by pointing out that he'd had her flesh, so the only reason to remain was for tender feelings.

"Why didn't you ask me what a Navigator is, or a dimension gate?" His words were guarded, almost like he dreaded her answer, which only added more fuel to her growing emotions. Darius Lawley had always been so untouchable, at least when it came to his opinion of her.

"Why does it matter that I didn't?" She turned her head to look at him. "Why does it bother you so much to discover I have integrity and won't demand you compromise your honor simply because we are lovers?"

She reached up and captured his hand. Oh, he let her do it, but she gave it a squeeze before releasing it. "There are some things high society and Illuminists have in common. My father taught me what honor was. I recognize it in you. The law book made it clear there are many levels to the Illuminist Order. Since I refused to take the Oath, I have no right to ask too many questions."

He drew in a stiff breath and pressed his thumb over her lips to keep her silent while he contemplated her.

"You're unique, siren. Very, very unique."

She turned away. "So everyone insists on telling me."

"That was a very personal compliment, Janette, one that has nothing to do with your blood." He dimmed the light, and she closed her eyes.

"In that case, thank you." Maybe it was foolish, but she wanted to enjoy the moment. Life had been too unpredictable lately, things she had depended on crumbling instead of remaining solid. Darius was the constant in her life. What she found endearing at that moment was more than tender feelings; it was the respect she'd heard in his voice.

⁓

She was under his skin.

His temper should have stirred. Instead, Darius felt his emotions heating in a very different part of his body. Her breathing slowed and deepened, granting him a measure of relief he was surprised he appreciated as much as he did. It had been a long time since he'd felt his control slipping. Tonight, it was shattered.

He studied Janette's face, the delicate pink of her lips, and ran his fingers gently along the surface of her cheek. From the moment he'd set eyes upon her, he'd known she was dangerous, in a purely personal way. At the moment, he wasn't agitated by that fact. Instead, he smiled as her scent drifted up and indulged in pulling her close enough to feel her heart beating.

Life was a fleeting thing, too often snuffed out by those trying to master the world around them. Becoming a Guardian had been his only way to interfere in that struggle. He just wished he wasn't so sure an epic battle was about to engage over the delicate creature lying in his embrace.

But he'd give his life for her, that much he was sure of.

He prayed it would be enough.

◦◦◦

"How magnificent." Janette leaned over the railing of the lower deck to see the islands below them. Sometime during the night, they had left the crisp air of Britain behind them. Now it was balmy, even as high up as they still were.

"Don't fall out."

Janette turned a sour look on Darius. "I am not a child, as you well know, Mr. Lawley."

His lips rose, his oh-so-complete control eluding him for just a moment as she witnessed a flicker of awareness in his dark eyes.

"Kindly spare the rest of us who regrettably spent the night alone," Lykos interjected.

Heat teased her cheek, so Janette returned to looking out over the railing. Below her was some of the bluest water she had ever seen. It made the coast of England look drab by comparison. It sparkled like a million diamonds as the sun shone down on it. Ahead of them, a huge caldera from an extinct volcano marked the edge of one of the Hawaiian Islands. Green tropical plants grew up to the edge of the sand beaches. That sand was purest white, too, like something in a children's nighttime tale.

"King Kamehameha the Third has recently been restored to his throne. We British aren't the most popular at the moment, since it was a British officer who deposed the king briefly," Darius muttered.

"The king finds the Illuminist mind-set more to his liking than the British high society," Marshal Agapitos informed her, his voice edged with enough pride for her to accuse him of arrogance.

Again.

The airship was steadily making its way toward the island. They crossed over the breaking waves and over the beaches. A station came into view with two other airships docked there. These airships didn't have escalators loading passengers onto them; instead, ramps were attached to them, and large crates were being loaded.

"Captain Kyros has dispatched me to escort you to the secured escalator for disembarkation."

The First Officer was just as official this morning as he had been yesterday. His jacket buttons gleamed from recent polish.

Darius reached for her arm but stopped before closing his grip around it. She could see him battling to stop before handling her. Instead, he offered her his hand, palm up.

She was already placing her hand into his before she finished enjoying the rush of delight spreading through her. She smiled, unable to stop herself from displaying her emotions to everyone around them.

But she was pleased, and for a moment, she could

see that Darius was happy with her response. It shimmered in his dark eyes, touching her deeply before he masked it and carried her hand to his arm.

Marshal Agapitos frowned at her when she turned and caught sight of him. Darius didn't give her the chance to remark upon it, though. He swept her past the Marshal, following the First Officer as Lykos and Decima neatly slid in behind them to keep Grainger and Agapitos from being directly behind her.

Bion led them past a security checkpoint; the men guarding it cradled long guns as they scrutinized her with narrowed eyes. She stared at the guns, trying to identify them, but they didn't look like any of the ones her father owned.

"It will be warm outside," Darius said. "You'll be glad Decima brought you linen to wear."

Her wool traveling suit was sitting inside a small traveling trunk that had arrived to the cabin at daybreak. Decima had also declined to wear her practical English wool in favor of some of the finest linen Janette had ever seen made up into clothing. Or at least outerwear. She had chemises that were soft and lightweight, but her new single skirt and jacket were also made of the flimsy fabric. It was sort of like wearing a nightgown and wrapper. She'd felt awkward stepping into the hallway, but now, with the tropical air warming her cheeks, she was glad she'd packed her wool away.

Darius and Lykos still had overcoats on. She recalled the chest harness Darius had worn all night and the small pistol he'd kept handy. There were other men who had discarded their overcoats and wore only vests over their shirts, but they also appeared more at ease than her companions.

A prickle of apprehension tingled up her nape.

Two large doors were open ahead, and the air blew in to tease the hair her hasty morning preparation hadn't captured. They moved closer to an escalator, the edge of the thing looking as though it simply dropped off into nothingness. Bion never stopped but stepped onto the moving contraption, and Darius took her along behind him. Once out of the airship, she looked back up at the marvel that had taken her halfway around the globe in a single day.

Navigator…dimension gate…

Questions flooded her mind, but instead of feeling frustrated, she was filled with a sense of adventure. So many more things to learn; she looked forward to a lifetime of being able to always discover new things.

As the escalator lowered them, the air grew warmer. By the time they stepped off and onto the loading dock, she was itching to remove her gloves. The dock had a large roof like a patio, but even standing beneath it, she was still uncomfortable.

A group of Guardians moved toward them with all the welcome of a firing squad. The Marshal inclined his head when they all offered him a stiff bow.

"Please escort Guardian Lawley and Guardian Claxton to the Solitary Chamber."

"I will be staying with my fiancée."

All cordialness evaporated. Darius gripped her wrist and twisted it just the right way to see her moving behind him without a single protest. It wouldn't have mattered if she had thought to endure the pain because

Lykos gripped her arms and helped pull her behind the back of his friend.

"You are allowed to accompany her, but not to the Crystal Fields," Agapitos declared gleefully.

"I am a head Guardian and, as such, have the necessary clearance to travel to the Crystal Fields."

"I have all the necessary men in place, Guardian Lawley. You may wait, as would any other intended spouse, for your fiancé to complete her duties."

"Like hell I will."

A light of enjoyment appeared in Agapitos's eyes. It reminded Janette all too much of the way Dr. Nerval had peered at her once his orderlies had secured her into the chair.

"Are you questioning my orders, Guardian Lawley?" Agapitos stepped up to Darius with a smirk on his lips. "Give me a reason to have charges brought against you. Nothing would give me greater satisfaction."

"Why?" Janette demanded. "Why is it so important for you to separate me from everyone I know?"

"A very interesting question."

The new voice was heavily accented. Janette turned to see who was interrupting because she couldn't identify the unfamiliar voice.

"Family is more important than ambition. This is a truth."

The man was dark-skinned, but not as dark as an African. He wore a pair of trousers and a shirt like Darius, and a vest but no overcoat. Instead, a blue sash with gold fringe crossed his chest. A large bone hoop dangled from one earlobe, and his hands had what appeared to be ink marks in patterns along the fingers.

The blending of primitiveness with modern clothing was amazing. He carried himself with an arrogance that suggested they were the ones falling under his authority. With the heat and the palm trees swaying in the distance, maybe they were. The civilization of Britain was very far away.

"His Majesty Kamehameha the Third has sent me to welcome you to the kingdom of Hawaii," he offered while staring at Janette.

Dark-skinned women wearing the simplest of smock dresses came forward. Their dark hair was free and flowing down their backs, and they held necklaces of fresh flowers.

With words of welcome spoken in a language she didn't understand, the women draped the flowers around her neck but ignored the others with her.

"Your presence is requested at the palace for supper with His Majesty."

"That is quite impossible," Marshal Agapitos insisted.

The Herald looked formal enough, but there was something very savage in his eyes. He smiled slowly, revealing teeth that appeared gleaming white against his dark skin. He lifted his hand, and twelve soldiers moved forward to surround them. They marched in time, their final steps echoing like a gunshot. Each man lowered his rifle without flinching.

"His Majesty finds himself short on trust when it comes to citizens of the British Commonwealth. This is the Kingdom of Hawaii, and his request shall be honored, or your Order will no longer enjoy the benefits of trade with us. The king will decide if your Pure Spirit will be allowed to hunt on our land. You will not take anything from his kingdom without permission."

"It seems there is yet another orphan eyeing me," Janette whispered. She didn't expect Darius to turn or to see amusement flickering in his eyes.

"One I invited to the table," he murmured, the hand on her lower back gently soothing her for a moment. It was a tender touch, one that warmed her heart.

She wanted to know how he'd managed it but merely returned his smile. The man truly was worthy of the title Guardian. For the moment, she trusted in him as she never had before, and she very much feared that she was falling in love with him.

৵৹

"Hale Ali'i is a modern palace, worthy of any dignitary visiting our land."

The Herald had never introduced himself but continued to speak on behalf of the king as they climbed into carriages. The vehicles were open-topped, allowing the warm air to blow Janette's hair about. Once the airship station was left behind, the jungle surrounded them. Islanders walked along the sides of the road, some of them carrying rolled mats or baskets on top of their heads. She bit her lip to keep from gaping at the women wearing nothing but long skirts. Their breasts were tanned from the sun, and their nipples, dark. Yet they smiled, waving to her as the carriage went by them. They pulled up to a gatehouse where more of the king's guards stood. It took only a moment for them to recognize the king's herald and open the gates.

"You will be very secure here and safe from all harm." The herald offered her an explanation as they passed through the gates.

The palace was no larger than her father's country estate, but it was also the only stone-walled building on the compound. It was a single story set with glass windows and large, ornately carved doors. Guards snapped to attention when they exited the carriage. There was a wide stone fence running in a huge perimeter around the grounds and numerous huts built several hundred feet away from the palace itself. Large trees with huge flat leaves offered shade.

"His Majesty has made arrangements for your comfort during the afternoon heat and will welcome you at sunset."

The herald clapped his hands, and the six women who had fallen into step with them the moment they left the carriage moved to flank Janette and Decima.

"The women will take you to the women's hut."

"It is our custom to accompany our women," Marshal Agapitos argued.

The herald offered him another challenging grin. "Any warrior who shares a hut with a woman is weak. This is a truth we hold scared. "

"That is not our way."

"Then you should have remained on your own land," the herald answered, his guards turning their weapons on the Marshal. "Besides, she is not your woman."

"She is my responsibility," Agapitos insisted.

The herald stepped up close to the Marshal, until they were nearly jaw to jaw. "Now she is mine. My king has sent for her to ensure your kind do not attempt to claim his land once more. You will not bring any Pure Spirit here without the permission of His Majesty, nor will you search for Deep Earth Crystals without permission."

He clapped his hands, and the women began to pull her and Decima away. Part of her was happy to leave the Marshal and Grainger, but she turned to look back, drawn by an overwhelming need to see Darius. The look on his face surprised her. He looked relieved.

Pain punched her budding tender emotions. It didn't make any sense, but she wasn't thinking, only feeling. The man was always too happy to be done with her. She shouldn't care. No, not a bit.

Yet you do…

⁓

"A risky gamble you took, my friend."

"I'm well aware of that," Darius answered as Lykos emerged from the lengthening afternoon shadows. Both men stared at the palace and the dinner that the king was hosting to welcome Janette. A meal neither Lykos nor Darius had been invited to share. Instead, one of the island women had brought them supper before departing to return to the women's side of the compound.

"My options weren't plentiful with the way Agapitos arrived. Kallias might have gray hair, but she is still as sharp as ever. I knew she'd understand what I meant when I told her to send a message," Darius stated.

The older Illuminist from the library had been a mentor for years.

"Odd that Grainger dismissed her so easily when she stood up to his men."

Darius nodded. "Another oddity. I'm becoming very curious about those charges against Janette's mother and just who lodged them."

"As am I," Lykos agreed. "Of course, we now have to survive and pry Janette away from a king. Considering we weren't invited to dinner, I get the feeling Kamehameha is planning on making that a difficult task."

The house was lit with the use of Deep Earth Crystals, and Darius could see the crystal sparkling on the table. There was all manner of finery inside the palace, forming a sharp contrast with the huts surrounding the stone building. The moonlight shone down on the palms used to cover the roofs, while only a few lights shimmered from inside their walls.

"Kamehameha might decide to keep her." Darius voiced what they were both thinking. "But I prefer him to Agapitos at the moment. Negotiations with him will be far more straightforward."

"At least his mistrust of Janette's arrival will provide us with time," Lykos remarked, but the Hawaiian guards watching the gate so silently drew his attention.

"Which means naught if we can't get a message out of this compound. Still, I'll rest easier tonight."

Lykos chuckled softly. "So would I, if I had such a delight to enjoy when the lights were extinguished."

Darius lifted the drink in his hand to his lips but didn't take a sip. He wasn't interested in brandy. No, what he wanted interfering in his clear thinking sat inside the palace. Through the window, he could see Janette was doing a fine job of charming the king. Darius smiled because Decima was digging her fingernails into her skirt beneath the table. Not Janette. She was poised and full of confidence as she batted her eyelashes.

He hoped she realized just how important her performance was. But for the moment, he was going to have to trust in her ability. It frustrated him, was threatening to drive him mad, but beneath both emotions was something else.

Appreciation.

He admired her, in spite of the dire circumstances. Damned if she wasn't holding it together. Locked beneath the delicate exterior was a spirit he was growing too attached to.

Lykos slapped him on the shoulder. "Don't look so horrified, my friend. Love isn't a fate worse than death."

"I didn't say I was in love with her."

His friend shook his head. "No, but your eyes do."

"We don't have time for nonsense."

Lykos sighed and drew a long sip from his brandy. "So Decima persists in telling me. But for once, I believe I am the only member of this group being honest." He offered Darius a toast before finishing his drink.

"Care to join me in an escape later tonight?" Darius asked. He was changing the subject, but his tender feelings wouldn't matter if the king maintained control of Janette. The man could easily have every Illuminist put off his compound, just as he was keeping them in the dark while Janette sat at his dining table.

Lykos grinned, but it was a savage sort of expression. "I thought you'd never ask."

"Bion is still clinging to Agapitos's heels."

Another interesting fact. Darius took one last

look at Janette. She was as secure as possible, but she wouldn't be staying safe if he didn't get to the Illuminists in the area.

But it still tore at him to leave her.

❧

"Come, lady…come."

The native women had no concept of personal space. They reached for her hands and all the way up her arms in their attempts to lead her. Four of them clustered around her the moment the king left the table. Decima wasn't faring any better.

"Come away now…"

Their voices were musical, the words coming out in a rhythm. Janette followed, eager to escape the king. Kamehameha was no fool. The man knew more about Illuminist matters than he admitted. It was clear enough in the way he'd watched her throughout the meal—like she was a commodity worth stealing—that he enjoyed a healthy knowledge of the power of Deep Earth Crystals, she was sure of it.

The women took her through the hallways of the palace and out the door into the yard. The night was alive with the sounds of birds and insects. Somewhere in the distance, thunder rumbled. She could smell the rain, but the air was hot and sticky.

"This hut is good."

The girls pulled her through a low doorway.

"Are there no bedrooms?" The moonlight was filtering through the places in the walls where the palm leaves were laced together. She felt exposed, which wasn't quite logical, considering the solid wall running around the palace grounds. But inside the hut, the walls were anything but solid.

"Too hot inside stone walls," one girl muttered as she and her companions began to pull at the lacing of the dress Janette had worn to dinner. The lace-edged silk would have pleased her father with its fan-pleated front and small bell sleeves. Her gloves were gone in a moment, and she couldn't help but sigh with relief. Perspiration was trickling down her legs.

"No one sleeps inside the palace."

The dress sagged, and they pushed her forward so they might draw it over her head. The silk rustled as it was taken away. The stiff petticoat went next, but Janette jumped away when they tried to loosen her corset.

"I'll sleep in it," she muttered with another look at the flimsy walls. Being daring enough to go without it in her chambers back at the Solitary Chamber was very different from being undressed completely here.

"No."

There was only a single lamp in the hut, but it cast enough light for Janette to see the wrinkles on her nose. The woman stiffened and shook her head. She was the oldest one among them and the other girls looked to her for direction.

"No good for the heart." She patted her chest. "The heart must have room to beat, not be kept inside a steel cage."

The other girls instantly responded by picking at the laces that bound her. It was a relief to feel the steel bones loosen and release her breasts, but it was also slightly unsettling. Her hair was next. Every last pin was pulled, and her braids were undone as well. Someone began pulling a comb through it until it lay just like the other girls', straight down her back.

"Good…good," the woman remarked. She and her companions wore only loose-flowing garments that didn't even look to be sewn, but the edges overlapped and tied around their necks to cover their breasts.

"Come and wash."

They tugged her outside to where smooth stones were arranged in a small circle. A small water tower was nearby with a piece of large bamboo running out and to a showerhead. The only light was from the moon, and it cast them all in shades of black and silver. The girls seemed at ease in the night, none of them hesitating.

"Come…come…cool water will feel good."

Someone tried to pull her chemise over her head. "Oh no, really." Janette hugged herself to keep the last bit of her dignity. Anyone on the compound might see her.

The older woman shook her head once more. "No good, washing with clothing on. Don't be like the missionaries. They do not smell very good."

The others laughed and wrinkled their noses. Janette lost the battle to not smile. Modesty might be considered proper, but it did make for more than one smelly matron.

"This is women's side of palace grounds. No men will come here. Bad luck for warriors to spend too much time with women. Our spirits will drain their strength so we can produce new life."

The moment she became distracted, the girls pulled her chemise over her head. One of them untied her knickers and pushed them down her legs. Janette let them take her stockings with a tiny sigh of relief. The stones were cool beneath her feet, and they felt wonderful. Her hair floated down onto her bare skin as the older woman nodded approvingly.

"If your God made you in his image, why do missionaries teach children to think their flesh is sinful?"

"Well...that is an excellent question," Janette responded.

Water began flowing, saving Janette from having to think. It was cool, but the air was remained warm. Still, goose bumps rose along her limbs, and her nipples puckered into hard points because she was thinking about Darius.

Would he like her without a corset to shape her?

In all the erotic texts, there had been nothing but the natural form of the body.

"You are thinking of your warrior."

The younger girls all leaned in, their faces bright with curiosity. The older woman offered them a knowing smile.

"The eyes...do not lie."

She waved her hands at her helpers, and soap was worked through Janette's hair and over her body. They didn't miss a single inch of her, making her grateful for the darkness because her cheeks were scarlet by the time they rinsed her.

They brought her a length of toweling, and the warmer climate soon had every drop of water gone.

"Now we go, in case your warrior comes."

The girls all giggled. They helped her into her chemise before they followed their mistress from the hut, but one hesitated near the wall.

"Sleep here, lady. Very nice for night rest."

What she pulled away from the wall was a net, or at least it looked like one to Janette. The girl smiled and lay back into the thing. It hung between two of the large support beams that held up the walls of the hut. Once in it, the net curled around her, and she swung gently back and forth.

"This is island way," she said before standing, then offered a nod and left. Janette stared at the net for a long moment before shaking her head.

Adventure. That's right. She adored it.

The cord the net was constructed of was quite soft. She spread it out, but it wanted to roll back up, so she sat down and felt a tingle of excitement race through her when the thing took her weight. She swung back and forth for a moment like she'd done on the back-yard swing in the summertime. A smile raised her lips as she smothered a giggle.

Lying back into it wasn't difficult. Soon she was nestled in it, the sides curling up to grant her a sense of security.

It was almost as good as Darius's embrace. But not quite.

"You look like a fae maiden."

She gasped but wasn't frightened. She turned to find Darius in the doorway, illuminated by the moon-light. He lingered there, almost as if he was making sure the native women saw him. Janette gasped again, this time shocked because she realized that was exactly his intention.

"Being seen in my bed…um…hut won't shame me into marrying you." Her voice was husky and teasing.

"Ah…" He moved forward, and she noticed he wasn't wearing anything over his chest. Not a single stitch. She could see the tiny strands of hair covering his breast.

"So you have fallen prey to the temptations of the pagan influence of the islands…" He was teasing her. He closed the distance between them, and her heart accelerated with every slow step he took. "Or might I indulge myself in thinking you have fallen to my skill of seduction?"

He touched her gently, just cupping her hips, but she quivered, sensation flowing through her like fine wine. Her chemise was thin, and the heat from his fingers nearly burned her, but she reached for him, laying her hands on his chest and smoothing a path through the crisp hair.

"Perhaps I want to seduce you."

He chuckled, guiding her closer and leaning over to press a kiss against her neck. "Among the Islanders, you are the flower I am expected to coax into accepting my seed." Another kiss and she stretched her chin up so he might trail more of them along her delicate skin.

He drew the chemise over her head. "Maybe I'm a fool to have done the honorable thing to ensure we don't have offspring until you ask me for them," he whispered against her ear.

Her belly tightened, a crazy bolt of excitement piercing her. It was an Illuminist man's responsibility to make sure his seed was sterile until his lover decided she was ready to carry a child. When controlled, the current from Deep Earth Crystals could ensure only planned pregnancies happened.

"You could never be anything less than honorable."

He slipped his hands over the mounds of her bottom and pulled her against his body so that the hard outline of his cock was pressing against her. He delivered another few kisses up her neck until she felt his warm breath against her ear.

"Ah…but you tempt me, Janette…beyond everything I believe I need to be."

She couldn't answer him because he kissed her. It was sweet and needy. This time, Darius savored the moment, sliding his mouth against hers in a slow tasting. Her breasts pressed against his chest, the perfect complement to his harder form. Need was nipping at her, centered deep in her belly this time. She reached for the opening of his trousers, fumbling with the waistband before discovering the method of opening them.

His cock was hard and swollen, jutting out the moment she separated the fabric restraining it. He cupped her head, continuing to kiss her while she stroked his length, fingering the smooth skin of his member. He shuddered, proving that her touch caused him the same riot of feelings as his did to her.

For the moment, that was all she wanted to think about. The way they affected each other, like two mirrors facing each other. He cupped her breasts, massaging each tender globe before brushing her hard nipples with his thumbs.

"One of these nights, I am going to have all the time necessary to make love to you." He leaned down and captured one nipple between his lips. She arched her back, offering her flesh to him. Pleasure twisted through her, traveling down to her clit, where it ignited an aching need.

"I have no complaints." Or any hesitation.

"Because I haven't been able to show you the difference between sating passion and making love." He drew in a harsh breath as her grip tightened on his cock. "But I vow to remedy the situation."

She stretched up onto her toes so she might whisper in his ear.

He slid his hands down her sides until he was clasping her hips. There was urgency in his touch now; she would have sworn she felt a current crackling between them.

He lifted her, and she clasped her legs around his hips. For a moment, his cock was between their bodies while he turned and placed her on the small table near the door. She had only a moment to notice the smooth surface against her bare bottom before he was pressing his member into her. Hard and promising, it burrowed between the slick folds of her flesh until she was once again being stretched.

"Put your hands behind you."

His voice was edged with need, and she never hesitated. He maintained his grip on her hips, holding her steady for every thrust.

"Close your eyes, Janette, and let it take control."

She wanted nothing else, and the moment she complied, her body became a receptor. Pleasure was urging her toward the rushing sensation she'd experienced before. Darius increased his pace gradually. By the time delight washed over her, she was straining toward him, desperate for release. It was blinding and tore through her like lightning, and she laughed as it wrung every last bit of strength from her. Darius jerked, and his fingers dug into her hips, but with the proof of his climax, something she craved. His seed filled her before he pulled her close and held her and then, after a few long moments, carried her back to the hammock.

Darius was torn. For the first time in too long, duty didn't offer him the same reward staying with Janette would. He wanted to join her in the hammock, hold her close, and inhale the sweet scent of her skin. He wanted to spend the dark hours stroking her and letting her awaken to his kiss.

But the need to ensure she was protected was more powerful, growing beyond the confines of duty or position. This was personal. So he spread a blanket over her and moved back into the doorway of the hut. The guards would expect him to remain, but he was not going to do what anyone expected.

Soon...soon, he'd be able to linger, but for tonight, he had someone to kill. He didn't bother to chastise himself for how violent his ideas were. When it came to Janette, he wouldn't be taking any chances.

The man who threatened her would die.

⁂

Janette rubbed her blurry eyes as the horizon began to lighten. Darius was nowhere in sight, and she found herself looking at the floor of the hut for any clue that he had actually been there. Her chemise was lying on the floor, sending color into her cheeks as she recalled exactly how it had ended up there. She was as bare as Eve beneath a thin blanket. She sat up and glared at her corset, trying to decide how to get back into it.

Maybe Decima would be up.

With a little hop, she landed on her feet and pulled her chemise off the floor and put it on. She reached for the corset off the shelf where it was resting. Beneath it, there was a folded envelope. A tingle of apprehension went down her spine.

Who could have left it?

Maybe Darius had left it.

Happiness filled her, and she picked it up, intent on reading the contents. But her eyes widened with horror when a small cameo slid out of it, the delicate carved-bone flowers on its front ingrained in her memory from the countless times she'd seen the cameo around Sophia's neck.

My dear Miss Aston,

You shall discover a way to conceal yourself in the king's party to escape the compound and join my compatriots on the north shore, or your friend shall pay the price of your disobedience. Alert your lover, and I shall be happy to put a bullet between her eyes before you can reach us, which will leave me ample opportunity to put a second one into the head of your Guardian Lawley. You will bring this note with you to prove you did not leave it for your lover to use as evidence to clear your name. Once you join me, the Illuminists will never welcome you back. In case you are considering acting the loyal Illuminist, be sure my next correspondence will include one of Miss Stevenson's toes.

Doctor Nerval

Her belly cramped, as though she might retch, but all the muscles did was fill her with pain. Nausea threatened to strangle her as she lifted the cameo, desperately searching for any hint of deception.

But she recognized it. Even the delicate silk ribbon that was creased where it had been tied behind her friend's neck.

Sophia.

Janette dropped the corset back on the shelf and reached for her skirt. She shrugged into the jacket and braided her hair before looking for her shoes. Memories of the clinic flooded her mind, tormenting her with details of just how horrible her friend's plight might be.

Well, she was going to do something about it. The doctor would keep his word that he would kill Sophia; she had no doubt about it. So she'd have to go alone and discover a way to free her friend. She refused to allow herself to worry. No, she was no longer the child her father had left at the clinic.

She was an Illuminist Pure Spirit.

Which meant she had to think when the times were hard. She looked around the hut and pulled loose one of the palms that made up the walls. It was dry and brittle. She stripped the dead leaves from it and knelt. Using the end of it, she began to write in the moist dirt floor, copying the letter word for word. Once she was finished, she left the cameo near the last line.

She stood and left before the dawn was finished breaking.

❧

"You're going to want to get up and close those trousers." Darius Lawley spoke from the doorway of the hut Marshal Agapitos had spent the night in. Darius enjoyed the moment of shock on the Marshal's face, savoring it as the man's face contorted with rage.

Agapitos closed his pants and snapped at Darius as the woman he'd been enjoying rolled over the back of the hammock. She landed neatly on her feet and hurried out of the hut.

"You have no right to invade my privacy."

"I have every right," Darius muttered softly. The early-dawn light illuminated the satisfaction on his face.

"How dare you?"

"You are to be questioned before the council of the local Solitary Chamber, Marshal Agapitos," Darius informed him. "Don't bother looking for your squad of Guardians. I have spoken with their superiors. They no longer answer to your authority, but to mine."

"You had no right!" Agapitos insisted. "I am a Marshal."

"You are a suspected Helikeian," Darius returned. "One I am going to personally enjoy bringing to justice. You and your father were the only members who testified against Janette's mother. Because you share blood, that is not sufficient. You tainted an innocent woman to separate her from the Order."

Past Darius, he saw Guardians moving outside, searching the compound for Janette and Grainger. But for the moment, none of them were watching what was happening inside the hut.

It was his chance, his opportunity to continue on for his cause. Agapitos reached into his pants pocket. Inside was a piece of level-four crystal carefully enclosed in a leather case. He always kept it near, just in case he needed it. Pushing the top leather piece aside, he held on to the other half of the case, which was a sewn into a handle. Pulling the crystal from his pocket, he shoved it toward Darius, aiming for the spot on his chest over his heart. It would burn through the chest wall and into the vital organ in mere seconds.

"You are going to die," he hissed as the crystal made contact, and he struggled to maintain his grip on it. "The Pure Spirit is ours, as surely as if we had bred her."

Pain burned into him. Darius reacted in a split second, striking out at the most vulnerable spot within reach. His training took control as he felt his chest burning. Agapitos staggered back, a solid blow delivered to his neck, crushing the bones. He gurgled and struggled to suck breath into his chest. Bright red blood coated his lips instead. His eyes bulged before he fell to his knees, the crystal rolling across the floor of the hut.

Darius rubbed the front of his chest, staring at the scorched fabric of his vest and shirt. Blisters decorated his skin, but he welcomed the pain. It meant he was alive.

"The bastard could have easily killed you," Lykos muttered as he arrived. Bending down, he picked up the crystal, careful to only touch the handle.

"Or any of us, for that matter."

Lykos studied the damage to his chest for a moment, but that wasn't what kept his lips in a hard line. His comrade was deadly serious when he made eye contact with him.

"Janette is missing. Along with Grainger and Bion."

Darius felt something move through him that he hadn't admitted to feeling in a very long time. It tore through his discipline and settled in his gut, where it felt like it was festering. He stared at Lykos, waiting for his friend to smirk and make some sarcastic comment to prove it was only a jest.

Instead, his fellow Guardian looked grim, his eyes full of another emotion Darius wasn't accustomed to either of them being caught in the hold of. His friend's eyes were full of defeat, but Darius admitted that what he was suffering…was fear.

Seven

ESCAPING THE COMPOUND WAS EASIER THAN SHE'D expected. The king was embarking on a morning expedition, just as the note had said. His servants were focused on making sure they had everything necessary for his comfort. There were carriages and wagons loaded with chairs and tents and every other manner of comfort.

Janette simply took a place inside one of the carriages with the other women of his household. Everyone was busy, their minds on their tasks. The women noted and smiled at her, clearly thinking she had been invited. Still, she fought to keep her expression serene when they began to approach the gates. The guards stood at attention as their monarch rode past and never gave the women riding after him even a glance. Some of the women in the other carriages were young, and she realized they were consorts.

The morning light was waking the inhabitants of the jungle. Colorful birds flew from tree to tree while butterflies fluttered about. The carriage rolled toward the coast, leaving the trees behind. The sound of the breaking surf filled the air as the carriage came to a stop. Everyone alighted and began to unload the wagons.

Janette pulled a parasol from the carriage and used it to hide her face as she wandered away from the king's party. For a moment, she faltered, wondering if she hadn't made a grave error in not waiting for Darius. But Sophia wasn't a member of the Order; it was very possible he'd consider the matter out of their control.

She couldn't take the risk, not with Sophia's life. Janette forced herself to walk farther away from the king's group, walking up to the tree line while searching for any sign of Dr. Nerval.

"So, you have loyalty in you." Grainger appeared from behind a palm tree. His vest was open, and his shirt too. "I wonder what your fiancé will make of your departure."

His lack of dress should have offended her, but she realized she was far more Illuminist than the daughter her father had raised to be a lady of high society because she didn't care a bit; her mind was focused completely on her goal.

"Where is Sophia?" she demanded.

Grainger offered her a smug look. "Are you sure we have more than her cameo?"

"She never lets it out of her sight. It was the last gift her mother gave her."

"How sweet," Grainger groused. "Disgustingly so. But beneficial to our cause. Where is the note?"

Janette pulled the letter from her jacket and tossed it toward him. The paper was too light and fluttered to the ground, but at least she had the satisfaction of watching Grainger stoop down to retrieve it.

"Did she follow instructions?" a new voice interrupted. One of the orderlies from the clinic appeared, shooting a hard look toward Grainger.

Grainger opened the letter and scanned it quickly. "Get the other one out of the pit. The doctor isn't a patient man."

Janette glared at the orderly, recalling the bite of the leather straps very well.

"I'm minding my post," Grainger insisted. He moved his hand, and for the first time, Janette saw the small pistol he held. He had the weapon's muzzle aimed at the ground. The orderly kicked at some dead palm leaves piled on the ground nearby to reveal an opening.

"I was going to enjoy shooting her, you know. She doesn't know when she's been beaten. Damned bloody nuisance."

The orderly reached down and hefted a bundle out of the pit the leaves had concealed. A burlap sack was over the person's head, and when he pulled it free, Sophia's blond hair shimmered in the tropical sun. She was gagged with a thick strip of fabric torn from the hem of her dress, and another length was wrapped around her wrists and body to keep her arms from being of any use. But her eyes were full of fury, proving the orderly true. Sophia hadn't been reduced to sniveling by her circumstances.

"You animals," Janette hissed.

The orderly was unmoved by her words; in fact, he appeared somewhat pleased.

"She's alive. That's what you've earned by coming." Grainger scanned the beach behind her for a long moment. "But she's only going to stay that way if you came alone." He pressed the gun into Sophia's side while glaring at Janette. "If your lover shows his face, I'm going to kill her."

The orderly grabbed Sophia's upper arm in his large hand. "Then let's go before someone comes over here to see what we're doing. We don't blend in here."

"No, we don't," Grainger agreed. He shoved the pistol into his pocket. "I can pull it out again in a moment, so do remember your dear friend is relying upon you to safeguard her."

Sophia tried to say something to him, her cheeks turning red as her eyes narrowed. Grainger tipped his head back and laughed. Janette yanked the gag off her friend but froze when Grainger leveled the pistol at Sophia.

"Not a single sound out of either of you." He gestured with the weapon toward the thick foliage of the tropical jungle. "And get moving before I have to start shooting you in nonlethal places just to keep you motivated. I promise the wounds will be excruciatingly painful and, in this climate, likely to fester."

"We're going," Janette retorted without a trace of respect in her tone. She grabbed Sophia and heard her friend cry out softly.

But the pistol was too real for either of them to ignore.

"What are we going to do?" Sophia whispered.

"I don't know, just keep moving. We'll figure something out."

Janette just hoped she could make good on her promise.

❧

Darius should have been furious. His honor should have been offended, but instead, he was stone-cold terrified. There wasn't a man alive he feared, but seeing the evidence that Dr. Nerval was indeed a Helikeian turned his blood cold.

"Someone needs to contact London. Once they have Janette, I expect they will dispatch someone to kill her parents to cover their tracks," Lykos said. "That way they can kill us and cover their tracks completely."

Guardian Cyrus Vettel of the local Solitary Chamber nodded. "My people will attend to it. As for the Pure Spirit, how many Guardians do you need to neutralize her?"

"She left in a blind panic. Neutralization isn't a foregone conclusion," Darius insisted.

Cyrus wasn't convinced; he knelt next to the writing Janette had left behind.

"This female was raised among high society." Darius pointed at the corset still lying where Janette had abandoned it. "She wouldn't have ventured past the door without that unless she was panicked."

"Yet she did refuse to take the Oath of Allegiance," Cyrus countered. "Since she is your fiancée, you should remove yourself from the search."

"She isn't my fiancée. It was a ruse to prevent Marshal Agapitos from using his authority to remove her from my sight," Darius answered smoothly. He ground his teeth together, frustrated by how much he had to struggle to maintain his composure. Janette undermined his discipline like nothing else.

"A clever one, too," Lykos added. "As a Marshal, Agapitos had the superior rank, and he knew it."

"I will need a full squad to rescue them both."

Darius didn't wait to see if Cyrus would agree with him. He left the hut and hurried to change out of his ruined clothing. Instead of the formal clothing they'd endured to impress the king, he put on canvas pants and a thin lawn shirt to protect his skin from the sun. The vest he reached for was all leather, with pockets and rings sewn into it for the tools he'd need to traverse the jungle. His hat was leather, and he made sure his goggles were in his pocket. The Crystal Fields were a dangerous place. He pulled on knee-high leather boots, but even the stiff leather might not be enough to keep him from being burned. He took his gauntlets with him as he ducked beneath the low doorway of the hut. Lykos was just finishing dressing himself but frowned when Decima appeared in a pair of pants.

"I am going," she announced in a clear and steady tone. She'd changed into serviceable clothing too.

"Women do not belong on a hunt." The king's herald appeared, the Hawaiian guards flanking him. "And you will not be departing from this compound with all your members. My king would be displeased to hear your Pure Spirit is hunting crystals while he has nothing here to ensure you will trade honestly with him."

"Leave the woman."

"They will not," Decima argued. "I belong on this mission as much as any other."

"Yet you are more valuable because you can produce new life," the herald informed her. "My king would insist on keeping you because your warriors will return for you."

"Bloody primitive attitude," Decima muttered softly enough to keep her words from drifting to the herald. "Talk him out of it, Darius."

The herald held his hand up, keeping the carriages waiting at the gate. These were Illuminist ones, with no horses pulling them.

"We don't have time to argue, Decima," Darius offered softly.

Her eyes narrowed. "Since you resigned your post, you do not have the authority to give me orders."

"But I do," Lykos answered. "I am your superior, and you will do your part by remaining inside this compound to satisfy the king. Is that understood?"

Decima was furious. Her green eyes flashed at Lykos. "It's understood."

A hiss and gurgle announced the arrival of the carriages. Darius turned to move toward the gate with the other Guardians falling into step behind him. The guards allowed them through, while he felt Decima's gaze like a dagger on his back.

"It will be better this way," Lykos muttered as the carriage pulled away.

"For everyone except you," Darius answered.

Lykos shook his head. "I disagree, my friend. I have no wish to be wearing the shoes you discover yourself in today." His expression tightened. "Our lives are too dangerous for anything beyond duty."

Darius understood his friend too well. The truth was coiled in his gut, slowly burning while he tried to think of a way to rescue Janette. He should have been considering the most effective method of neutralizing the threat she posed to the Order. His emotions shouldn't have been involved beyond a slight recognition of the fact that it was a waste of a valuable resource.

Instead, he heard her laugh and recalled the way she'd demanded to ride him. He saw her blond hair lying over her shoulders like a shimmering curtain and remembered the silky texture perfectly. Her scent, the sound of her breathing when she was asleep in his embrace, and a hundred other details flooded his mind.

But what bothered him the most was the fear that he'd be unable to reclaim her. For years, he'd thought his heart was dead. It wasn't. He'd just walled it up behind his duty, and it had taken a slip of a society girl with a spirit that wouldn't be intimidated by his strong exterior to break through the barrier.

Damned if that didn't make him adore her even more.

～

Dr. Nerval was pleased.

Janette studied the arrogance in his eyes, wanting to memorize it. She needed to hate him. She needed to overcome years of teaching that had whitewashed her thinking, because she wasn't safe in some high-society house where things like kidnapping were fiction.

The doctor looked at the Illuminist pin on her lapel. Hatred flared up in his eyes. "You are my discovery. It will be the Helikeians who reap the benefits of your abilities. A fact you would have been wiser to learn while at my clinic. Now, due to your disobedience, there is someone else involved."

"Don't you dare try to place the guilt for your crimes on my shoulders," Janette argued. It felt good to speak her mind to him, but the orderly standing next to her reached out and backhanded her.

The doctor smiled, satisfaction shimmering in his eyes. "Thank you, George. As you can see, she shall require firm handling. I'll expect you to attend to that need most intently. Our purpose shall not suffer further setbacks due to emotional outbursts."

"Animal," Sophia sputtered. She turned to stare straight at George, never flinching when he delivered a solid blow to her cheek. Her head snapped to the side, but she righted herself quickly and sent the doctor a hard look.

Dr. Nerval sat down in a large chair. The hut they were in had window shutters, but they were closed to conceal what the occupants were doing. It made the structure stuffy and hot.

"Now. To the matter at hand," the doctor began. "Beyond the boundaries of this settlement, there is a recent lava flow. The eruption has ceased, allowing us the wonderful opportunity to search for new crystals."

"It takes hundreds of years for Deep Earth Crystals to grow."

The doctor nodded. "Yes, but lava accelerates the process. If magma flows over the seeds of a crystal and the conditions are perfect, stage-four crystals can grow in a matter of months. We might even be so fortunate as to discover a root ball."

"What is that?"

The doctor's eyes glowed. "The root ball is absorbed back into the crystal when it grows at a normal pace. Beneath a lava flow, they are sometimes still intact. When broken, a root ball will release a pulse of light capable of causing mutation in the cones of the human eye that will allow that person to see the dimension seams."

"So that is how one becomes a Navigator."

"Exactly." The doctor tapped his cane against the floor, but the packed earth beneath their feet only offered a dull sound. "A Navigator is a self-made man. Like Bion Donkova there. You are proving your worth well."

The First Officer nodded. He was standing near the door, his arms crossed over his chest. The pose reminded her of Darius too much—except for the fact that Bion was clearly a traitor to the Illuminist pin he was wearing. His crimson coat was open now, showing his lack of regard for the formality of the uniform.

"If she finds a root ball, it's mine," he insisted.

The doctor frowned, but Bion abandoned his lazy stance, moving across the hut with clear purpose. "I am not jumping ship for just any reason. You told me any root ball discovered would be mine to make use of."

"You are not the only one who wants the root ball."

Grainger raised his pistol, but Bion only grinned at him. It was an arrogant expression, making it clear that the First Officer didn't think much of the threat.

"You have no choice but to take whatever I offer you," Dr. Nerval spoke firmly. "Your absence will be noted by now."

Bion chuckled softly. "Care to try my nerve, Doctor?" There was only the softest of sounds as his foot connected with the pistol. It was an expert Asian fighting-arts kick, and the weapon went skidding off into the wall.

"You bastard!" Grainger snarled. He launched himself toward Bion but ended up sprawled on the floor after one solid strike to his neck.

"The root ball is yours," the doctor insisted.

Bion froze, his arm raised to deliver another blow to Grainger's temple. He had the man's arm pulled and twisted up to his hip, rendering him immobile. He leaned against Grainger's arm, drawing a groan from his victim.

"You have my pledge," Dr. Nerval said solemnly.

"Then we have a deal," Bion muttered before releasing Grainger.

Grainger rolled over and stood tall. "I won't forget that."

"Good," Bion shot back.

"Enough," the doctor interrupted. "We are becoming distracted. Take them both up to the lava flow and put them to work."

He pointed his cane at Janette. "Run, and your friend will suffer for it. Decide to sacrifice her, and you will suffer." He smiled, the cold twist of lips she recalled from the clinic, which evoked the memory of Darius telling her this man had ordered five other women lobotomized.

"Do not underestimate my ability to cause suffering. I assure you, I am very good at it. George? See that she is secure."

The orderly pointed toward the door. Janette was all too happy to leave the hut. Outside, the island was a tropical paradise. Huge trees grew high into the air to compete for sunshine. The sound of birds filled the afternoon air as the wind tugged on the hem

of Sophia's torn dress. The soil was rich and black.
Janette could see why. Ahead of her was a barren
expanse where lava had recently covered the jungle.
It looked like hell on Earth: no hint of life anywhere
on what looked like an endless expanse of solid rock.

"Now prove you are worth the trouble I have
gone to."

The doctor had followed them. The tip of the
cane jabbed her in the lower back, sending pain
down her legs.

"Go!" His voice was long and thin now, almost
giddy. "Listen for the crystals, and harvest what my
brethren need to be strong."

"I'm going, but only to be away from you." She'd
have been wiser to keep silent, but it felt too good to
speak her mind.

"A fine idea," Sophia agreed. "You have always
been a fine judge of character, Janette.

George turned and slapped Sophia. Janette turned
on the doctor when he began chuckling.

"I do enjoy it, you know." He leaned on his cane
while staring at the red mark on Sophia's cheek.
"Send them out without hats today," he ordered
George before looking back at Janette. "The tropical
sun is harsh. It will burn your skin quickly and leave
you scarred for life." He looked up, past the brim
of his hat. "There are enough hours of light left to
ensure your night is not a restful one, but perhaps
you will recall your manners tomorrow morning
after sampling some of the pain I've promised you
for disobedience."

He lifted his cane and motioned them toward the

lava flow with it. George reached for her upper arm, but Janette moved before he touched her.

"We're going."

She picked up the hem of her skirt and climbed onto the surface of the lava. It crunched beneath her shoe, and the scent of sulfur teased her nose.

"Don't despair."

"Are you comforting me or yourself?" Sophia asked as they climbed farther onto the rock.

Truthfully, Janette wasn't sure. Fear gnawed at her, but it wasn't worry about anything Dr. Nerval might do to her. What sickened her was what Darius might make of her departure. He was a noble man, one who wouldn't forgive a slight, even for the most desperate circumstances. He'd always been clear on that matter, and she felt tears stinging her eyes as she moved out onto the lava flow.

He'd never forgive her for turning over a Deep Earth Crystal to the Helikeians.

Never.

❧

"Captain Kyros cannot delay departure. It is time for you to depart, Doctor."

Dr. Nerval snorted, but Bion didn't shrink away from him.

"I suppose you are correct, compatriot. We need to rename you. Your Illuminist name is foul upon the lips."

"I only care that you call me Navigator," Bion replied. "But the matter at hand is your departure. Captain Kyros will risk discovery if he delays departure for London, and your true identity will be unmasked if you are not at your clinic. You need to leave if you intend to be aboard the airship when she leaves the station."

"Yes, he is correct. Which of course accounts for how he has risen to such a high rank without being discovered," the doctor muttered. "A keen intellect."

"You're leaving?" Grainger demanded. "Before she finds anything of value?"

"Yes," the doctor informed him. "I need to report to the council personally. Finding her has been a triumph I have no intention of being deprived of telling them personally, and our soon-to-be Navigator makes an excellent point. I will continue to use my clinic to find more assets." He looked up to where Janette was picking her way over the lava flow. "You shall be personally charged with ensuring she produces what is expected of her."

Grainger protested. "Why? I've proven myself already. Bion should have to earn that reward he demanded of you."

"He has earned it by jumping ship. It was a sacrifice, actually. Keeping both Kyros and Bion in their positions would have been best."

"Too bad. If your compatriots are going to demand such dedication from me, there was no way I was going to set course back to London while the first Pure Spirit we've discovered goes into the Crystal Fields without me," Bion argued.

"Root balls can be transported," Dr. Nerval insisted.

Bion crossed his arms over his chest again. "That they can. But not necessarily to me. Do I look like an untried boy to you? I'm not the only one who will want a root ball if she discovers one. I plan to stay right here to make sure I receive my price."

The doctor wasn't pleased. He pressed his lips into a hard line but finally nodded. "See that she is diligent. Give them hats tomorrow. Heat stroke will sap their strength too much."

Grainger and Bion watched as the doctor departed. Grainger turned a hard look on Bion the moment the doctor's carriage left.

"You are not in charge of this operation," he insisted.

"Neither are you," Bion answered.

Grainger stiffened. "You think you know so much, but you understand little. That bitch is the child my father always wished I was. My family has been charged with recovering her bloodline for three generations. Once she bleeds, I'm going to breed her, so keep your cock away from her."

Grainger turned his back on Bion. He had his family honor to restore and bring glory to.

❧

"There are two fresh lava flows and the known Crystal Fields," Guardian Cyrus offered. "My suspicion is that they would go to one of the recent flows because there are fewer Illuminist teams in those areas."

"Why?" Darius inquired. "Recent flows have other resources to offer beyond crystals."

"Yes, but they cool unevenly. It makes them dangerous to traverse. The rock can appear cool but in reality only be a few inches of solidified rock. When you step on it, it can fail and send you into the molten lava or release a toxic-gas geyser."

"And Janette knows nothing of the dangers of the Crystal Fields, thanks to Agapitos and his plot." Darius ground his teeth as frustration threatened to drive him mad. He'd never felt so helpless. Time felt like it was crawling, each mile taking too long to cover. The islands were small compared to the rest of the land masses in the world, but today, they seemed massive.

"She had managed to surprise us a few times with her cunning," Lykos offered.

"Yet you still believe her innocent of planning this entire event?" Cyrus inquired.

"I do," Darius insisted. "She could have departed for the Crystal Fields with Dr. Nerval without being rescued from the clinic. There would have been no reason for Sophia Stevenson to bring Janette's imprisonment to my attention. Janette is innocent; I'll stake my future on it."

Guardian Cyrus nodded reluctantly. "I could wish that were not a fact, but it is. You'll end up before a Marshal before this is finished, even if you end up neutralizing her to protect our interests."

Darius stiffened. Understanding was clear inside the carriage. Every Guardian had to come to terms with the necessity of protecting the Order above any remorse they might feel personally. It was a greater sacrifice than giving one's own life in the service of the Order because one would have to live with the knowledge that they had taken the life of an innocent.

For the most noble of reasons, but an innocent nevertheless.

❧

"I thought that blasted sun would never go down."

Janette glared at Grainger. The man had a wide-brimmed hat on and sipped a glass of water. He handed it off to a native man who was wearing only a length of fabric wrapped around his groin.

"I suppose I should take you in for the night, even if you have produced nothing of value."

Her mouth was as dry as winter wool. She wanted to rub at the prickling along her forehead but knew better. The skin was tight and burned. One slight touch would send pain rippling through her. Sophia had fared no better. Her friend was red everywhere her dress didn't cover. Janette even discovered herself longing for her gloves. They would have been hot and stifling, but at least they would have protected her hands from the sun.

"I have never done this before," Janette insisted.

"Then you had best prove a quick learner, if you plan to continue eating."

Grainger gestured toward the edge of the lava flow. It was slow going, but she went gratefully. Grainger locked them both inside the small hut she'd spoken to the doctor in. The inside was still warm from the afternoon sun, but at least the walls were only made of stacked-up lava stone. The wind whistled through the gaps, carrying away the heat.

"What a toad," Sophia muttered. "You really shouldn't have come, Janette. I hoped you wouldn't."

"Of course I would come after you," Janette insisted. "He promised to cut off one of your toes to send with his next letter."

Sophia snorted. "Yes, he delighted in telling me so.

Toad. I would not have made it simple for him, and I would have endured if necessary."

Sophia walked toward the back of the hut, where a large rock with a flat top had baskets sitting on it. There was one large bottle, and she lifted it to her lips for a drink. She had to force herself to stop, and water dribbled down her neck before she managed to overcome the urge to gorge.

"You should have to. This is all my fault." Janette reached for the bottle, and her hands trembled because she was so parched. It seemed forever since her last drink of water, but when she began swallowing, her belly tightened around the first few mouthfuls, making it impossible to swallow any more. She sputtered and ended up wiping water off her chin as well.

The baskets held a meager offering of food, but the fruit looked delicious. Janette didn't recognize most of it, but she could smell the sugar in it.

Her friend scoffed at her after taking a bite of a golden fruit with a prickly exterior. "It is not, Janette, and don't you dare quibble with me. Not knowing what had happened to you was killing me. I arrived at your house just in time to follow you to that clinic. Well, I went straight home and changed into those cycling pantaloons so that I might tell Mr. Lawley—and I am glad I did. I would not have regretted it even if that toad had cut my toe off."

Sophia aimed a determined look at her as they finished off the meal.

Long after they'd both crawled into the sleeping nets, Janette found her thoughts lingering on Sophia. But no way to free her friend presented itself. Instead, she fell asleep, and her dreams were full of the man she'd broken her word to. At least that was how Darius would see it. Tears stung her eyes because she knew in her heart he'd never forgive her for leaving the royal compound. Understand, perhaps, but even if he was noble enough to forgive her, the Order would not. A Marshal would brand her a traitor just as quickly as her mother had been. Tears slid from the corners of her eyes, stinging her burned cheeks.

Darius might forgive her, right before he was ordered to execute her.

✎

London

Compatriot Heron was pleased. Dr. Nerval savored the moment, drawing in a deep breath and holding it while he allowed satisfaction to sink into him.

"You have no right to praise this relic of an operative," Compatriot Peyton announced. "He has allowed the Illuminists to know his position."

Compatriot Heron lost much of his beaming expression. Dr. Nerval felt his control slipping for the first time in years. He thumped his cane against the floor. "I have brought you the first Pure Spirit in a decade. Now that she has been secured, it will take but a few more actions to make her removal from society complete. This council should reward me with the Sapphire Phalanx. It is my turn to be recognized by every member."

Dr. Nerval stared at the brilliant blue sashes each man in front of him wore. They were symbols of the honor he'd spent years earning.

"I would never vote for such a thing," Peyton announced.

"Yet I will," Compatriot Heron remarked and looked at Silas, who nodded. "I suggest you reconsider your position, Compatriot Peyton, for you are in the minority. Never a wise position to linger in."

Peyton grimaced; his lip rose, and the muscles along his neck drew tight before he bent and nodded. "I see the wisdom in my fellow compatriots' decision."

"Excellent," Compatriot Heron muttered. Two lower members brought forth the sash. The doctor's legs wobbled just a bit as he stood to receive his honor. The sash was lifted over his head before being settled perfectly across his heart. Heron stood and approached with the sapphire pin that could be worn at all times as a symbol of his new honor. Heron attached the small symbol of a javelin held in the grip of a snake to his lapel.

"Now, return to your clinic," Heron said softly. "I will hope to hear from you again soon."

The lower member followed him from the chamber after a flick from Heron's hand.

"That was too generous." Peyton argued.

"The gesture was not for him, but for those members watching him and how we respond to those who bring us what we want." Heron cast a doubtful look at Peyton. "You seem to fail to grasp the long-term effects of our work here. That bothers me immensely."

Peyton stood, offering the expected bow as his senior compatriot left the chamber, but he was fighting to maintain his composure. His temper flared, his pride suffering from the memory of seeing the sash bestowed on Dr. Nerval.

Janette Aston should have been his daughter.

Damn Mary and her mother for being crafty enough to escape his so brilliantly executed plan. Even twenty-five years hadn't been long enough for the sting of Mary's rejection to dim.

Peyton would be damned if some doctor was going to enjoy any benefit from the work he had done. The glory of producing a new Pure Spirit was his alone. Janette was his creation, even if she was not his daughter. In time, she'd bear his grandchildren, and they would be raised as Helikeians.

Compatriot Peyton left the nondescript building where the Helikeian council met and resumed his position as Marshal Photios. The sun had set, but his driver waited at the arranged spot. As a Marshal, no one questioned him. Not now—or twenty-five years ago when he'd overlooked the lack of evidence against Mary Aston.

He sat back in the dim interior of the carriage as the sound of steam filled it. The driver took them toward the outskirts of town with an expert hand.

Mary, or Zenais as he'd known her, was still able to impress him. Her intelligence had drawn him to her just as surely as her bloodline. They would have been magnificent together.

Bitterness filled him. Zenais had escaped him so very completely, but there was a satisfaction in knowing her daughter was her undoing. Photios grinned as the carriage swayed. Yes, Zenais had clearly raised her daughter with the same educational goals she had been raised with. That was her undoing in the end. Instilling a love in her daughter for the one place she had been banished from. Dr. Nerval was only a lucky man. Janette Aston had always been destined to seek out the Illuminists. The doctor had had nothing to do with it. All of it was the culmination of the plan Photios had put into motion twenty-five years before.

So the glory was going to be his too.

"Wait here."

Photios received only a nod from his driver. The man didn't look at him or which direction he went—such was the posting of a driver to a Marshal. He had complete authority, and his comings and goings were not subject to question.

Blind, trusting Illuminists. He was going to enjoy watching their kind fall. Soon, their Solitary Chambers would belong to the Helikeians, and it would be a glorious day indeed. With enough Deep Earth Crystals, they would arm their men with weapons the Illuminists refused to create in their noble determination to use their knowledge for the benefit of all mankind.

Photios snorted on his way through the back streets. They were narrow and used by supply carts and delivery boys. The well-worn paths used by the servants stood out clearly with the help of the moon. His cloak covered his suit, making him shapeless in the night. Once he reached the back door of the doctor's house, he lifted his walking cane and rapped on the door with the solid brass ball on the cane's end. The door was opened by a scullery maid, who hurried away when she saw the pin on his lapel.

Photios smiled. It was a smug expression, he knew,

but merited because there were no servants in the doctor's house who did not serve the Helikeians.

The cook appeared before him. A rotund woman, she didn't say a word but waited for his instruction.

"Put this in your master's drink. Tonight." He extended his hand, a small glass vial in it. She took it without comment. "Do it yourself, and present yourself at this address tomorrow for a new position. Bring the girl who answered the door."

The cook slipped the vial into her pocket. Photios turned in a swirl of black wool. He heard the door shut behind him. Let Dr. Nerval enjoy his new honor.

It would be his last triumph.

◦~◦

"Uncomfortable night?"

Janette jumped. The net swung with the sudden motion, and she spilled onto the dirt floor of the hut. Sophia jerked awake and ended up sprawled next to her.

Grainger watched from the doorway. "Another few hours without hats and you'll both blister."

Janette stood. "Whatever sort of satisfaction you're hoping for, I doubt you'll get it from either of us."

His lips twisted into a smile, but it wasn't a kind expression. Instead, it nauseated her, because along with it, his eyes narrowed and his gaze swept down from her face to settle on her breasts.

"As soon as I have confirmation that you aren't carrying your lover's bastard, I plan to satisfy myself as often as I please between your thighs." The tip of his tongue swept over his lower lip.

"What a blessing that I haven't had breakfast," she muttered. "I'm sure I would have lost it in response."

He raised an eyebrow. "In that case, you can get back to work with your belly empty."

Grainger moved out of the doorway. "Find something if you want water." He snickered at them. "You won't live very long without it, and I won't be bringing it to you without a very good reason."

"Pay him no attention, Janette." Sophia swept her past the man, using her body as a shield.

"I have to. We will die out there without water."

For the moment, they had only each other, but Janette felt strangely strong. Maybe it was the training she'd had in the few months since passing the exam or just the comfort of having her friend near. Maybe it was the way Sophia faced their dilemma without tears shimmering in her eyes. Whatever the reason, Janette looked out toward the lava with her chin held steady.

They would find a way to survive. *She* would.

It looked as if the hand of Satan had reached up from the bowels of the Earth to claw at the peaceful perfection. The dark red rock rested in long fingers among the lush tropical foliage where it had flowed before cooling. Steam rose from it in little wisps, and the scent of sulfur was strong.

"Shouldn't we stay close to them?" the orderly asked.

"I can shoot them from here." Grainger lifted his rifle and looked down the barrel at Sophia. "There is nowhere for them to hide. So I don't need to roast out on that damned rock."

"Come away, Janette. Let us improve our view," Sophia muttered with enough sweetness to please even the sourest spinster. Grainger scowled at them, but Janette followed her friend.

"Have a lovely morning, ladies," he called after them.

Janette concentrated on finding good footing. The lava still steamed in places, and it was like molten ocean waves had frozen. There was nothing even about it. They had to pick their way across it, their shoes slipping on bits of gravel and threatening to send them tumbling. At least they had hats today. Made of braided palm leaves, the wide brims at least made the sun bearable.

The humming began when Janette was shaking off a twist in an ankle. The pain gave way to the rhythmic sounds pulsing in time with her heartbeat. Steady and strong, they grew louder with only a single step.

"You hear one, don't you?"

Janette nodded, biting her lip. "I'm going to have to get better at hiding my feelings."

She stopped and looked at her friend. "How did you know—"

"Because that man never stopped talking from the moment his ruffians kidnapped me," Sophia explained. "Mind you, I'm sure it's due to the fact that they expect to kill me at some point, but still, you'd think members of some secret order like theirs would be a little less talkative around a nonmember. No one is perfect, after all. One or two captives are sure to escape having their throats slit from time to time. It's simply a matter of averages."

Janette wanted to be horrified; instead, she discovered herself grateful for her friend's humor. "You never do take anything seriously."

Sophia widened her eyes innocently. "That isn't

true, and you know it. Why, I take the threat of being sent to the Highlands very seriously, Janette. You know I detest the rain."

"Cold rain, anyway." Janette looked at the clouds around the peak. Yesterday, they'd grown until they covered the lava flow and dumped warm rain on them. It had been a welcome relief.

But she couldn't count on there being rain today. Grainger's threat hung over her like a stone, ready to crush her.

Janette walked closer to the crystal, fighting off the urge to sway in time with the humming. It filled her head, leaving little room for any sort of thinking.

Sophia hooked her arm and pulled her forward. "I do believe it is a good thing I am here. You need a steady hand for this crystal hunting."

They climbed over a large finger of lava, and on the other side, water rushed by. It was like heaven and hell were side by side. On one side, nothing but endless dark brown lava rock with the scent of sulfur, while on the other, the lush jungle with its plants all green and sprouting flowers. Through it ran a river. The water rushed down from the top of the mountain where the lava had erupted. It was a torrent now because up near the peak, clouds had gathered and were dropping the rain that fed the stream. The water was moving fast enough to fill it with tiny bubbles, which gave it a white appearance.

"Water."

They both climbed down, eager for a taste. Neither one gave any mind to their hems but waded right into the water to scoop handfuls of it up.

"I never thought water could taste so sweet," Sophia muttered.

Janette agreed, but she was distracted by the humming. Once her thirst was sated, she turned practically hypnotized by the rhythmic sounds.

"You hear one?" Grainger appeared on the top of the lava flow with Bion close on his heels. "Don't you?"

Janette stumbled, instinctively moving away from Grainger.

"She did until you interrupted," Sophia scolded him.

"Shut your mouth—" Grainger ended up following his own orders when Janette looked away from the rock to glare at him. He was furious but gestured with his hand for her to seek out the crystal.

Part of her wanted to refuse on principle, but there was another part of her that refused to give up on life. Grainger had a long rifle propped against his shoulder. The barrel was pointing at the sky, but that could change so quickly.

"Let Sophia go." She wasn't sure where she got the idea to bargain with him, only that it erupted from her and there was no controlling it.

"You're mad if you think I am going to get rid of the single hold I have over you." Grainger reached into his vest pocket and pulled out a small pistol. It was tiny, likely a lady's muff weapon. His lips twisted slightly before he aimed the barrel at Sophia.

"Don't be an idiot!" Bion lunged at him, but it was too late.

There was a puff of black smoke and a squeal from Sophia as the bullet tore into her leg. She fell into a heap, clutching at her calf while Janette dragged her out of the water before the current pulled her down-river. Janette shoved her petticoat aside to stare at the groove left in her friend's flesh from the bullet.

"That wasn't necessary," Bion said.

Grainger's eyes narrowed. "I disagree. If you're too soft to witness the methods necessary to keep this Pure Spirit in line, I suggest you leave. I've never had much taste for traitors myself."

"I don't find enjoyment in tormenting females." Bion pulled his arm back and sent a solid blow toward Grainger's jaw. It connected with a harsh sound of flesh hitting flesh. Grainger stumbled backward, and the back of his head collided with the lava rock.

"You...bastard..." He mumbled but collapsed in a heap as he rubbed at the back of his head. He still held on to the pistol, though, even as he seemed to lose track of what was happening.

"Damned idiot," Bion muttered before dropping to one knee beside Sophia.

"We don't need your assistance," she snapped, but the First Officer paid her no mind. He pulled her leg out so he could look at it, without a care for how forward his actions were. Not that either of them should have been shocked, considering the circum-stances, but Sophia sucked in a deep breath and her eyes bulged. She likely blushed, but with the sunburn, it was impossible to tell.

"It's only a flesh wound. You're lucky." Bion grabbed her skirt and tore another length of fabric off the already-mangled hem. He wound it around the wound before tying it securely. "But it's going to hurt like hell."

"Good," Grainger snapped.

Janette turned to see the muzzle of the pistol aimed at Sophia again. Grainger's eyes were glittering with rage. Blood trickled down his chin, and more had soaked into his collar from the back of his head. Fear tingled through her because he looked far more dangerous wounded than he had ever looked before. There was desperation in his eyes now.

"Get that crystal, or I will put the next bullet closer to her heart."

Bion moved, but Grainger followed him with the rifle. "Stay right there! I'll shoot you too. Actually, first, because it would please me greatly to be rid of you…traitor."

Bion froze, but his gaze was on Grainger, judging the distance between them.

"I'll get off a shot, Bion, and that's a promise." He stood, using the lava rock to support his body. "Now get me that crystal. I know you hear one. Dig it up, or enjoy having your hands stained with blood."

"Don't do it, Janette," Sophia muttered.

Bion reached out and covered her mouth with his hand. "He's not in his right mind."

"I am indeed in my right mind!" Grainger insisted. "Get me the crystal!"

His finger moved on the trigger, his eyes glowing with some insane light.

"I'm going," Janette announced. "Look…I'm going now…just be patient."

"I am the one giving orders here!" Grainger yelled.

"I can't hear it," she shouted back at him. Her heart was racing, sending blood pumping through her ears.

"I just need to listen—and everyone needs to stop shouting, so I can hear it."

Grainger ground his teeth. His nostrils flared; he looked like he was losing control.

"Do it now," he told her in a low growl.

Panic threatened to grip her, but she fended it off. Sophia shook her head, but Bion pulled her against his body to keep her still. The sound of the crystal rose above the water, drawing her to the edge of the lava, where the river rushed around it.

"Yes…yes…crystals need water to grow…" Grainger mumbled.

Janette waded into the water. The current pulled at her skirts, but she bent down and dug into the black sand beneath the surface. Pieces of lava stone bit into her fingers as she pulled up handfuls of mud until she felt the tingle of power traveling through her body.

"Yes!" Grainger shouted with glee. "Bring it to me!"

"It's stuck," Janette insisted. "I can't free it."

He glared at Sophia. "Give her your gloves, Bion, and do so slowly."

"They won't have the strength to harvest it," Bion argued.

"They'd better." Grainger refused to budge. "Give her your gloves now, or she can take them after I shoot you."

Bion's expression tightened. A muscle along the side of his jaw twitched. "I believe I'm going to enjoy killing you."

"Not while I have the gun." Grainger snickered. "Give her the gloves."

"I believe I am going to enjoy watching the pair of

you fight over that damned crystal," Sophia remarked as she took the gloves Bion held out for her.

"I agree," Janette added. She was beginning to shake, the water stealing every last bit of warmth from her legs. It felt like the blood running back up to her heart was cold too.

"Shut your mouths. Women never know when to be silent."

Sophia rolled her eyes when she reached Janette. She limped and stood at an odd angle to favor her injured leg once she was next to her friend. They reached beneath the water, Sophia feeling about until she had her hands on the crystal. Sophia jerked but didn't let it go. They pulled, combining their strength until it came free. They both lost their footing and sprawled into the middle of the rushing water.

"Hold it right there!"

Janette jerked her head around, sure she was hallucinating because she heard Darius's voice loud and clear in spite of the rush of the water and the crystal humming inside her head. She quickly righted herself. She had it in her hands—it was an inch wide and four inches long.

"Don't move, Grainger. Not an inch, or I'll put a bullet between your eyes."

It was Darius.

She turned her head and found him standing on the other side of the river. He was waist-deep in the water with a pistol leveled at Grainger.

"I'll kill her," Grainger threatened, the muzzle of his rifle aimed at Sophia.

Bion launched himself at Grainger while everyone was

looking at Sophia. The gun went off, but the bullet only hit the water as Bion tackled Grainger to the ground.

The current was much stronger than Janette had realized; it was pulling at her. She struggled to stay on her feet while holding the crystal.

"Janette…give me your hand…" Sophia lunged toward her, grabbing her hands and pulling the crystal closer to the water.

The moment the crystal hit the water, there was a sizzle and an explosion. Whatever had been in her hands vaporized like it was scalding-hot and the water had cooled it. The white steam rose into Sophia's face, while the force of it sent Janette back into the strongest part of the river. The current swept her off her feet, tumbling her like a stick. It sucked her down, filling her mouth and nose, encasing her in a swirling white environment. She couldn't tell which way was up or down. She felt the water suck her down, pulling her body away from the light. Her lungs began to burn, and she fought, but to no avail. Darkness began to crush her in its grasp, but she fought against it, struggling to escape the hold of the current. Where her mind was willing, her body couldn't maintain the battle without air. Her muscles refused to obey her as her mind began to succumb to the darkness.

Darius had come for her. Maybe to kill her, but at least she'd seen him one final time.

❦

"We must go after them." Sophia's voice was a mere croak, her throat feeling as raw as her sunburned face. "Before they drown."

Tears streamed down her face in spite of her resolve to maintain some dignity. It certainly wasn't easy. Men surrounded her—Lykos and others who seemed to be working with the Illuminists. Sophia sat on a rock and tried to recover from whatever had happened to her. She rubbed her eyes, trying to restore her vision.

"She must have had a root ball," Bion remarked near enough for her to hear him. Sophia looked up, but her vision was blurry, and all she saw were unrecognizable shapes.

"It was a bunch of tiny crystals, hundreds of them," she informed him. "But they turned to steam when Janette got them too close to the water."

She heard Bion mutter something under his breath and slapped her knees with frustration. The wet fabric of her dress and petticoat sloshed, but she didn't dare stand, because she didn't know which way to go.

"Stop whispering—at least so long as we are discussing my eyes. Even if what happened is part of your secret Order, it happened to my eyes. You can't take them with you." She stood but stumbled as her blurred vision disoriented her. Bion wrapped an arm around her waist. It was horribly improper, but she would have fallen without his assistance. She bit her lip.

"What we need to do is cover them before the sunlight damages them."

"What we need to do is go after Janette—she isn't the best swimmer, I can tell you."

"We'll see to Darius and Janette. You need attention."

Bion picked her up. Swung her right up into his arms as if she were a child. A harsh gasp got past her lips in response.

"You cannot be so forward with me."

"For the moment, it cannot be helped." Bion deposited her back on the rock she'd been sitting on. He covered her eyes with one large hand, sweeping it downward to close her eyes.

"Why aren't you in chains or dying like Grainger?" She was being rude but couldn't seem to control the urge to snap at him.

He ripped another strip from her dress, making her sigh. "Your dress is beyond repair, Sophia."

"I know." But she didn't care for how defeated she sounded. "You didn't answer my question." At least returning to her demanding questioning was better than sounding like a lost little girl.

"Keep your eyes closed. You'll have to endure being blind until we can get you some glasses." She heard him dunk the fabric in the water a few times before squeezing it.

"So answer my question."

He began to wind the fabric around her head. It was a long strip, and soon, every bit of daylight was blocked out.

"Why can't I know? It seems only fair to know if I should thank you or curse you."

He tucked the edge of the strip in. "I doubt you'd know many curses."

"I know a few," she groused, the wound on her leg beginning to throb. Fear was trying to strangle her. "Please tell me what happened to my eyes. I'm a tailor…you see. My father needs me."

"You won't be blind," he offered softly.

"Don't coddle me." She stood again, needing to

prove she wasn't weak, but her leg crumpled. Pain bit into her so hard she couldn't breathe. She ended up cradled against Bion's chest again. It should have horrified her. She should have been offended or angry with just how familiar he was being.

Instead, she felt comforted as her mind shut down and she sank into oblivion.

"She lasted longer than most," Lykos remarked.

"She's a bloody big problem now," Cyrus muttered, "but I suppose she'll find it rather fortunate, considering she's best friends with the Pure Spirit. They can continue their friendship now."

"That's assuming Janette and Darius are still alive."

Lykos looked down the river. There was no sign of Janette or Darius, and he knew the water wound its way through the jungle all the way to the coast. Two hundred feet into the foliage, the river split.

As if they didn't have enough complications as it was.

"This case is cursed," he announced, not really talking to anyone in particular. "We still haven't recovered our Pure Spirit, and now we have a Navigator who isn't a member of the Order."

"She might not be a member of the Order but we're going to have to explain what's happened to her." Bion peered down at Sophia. Bitterness welled up inside him as well as anger. She was a mess and an innocent.

"You recovered her alive. It's more than some have been granted," Lykos muttered nearby.

"I'm no more happy with that than you would be. But the light is fading, which means we're going to have to leave the search until tomorrow."

Understanding dawned in Lykos's eyes. Bion turned

and began carrying Sophia to where a carriage waited. He expected better from himself. Lykos was the sort of man who recognized the trait because he held himself to higher standards too.

It was not good enough. He'd fallen short of his mission.

Eight

SHE WAS STILL ALIVE. SOMEHOW, SOME WAY—AND part of her resented it because there was pain in living.

The water still roared with a deafening sound. Now that she'd listened to it for so long, it was becoming soothing.

"Wake up, Janette." Darius slapped her cheek gently. "We can't stay here."

She reached up to rub her eyes. They felt full of grit, and her tongue was coated with the same. But memory rushed through her, clearing her mind, and she sat up. Her head collided with Darius's, sending another jolt of pain through her.

"How did you..." She looked around, confused. "How did we get here?"

Darius's clothing was filthy. His once-fine lawn shirt was full of dark volcanic sand that made it look charcoal gray. His hat was long gone, and his hair was drying in soft curls.

"I followed you with some notion of rescuing you, but the river got the best of my intentions," he remarked as he hooked his hand under her arm and lifted her to her feet.

His grip was solid and real, sending a rush of relief through her. "How did you find me?"

He turned his dark gaze toward her, the intensity of it sending a ripple of sensation down her spine.

"You left the note behind." His eyes narrowed. "What you should have done was brought it to me."

"I was not willing to risk Sophia's life or her toes."

"It was foolish of you, Janette. It nearly drove me mad to think of you out with that monster with no way to protect yourself."

"I'm not so helpless, you know." But she was glad to see him, and her voice was full of relief.

He was frowning, but in his eyes was a flicker of relief as well. His stony expression crumbled as he grinned. "I know you aren't. In fact, your ability to undermine my self-discipline is quite remarkable."

He managed to deliver his comment in a dry tone, worthy of any high-society drawing room. Coupled with the tattered clothing and filth, it struck her as so funny that she laughed out loud.

He reached out and grasped her arms. She wasn't sure if he stepped toward her or pulled her into his embrace, but his lips claimed hers. His kiss released all the tension that had been balled up inside her for the last day. The sweetest relief flooded her as his mouth claimed hers in a hard kiss.

He kept her still with one solid arm across her back, while capturing the back of her head in his other hand. His lips took hers, slipping along the delicate surfaces and pressing her to open her mouth for a deeper taste. The moment she surrendered, his tongue thrust deep, sending a spike of need through her that was white-hot. She curled her hands into the lapels of his vest, pulling him closer even though there wasn't any space left between them. Need was building inside her again, and she welcomed it because it burned away the uncertainty that tormented her.

"Damn it, Janette." He put her away from him while muttering a few more phrases no gentleman would utter. "Swear you will never face something like this alone again."

He cared. She heard it in his voice, and there was no disguising the need in his eyes. Heat touched her cheeks, and she realized it was guilt, but at the same time she was happy because he truly cared. She cupped his cheek, smoothing her hand along his jaw, and felt him shiver. He drew in a deep breath before placing a kiss into her palm and turning to scan the surrounding jungle.

"Let's get moving before I forget what it is I'm supposed to be doing in favor of what I'd like to finish with you. We have a limited amount of daylight left to find shelter. The jungle is rather unsavory after dark."

He reached for her bicep, but she stepped forward before he closed his grasp.

"I believe I can do without any more unsavory experiences for a bit." She yanked her water-soaked skirt out of the way of her feet.

The jungle grew thick the moment she made it beyond the edge of the riverbed. Darius moved past her, cutting a trail.

"We won't make it out of this jungle before night-fall." He braced his arm against a thick branch to hold it out of the way for her.

She stopped, staring at the wall of vegetation in front of her. "Where are we going?"

"To the village. Follow the trail."

She stared at the huge green leaves. There were at least twenty different shades of green, and all of the foliage was larger than any plants she'd ever seen. A warm hand captured hers and tugged her gently behind him.

"This way."

What Darius perceived as a trail was nothing more than scattered bare patches of earth. Left to herself, she would have been completely lost. Yet he seemed at ease, threading his way through the labyrinth while tugging her behind him. She stared at his wide shoulders, slightly stunned by his skill. The man was still wearing a pair of trousers and a vest any Londoner would have considered civilized, yet he was making his way through a primitive landscape with ease.

She smothered a dry chuckle, but he heard it and turned to investigate what she found so amusing.

"You surprise me, Darius, and yet maybe I'm being thickheaded not to admit it's your ungentlemanly side that draws me to you."

For a moment, he allowed her to see his boyish nature again. A slightly mocking grin, which gave her a brief glimpse at his teeth, and playfulness lit his dark eyes.

"We seem to be counterparts to each other, Janette, for it's your spirit I can't seem to ignore."

"You needn't sound like that is such a burden." Her tone was wounded, allowing him to hear how

much her emotions were entangled in their relationship. "Being lovers shouldn't be so much for you to
worry over."

She tried to walk past him, but he twisted her
hand slightly, locking her elbow so that she was held
close to his body. His black eyes were hard, glittering
with emotion as thick and choking as those she felt.
For one moment, it felt like they were soul mates,
like they were counterparts and not whole without
each other.

"It was a burden to think of you in the hands of
a Helikeian, and it had nothing to do with the fact
that they are my enemy, only that I know what they
are capable of doing to anyone they want to control.
Death is not what your friend had to fear, and it put
me through hell to think of you in that situation."

"I…" She shut her mouth, her emotions surging
up and making it impossible to think or decipher how
she felt.

"You what, Janette?"

"I don't know…" She pulled on her hand, but
he maintained his grip and cupped her chin to keep
their gazes locked. "I don't know how to feel about
you, Darius. It's like you're two different men—one
who threatens to kill me, while the other rescues me.
You warn me to stay away and then show up in my
room to soothe my bruises before grumbling about
how much of a burden I am. I don't know who
you are."

"In that case, Janette, I'll make sure you understand
me before we leave this jungle."

His face became a mask of determination, and

she saw something in his eyes that sent her belly fluttering—something that looked like a promise.

And Darius always kept his promises.

✧

"I didn't expect to have the privilege of your company again so soon, Dr. Nerval."

Captain Kyros stood in the lobby of his airship while passengers boarded. He didn't miss the new pin on the doctor's lapel. The javelin in the grip of a snake drew only a few curious glances from the surrounding population, but his Compatriots knew what it symbolized. The fact that he could not wear his blue sash in the open did not stop him from gaining recognition of his new award.

"You will not enter my name into the passenger log."

The captain nodded as the doctor passed by with his personal servants behind him. A plump woman trailed the butler and undergrooms. She was busy twisting the tassels of her shawl and snapping her fingers at a younger girl.

The captain turned his back. For those wearing the pin of the Sapphire Phalanx, there were no questions. Dr. Nerval was set above others now, and if he wanted his name absented from the passenger log, it would be so. Kyros saw to it personally—savoring the moment, because such times were rare when he could enjoy being Helikeian. Someday his service as an agent among the Illuminist enemy might well be rewarded with the Sapphire Phalanx. Such an honor was a lifetime's work, and it would glorify his name into the generations of the future.

❧

"Madam…the Master did not tell us to expect you."

Mary Aston swept into the house she'd called home for twenty-five years. She could hear the cook pulling the cords in the kitchen to alert the upstairs staff to her presence.

"Howard doesn't know I've returned." Neither had he given her permission, but her husband was about to come face-to-face with the woman she'd been forced to bury so many years ago. By God, she was an Illuminist, and her husband would answer for sending their daughter to an insane asylum.

"I intend to speak with my husband directly." She pulled off her gloves and dumped them on the tray the downstairs maid had managed to fetch in spite of the late hour.

Giles appeared, a single loose button on his vest the only indication that she'd arrived after her husband had retired for the evening and his butler had taken his leave. There were hurried steps on the wooden floorboards as her maid came down the main staircase instead of taking the back stairs, which would have taken longer.

"Welcome home, madam. I've set the girls to preparing your chambers."

"Thank you, Alice, but I will see my husband first."

"The master has retired for the evening," Giles informed her.

Mary looked the man in the eye and smiled knowingly. "I owe you an apology, Giles."

"You do, madam?"

"Yes. For you see, I am not the simpering fool I have always portrayed in your presence. Go up those stairs and tell your master to turn his lover out of his bed, or stand aside as I do. Either way, I am going to speak with my husband."

The tray with her gloves on it clattered to the floor. Alice covered her mouth as Giles tried to think of something proper to say to her.

"Never mind," Mary muttered. She yanked a handful of her skirt out of the way and mounted the stairs.

"Madam...you mustn't!" the butler called after her, but his shock had paralyzed him too long to stop her. Mary was already on the upper floor when the man gave chase.

"I disagree," she muttered before reaching the large double doors of her husband's rooms. She threw them open and marched through the dressing room to the second set of doors that led to the bedroom.

She hadn't seen it in years.

"My goodness, Howard, whatever are you doing?"

Her husband had a pretty little maid in his bed all right. The look of pleasure on his face made Mary's temper sizzle.

"Out," she ordered the girl.

"What...? What are you doing?" Howard sputtered.

The maid let out a shriek and scampered off the huge bed. The girl gathered up her clothing, and her bare feet slapped against the polished wood floor as she fled. Leaving Mary's husband to deal with her.

"What are you doing, *madam*?"

Mary moved forward, her steps slow and confident. "Interrupting your liaison, dear husband."

Howard grabbed the neatly turned-down bedding to shield his pride.

"I will not stand for this…this disruption, Mary."

She'd reached the ornately carved footrail of the bed and wrapped her bare hands around it and leaned toward her husband.

"Mary! You will cease this…forwardness immediately."

"Yes, of course, Howard, that was always our agreement, wasn't it? But I must tell you…" She tapped her lower lip with the tip of her finger suggestively and had the satisfaction of watching her husband swallow. "It was dreadfully disappointing. I never climaxed in this room. Maybe you should have let me ride you."

"Madam!"

Mary frowned at his outrage, aiming the full strength of her temper at her husband for the very first time in their marriage.

"You're a selfish man, Howard, and your high-society friends are selfish to pump their wives until they feel the bite of climax, while lecturing their female companions on the merits of abstaining from pleasures of the flesh. You get to spend, but I must act as though I have never felt passion or desire."

"Mary! You are my wife."

"Yes, I have been your wife, but you made a promise to me, Howard, one you broke when you sent our daughter to that clinic." Mary turned the full force of her fury onto her husband. "I agreed to every one of your stipulations, and I have upheld my promise, but you broke your word to me. You swore an oath to me that you would never treat me or any female children I gave you like chattel."

"Janette needed treatment…"

"For what? For not behaving like a mindless fool?"

Mary took a few steps back toward her husband, unable to resist the urge to shout at him. "You arrogant toadstool! How dare you have my daughter locked up for being intelligent? We had a bargain, and you have broken it. So I will no longer obey you."

"Really, Mary." Her husband was on his feet now. "And this display of gutter behavior is your way of getting even with me?"

"No. Leaving you is." Mary regained her composure. "I am returning to face the charges against me."

"You cannot. I forbid it."

Mary reached for the door handle. "You have lost my allegiance."

"Janette is fine and safe!"

Mary turned on her husband. "She is halfway around the world! Being fought over by ruthless men. I am a fool to have gone to the country while you sent her to that Helikeian devil! How could you send your own child to a stranger?"

Mary didn't receive an answer. Howard sucked in his breath, as though in pain. Her hand was on the doorknob, but his lips moved, and no sound emerged. He kept trying to say something while reaching for his chest. A solid foot of a rapier protruded from his chest; in the darkened room, a man had moved up behind him without their noticing.

"You won't be facing those charges, my dear Zenais."

Photios pushed Howard off his rapier. Mary's husband fell to the floor with a dull sound, rolling over and lifting one hand to reach toward her. But a trickle of blood ran across his bare skin, telling her his lung was filling with blood from a puncture wound.

"It was charming to witness your little fight with your husband, and quite fortunate you allowed the maid to witness your arrival." He dropped the rapier on the floor and lifted his hands. "It will be quite believable when the constables find your husband run through with his father's dueling rapier, and you strangled nearby.

"Where is my daughter?"

Photios smirked at her, clearly confident that she was at his mercy. "In the Crystal Fields, harvesting for the Helikeian Order. She could have been born into our ranks if you had only seen the wisdom of wedding me. She would be so much happier right now."

"I knew there was something dishonest about you. It was in the way you always made sure I couldn't even talk to another male Illuminist."

"You were to be mine," Photios declared. "Your blood and mine would have produced Pure Spirits. Fate still favors me—your daughter will bear my grandchildren, and they will be proud Helikeians."

He raised his hands, his fingers forming claws. "I didn't want to kill you, but it is the only way to cover taking your daughter."

There was no way to open the door, no time, so Mary sent an Asian back kick toward Photios. Her skills were rusty, but they proved solid, and her foot landed on his belly. The force of her kick sent him stumbling backward. It gave her enough time to open the door and dash through it.

But the house was dark, the servants having fled to avoid dealing with the master's displeasure over her arrival. Photios was behind her, his footfalls gaining on her, so she crunched herself down at the top of the stairs, hugging her knees and tucking her chin against them. Her attacker let out a hoarse cry as he hit her body and flew over her. She heard him crashing into the stairs on his way to the bottom floor. Raising her face, she watched the way his body flailed, frantically trying to stop until one loud crack signaled the end of his struggle.

Photios rolled down the last few steps in a lifeless heap. His body sprawled at the base of the stairs, his lifeless eyes staring up at the ceiling. The silence was nearly deafening, but satisfaction began to grow in her belly.

At last…her life was her own again.

❧

"Where are we?"

Janette couldn't stop herself from sounding intrigued. Darius pulled her a few more steps into a clearing before stopping.

"One of the tribal villages," he muttered. "My pronunciation of the name would be insulting to the inhabitants."

The people in question were watching them. The warriors of the tribe picked up their spears and sent their children scurrying back to their mothers.

"Stand still. Don't move until they welcome us."

"I don't believe I needed that warning, Darius."

The warriors came closer, keeping the sharp points of their spears pointed at them. Darius waited until one of them spoke, and then stunned her by answering the man in his native tongue. A few moments later, the spears were lowered. Darius turned a smug look toward her.

"You might have told me you could speak their language."

His lips remained raised in a smirk. "Ah...but where would the fun have been in that, sweet siren?"

Janette straightened her back and gave him a hard glare. "And when, pray tell, did we begin having fun?"

He stepped close and cupped the back of her head with one hand. So simply, she was in his power once more. His eyes were full of mischief, and he pressed a hard kiss onto her mouth. The warriors cheered him on as she pushed against his chest. He released her with a chuckle.

"I brought you here to begin having some, siren."

Disbelief held her in its grasp. "You did what?" she demanded, without a care for how shrewish she sounded. "What happened to your devotion to duty? And the expectations set out for me?"

He reached out and stroked the side of her face. Sensation rippled down her body in spite of the warriors watching them with keen interest. They might not have any reservations about witnessing such intimacy, but Janette stepped back.

Darius followed her, grasping a handful of her filthy skirt to hold her still.

"I decided I agreed with you."

His eyes had narrowed, and his voice turned hard. She could feel the tension in him but couldn't decide what the reason behind it was. "On what topic?"

"That you don't know who I am, so I've brought you to a place where no one will interrupt us while we get to know each other. You've met the Guardian, Janette, but there is part of me that clings to the Order because it allows me to witness life in different forms. If you want to return to something more familiar, you have only to ask—but I will never fit into the mold of a gentleman. It isn't in my nature."

Cryptic and confusing, his words left her stunned. He used the moment to kiss her once more before he was pulled away by a group of women. He laughed at her, more at ease than she saw him most of the time. Only in those few moments before he'd left her rooms had she seen this side of him, and yet there was something new too. A look of freedom in his eyes she'd never seen before. Yet there was also a challenge. Darius watched her, his dark eyes intent on her reaction to the women surrounding her.

Part of her was looking forward to getting to know this side of his nature, and that was a solid fact.

～～

The women took her to another river. Janette stared at it with trepidation. A shudder shook her, but her escort didn't pay it any mind. They cheerfully stripped her and pulled her toward a deep pool. The women wore only short pieces of fabric wrapped around their loins. Many had necklaces of shells around their necks, but every one of them was nude from the waist up. Their nipples were dark, and they giggled when her rose-colored ones were exposed.

They all wanted to touch her, stroking her softly with their fingertips as more women came to join them. They pulled the remaining pins from her hair and combed it gently before washing it. The soap was held in coconut shells and smelled like the fruit too. By the time they finished bathing her, there wasn't part of her they hadn't touched.

She should have been mortified; instead, she was intoxicated by the uniqueness of the moment. It was like being back in the Garden of Eden. There was no shame, only playfulness. Little girls scampered about, no one snapping fingers at them to be silent. Instead, their laughter made Janette smile. The air was balmy and warm, making clothing unnecessary.

Janette couldn't seem to soak up enough details; there were so many differences between them that she found fascinating. She wanted to know everything in a moment, wanted to absorb the feeling of the water and the sand beneath her bare feet, and even the way her body felt without anything but the sunshine against it.

Fine, she was wicked, and yet she couldn't agree with what she knew her society would have said about her. What made England's view on propriety any more correct than the native girls surrounding her with their seashell necklaces and bare breasts? The truth was she was enjoying her adventure too much to judge it.

Once she was clean, the girls pulled her up and onto the rocks so that her hair would dry. The sun began to sink on the horizon as the birds called to one another. The girls were all excited, chattering and giggling. They added flowers to their unbound hair and to hers as well. Other women were weaving long strips of leaves into skirts the girls tied about their hips. They shook from side to side, sending the strips of leaves swishing, and the air filled with a rustling sound. Once it was dark, drums began to beat back at the village. Crimson light flickered on the trees to announce a fire.

"Come…come…" Janette felt the first stab of concern puncturing her moment of enjoyment. The village was full of men, and she had only a loincloth on.

But the girls were clearly excited. They smiled and took her along with them as the light of fires shimmered ahead. Straight out of a fiction novel, the village looked like a savage stronghold. The red and gold flames sent dancing light over carved images of pagan idols. In the darkness, the stones set into the eyes of the wooden masks glittered in the firelight.

The beating of the drums added to the moment, easily carrying her away on a pounding that was in time with her own heartbeat. The girls all began to keep rhythm with the drummers, their hips jerking and moving as the men used bare hands to play the drums. She was caught in the middle of them, moving along almost without consent as they increased their dancing in response to the tempo.

It was wild, and in the middle of it, Darius sat near an older man who looked important. He had a silver chain around his neck and a headdress adorned with what looked like tusks of wild pigs. Darius sat in the same manner as the man next to him, with his legs folded, on a mat woven from dried palm leaves. The firelight illuminated his bare chest, sending a bolt of desire through her. It was twisting inside her like some living force.

He sat watching her—not the women performing with far more skill, but her. His dark gaze was on her breasts and her hips. Heat spread up her body, and she felt need building inside her. She wanted to entice him, wanted to inspire lust in him. Wanted to be only herself, not the person she'd always been groomed to be. Just a woman, free of society, because deep down inside, she was the same as every woman before her— from any society throughout history.

The women all jerked and swished, their breasts bouncing with their motions, and it set off an intense desire inside her. It began to pound through her blood, her nipples hardening while her clitoris throbbed. She finally understood what the matrons referred to as *brain fever*. It consumed her, driving away all thoughts of decorum.

And she didn't care.

Like any lunatic, she was happy in her insanity. In fact, she was proud. It was primitive, this desire to have Darius as her lover once more. Her passage heated, the folds of her sex becoming moist. She lifted her arms, reaching for what she desired as her hips mimicked the motions of making love.

Darius surged to his feet. The older man beside him laughed, but Janette didn't have time to look at anyone save Darius. He closed the space between them, the women parting to allow him a path to her. They didn't stop dancing, though. They raised their arms to the night sky, and the drums continued at a frantic pace until Darius hoisted her off her feet and spun her around.

Her unbound hair flew in a wide circle before he lowered her. But her feet never touched the ground.

He cradled her against his chest and carried her away from the dancing and into one of the huts that ringed the center of the village.

The sound of the drums followed them. It was so loud, it felt like it shook the very air around them. Janette wanted to remain immersed in the pounding tempo. She reached up, sliding her hands along the column of his throat before pressing a kiss to his warm skin. A soft growl was his response, and it fanned the flames of her desire. She reached for his shoulders, gripping them to pull herself up and kiss farther up on his throat.

He gripped her hips and pressed her back against a thick support beam, spreading her thighs with his body to the delight of her raging need. Her clitoris ached, her passage feeling empty. The hard bulge of his cock was pressing against her slit, teasing her with how swollen it was. The thin layer of his loincloth was suddenly frustrating her to the point of desperation.

"I need to be inside you, Janette."

He was growling, and her kisses turned hard.

"Then be inside of me," she answered. It was a demand, rising from the wildness surging through her. There was only her need for him, being driven by the pounding drums. She thrust toward him, grinding against his erection.

"Yes, ma'am," he agreed before pushing her back and ripping the fabric out from between them. He pressed her against the beam at her back with his chest, flattening her breasts and sending another white-hot shaft of need through her.

"Tonight is perfect. You are perfect."

He thrust deep, sending pleasure through her. She groaned, too caught in the web of sensations to remain silent. Her spine arched, and her head tipped back. He pulled free before returning to her with a hard motion of his hips.

"Together, we are perfect…" she purred.

He said softly, "Exactly."

Their skin slapped together, adding to the intensity of the moment. There was only pleasure and the hard motion of his hips, driving in and out of her body. She met him on every thrust, moving in time with the music and his demands. Her need had become desperate, the churning desire tightening beyond anything she'd felt before. Every muscle she had felt tight enough to snap, and still he continued to thrust against her. She could feel the pleasure waiting to burst, but it held off, making her frantic for release. With a final effort, it spilled over her like a cauldron of hot water, burning a path along her body, not missing a single inch as she twisted and contorted.

Darius tightened his grip on her hips as his seed began to fill her. She gasped again, a second wave of delight ripping through her belly. This one was deeper, the walls of her passage tightening around his cock to pull every last drop of seed from it. Her head sank onto his shoulder, her body a quivering mass as she tried to breathe. Beneath her hands, she could feel him shaking too.

He pressed a kiss against her neck, and she heard him draw in a deep breath before he straightened.

"So now you know, Janette. I am no gentleman, and quite happy about it. You wondered why I always warned you away? It's because I will embrace the moment, and I will not apologize for it."

He cradled her against his chest, walking through the dark hut and laying her in a sleeping net. He stroked her face, his touch gentle and tender.

"But that's what draws me to you, Darius. You offer me freedom, and I adore it."

The net swayed, making it impossible to resist falling into sleep. The drums faded into the distance as satisfaction carried her off on tiny ripples of pleasure.

Darius stared at her. She didn't mean it. Couldn't have.

Doubt was a vicious demon, and it was running loose through him in that moment. It tore at the firm conviction that no lady could accept him just as he was. Tomorrow, when she was back in civilization, she'd turn her nose up. All he'd be left with was the memory of how free she'd been while no one was looking.

But there was part of him demanding proof that she wouldn't accept him. It became a challenge that burned through his doubt, and he looked back at her sleeping form.

Tomorrow. Morning light would show him the truth of the matter.

⤜⤏

She heard the crystals.

Janette opened her eyes to see that the sun wasn't up enough to light the inside of the hut very well. But she heard the humming. She rolled out of the sleeping net and landed on her feet. She'd slept in only the loincloth, and her breasts were still bare to enjoy the cool morning air.

"You'll want to cover up."

Darius was outside the hut, but he'd heard her.

"I hear crystals."

He moved into view and pointed up. "Lykos has sent out small airships in search of us. They had to wait until first light, though."

Good.

Her cheeks turned pink as the memories of last night erupted in full color. Darius didn't miss her blush.

"I'll see what I can find for you to wear. Your clothing was tattered, and I believe the women tore it up to make good-luck charms. They believe you were sent by the water goddess Kapo, and I am your lover consort, Kanaloa."

"That's the first time I've been royally treated." She heard the hiss of steam and stepped toward the doorway. Darius put his arm out to bar her way.

"I'll find you something."

"Why?" she demanded before ducking under his arm and walking into the morning light. "You aren't wearing any more than the village men. I'd rather not have them thinking I'm a prude. Or that I can't keep pace with you, Darius Lawley."

She hesitated for only a moment before enjoying the warmth of the sun on her bare chest. *Wicked.* But she would not be called a coward. More importantly, she would not lie on her deathbed lamenting the adventures she'd turned her nose up at. Darius chuckled, and she turned to find him watching her. There was a sparkle of enjoyment in his dark eyes, which thrilled her.

"You are perfection, Miss Aston."

She wrinkled her nose. "Formality is somewhere"—she waved her hand in the direction of Britain—"very far away. Call me something…more personal."

One dark eyebrow rose. His eyes narrowed. "Mine," he pronounced with a clear ring of savageness in his voice.

She clapped her hands together. "Perfect."

High above, a smaller airship was drifting toward them. Thick columns of steam rose from twin stacks on either side of the passenger compartment. Several of the windows were propped open, and men leaned out with binoculars.

Darius raised his arm, completely at home in his native attire. She stared at him, absorbing the raw magnetism. She could feel it—actually taste it—and when he turned to stare at her, she felt her pride rising. Reflected in his eyes was approval.

"I suppose we must return."

His expression tightened. "Regrettably, yes."

He reached out and stroked her cheek. "You wouldn't be safe here, but the idea of remaining is still intoxicating."

There was another blast of steam and a long hissing sound. The airship descended, sending the villagers scattering. A ladder was pushed over the side of the passenger compartment. Darius reached up and grabbed it.

"But everything ends," he announced before the ladder lowered enough for her to grab it. His tone was tight, and by the time she reached the top of the ladder, his stony expression was one she recalled too well. The duty-bound Guardian had returned, and it seemed she was once more just another task on his list.

Pain tore through her. It centered over her heart, and there wasn't a single glimmer of hope in his dark eyes to relieve it.

"The ride will be intense, but it will have to end eventually. Reality will be waiting, I assure you. The sun will rise, and consequences will be illuminated."

His words rose from her memory, and she felt the harsh bite of consequences taking their toll. The passenger compartment of the airship was full of Guardians, their badges pinned to their vests.

Yes, reality had certainly arrived.

❧

"You're young and impressionable," Guardian Cyrus Vettel offered.

"You needn't make it sound like an accusation." Janette found herself uncomfortable in the dress and its layers of undergarments. It was certainly a curiosity how quickly she had become accustomed to wearing none of it.

"You were hunting crystals for the Helikeians," Guardian Cyrus Vettel muttered drily.

"She was attempting to rescue her friend," Darius interjected.

They weren't in a true Solitary Chamber. Instead, they stood near the doorway of a building under construction. But the makeshift hearing lacked none of the tension she would have felt if it were being conducted back in London. Guardians were set to guard her as Guardian Vettel considered her from behind a stone-hard expression. Lykos and Decima silently surveyed her as well.

"If you hadn't refused to take the Oath, I might be more inclined to be sympathetic."

"If the lot of you would stop viewing her as a commodity instead of as a person, my fiancée might be more inclined to pledge her life to the Order."

Guardian Vettel pointed a finger at Darius. "Is this man your fiancé or not?"

"I am," Darius confirmed.

"I will hear it from her lips, Guardian Lawley," Vettel insisted.

Janette suddenly laughed. Darius and Vettel eyed her disapprovingly. "You will not hear anything of the sort because who I choose to have in my bed is none of your Order's affair."

Guardian Vettel opened his mouth, but Janette interrupted him.

"As for the Oath of Allegiance, I will complete my training year. That is my right, laid down in the laws of the Illuminist Order. As for any of you who do not care for my choice, I suggest you invest more time in treating me like a member instead of a thing to be controlled. Now I am going to see my friend."

She turned her back on them and their impromptu trial. It was a daring move, but the Guardians moved out of her way. Each step took her farther away from Darius. Her feet felt heavy, but she continued onward.

She was an Illuminist—she had rights, the same as any male member of the Order.

You're a woman in love…prey to the same weakness as other women…

A hard hand caught her upper arm. Darius spun her around to face him as Lykos and Decima sent the others away from them. He pulled her around the corner of the building.

"Damn us both, Janette."

She pushed at his chest, but he held her tight. "So you've told me, Darius." She wanted to push him away, wanted to insist he release her, but instead, her hands curled into his vest. "I won't take the Oath now. Nothing you say will change my mind."

Surprise lit his eyes for a moment before savageness flickered in them. "I don't give a damn about the Oath."

"Then why are you stopping me from seeing if Sophia is well?" Why was he insisting on tormenting her with his touch? It seemed unbearable now.

"If you're going to reject me, Janette, do it to my face."

He was growling, and suddenly her temper flared up. She lifted her arms and brought them down on top of his wrists just like she'd learned in Asian fighting class. He let out a profane word as his grasp on her biceps broke.

"Reject you?" She stabbed him in the center of his chest with one finger. "You're the one who continues to warn me away."

"You are the one who just refused to acknowledge me as your fiancé."

She felt like steam could have risen from her ears, her temper was so hot. "You never asked me to marry you, Darius. You just said it because you were doing your duty to protect me. Well, I'm going to be an Illuminist, and marriage is only for love. I don't want to be your duty wife."

"It wasn't duty that prompted me to say such. It was the fact that I just couldn't tolerate having you taken away from me." He leaned closer, pushing her back with his superior size. "Tell me you don't love me, Janette, and I'll walk away, but it will tear my heart wide open because I sure as hell wouldn't have said we were engaged if I didn't love you. Soft, flowery words are not my way."

He captured her arms again, pulling her against his chest before planting a hard kiss against her surprised lips. She was slow to respond because she was too busy sorting through what he'd said. But her body knew what it wanted, and it was deeper than just desire. She reached up, wrapping her arms around his neck, and trembled as she kissed him back.

"Why are you kissing me back, Janette?" he asked, but there was a need in his eyes that betrayed him.

She had never seen anything so sweet. She tilted her head and kissed his hand where it was still holding her neck. "Because I love you."

Surprise registered on his face. "But—"

"But nothing, you arrogant man," she admonished him softly. "Do stop telling me what to think, Darius."

He shook his head, but she cupped his face. Rising onto her toes, she pressed a soft kiss against his lips. She slipped out of his embrace and walked around the wall. The rest of the Guardians were clearly waiting for her.

"He is my fiancé."

Her choice, her lover, and the man she loved. Perfection truly could be found on Earth.

❧

"These glasses are too dark," Sophia muttered.

"You can change to lighter ones in a week or so," Bion told her.

Janette watched her friend aim a frustrated glare at the First Officer—except Bion was a passenger now. They were returning to London on a different airship than the one they'd arrived on.

"But I can't make out the dimension gates. You said that root ball restructured my eyes. Why aren't they working?"

Bion looked at Lykos instead of answering. Sophia's eyes narrowed behind the pair of dark purple glasses she had perched on her nose.

"Don't you dare side with him, Lykos Claxton. I have to needle every bit of information out of him. It's shameful, really. These are my eyes." She stood and walked toward one of the large viewing windows.

"I recall that feeling myself," Janette muttered.

Lykos lifted his hands in mock surrender. "I am not responsible. You are Darius's problem."

"Trust a man to call a woman's questions a *problem*," Decima remarked. She was leaning against a support beam. She sent a glare toward Lykos, who returned it.

"Good night," she muttered before Lykos could answer her.

"Now, just wait—"

Decima turned her back on Lykos. His lips thinned, and no one at the table missed it.

"Go on," Bion offered. "I'll babysit our foundling Navigator."

Sophia heard him and turned in a flare of her skirts. Janette tugged on Darius's hand.

"What's the hurry?" he demanded.

"Trust me, this is not going to end well," Janette answered as she tugged him way toward the passenger cabins. "Sophia is a redhead masquerading as a blond. Bion is about to be skinned alive."

"He might enjoy it. The man has the heart of a pirate." Darius produced a key and opened the cabin for her.

"Then again, maybe you were simply impatient to be alone with me," he said as she passed into the room.

Janette sighed as he closed the door. "There you go again, Mr. Lawley, making assumptions on how I feel. Haven't you learned your lesson?"

She opened her top, revealing the swell of her breasts above the edge of her corset. His dark gaze followed her fingertip as she stroked one soft mound.

"I stand before you a reformed man, madam." He deposited his overcoat and vest on the wall hook before shrugging out of his chest harness. "But I confess I am still a needy one. Tell me again how you feel because I'm failing to believe it."

"Rogue," she accused. "You are supposed to mutter endearments in my ear, to earn my surrender. Not beg for compliments to shine your ego."

His shirt followed, and her breath caught, desire rising up to fill her mind. She enjoyed its slow burn, feeling no shame, only a sense of rightness.

Her husband propped his hands on either side of her, pressing his palms against the wall.

"I love you." He pressed a kiss against her neck. "I adore you." Another kiss landed on the opposite side of her throat. "But most importantly, I thank you for proving me wrong—and that, Miss Aston, is the greatest compliment I have ever paid anyone."

"I believe you." She slid her hands along the warm

column of his throat, shivering as sensation rippled along her arms and down her body. "And I love you."

Neither of them noticed when they went through the dimension gate. They were both far too busy enjoying the perfection of each other's embrace. Janette snuggled against her lover, basking in the glow of his declaration.

Perfection.

∽

Sophia didn't sleep; she wandered around the dining area of the airship well after it was deserted by the other passengers.

It wasn't the pain in her eyes that kept her awake, although it was more of an annoying itch now. Keeping her hands away from her face took concentration, and she'd woken up more than once with tears on her hands because impulse took over once she was asleep.

Her father needed her—that was the thought hounding her.

"You need rest to heal."

She turned to see Bion moving toward her. The man was too large for her liking, his shoulders too wide. "What I need is for you to stop shadowing me like some nursemaid. Where do you think I will go?"

Sophia opened her hands to indicate the inside of the airship passenger area. The engines droned with a low rumble, while outside the windows, the clouds let in slivers of moonlight.

"I was hoping you'd get some sleep, so I could as well," he muttered too softly for her caring.

"Save your pity."

Everyone could save their coddling and sympathy. It turned her stomach. She turned to brush past Bion, seeking escape from his presence, when he reached out and captured her wrist. Without a glove, his hand wrapped around the tender skin, sending a jolt of awareness up her arm.

"You mistake me greatly," he informed her firmly. "Pity is the last thing I feel for you."

There was a strength in his words she was tempted to lean on. Her life was suddenly shattered into pieces, and she wasn't sure how to sweep them up or put them back together again. But she would muster her courage; she had to or risk becoming one of those delicate creatures she and Janette had always deplored.

"Good. Excellent." She pulled her hand away and walked toward her cabin. But she felt Bion watching her. Of course, it was only because he was duty-bound to watch her. There could be no other reason. She rubbed at her wrist, trying to erase the feeling of his skin against hers.

There was no other reason for his presence. None.

৵৶

"I swear to uphold the laws of the Order, to defend its ideals and maintain my duty."

The inner chamber of the Solitary Chamber was brightly lit, and Janette waited for the three Marshals to accept her pledge. Tonight, she'd take her Oath and become an Illuminist.

"Upon my honor, I swear to maintain secrecy, even if it should cost my life."

There was a nod and then another and at last a third

before applause filled the room. She stood, her knees aching just a tiny amount before she was distracted by the middle Marshal standing up. He moved toward her, carrying a gold Illuminist pin. Excitement rippled through her, but what she noticed most was the sense of achievement. It was like a candle flame burning brightly inside her. For the first time in her life, she had set a goal and earned an honor that was entirely her own. In spite of her gender, she was an Illuminist because she had chosen to be.

Her husband stepped up as the pin was placed on the lapel of her vest. The satisfaction in his eyes had nothing to do with her hereditary ability—it was because he loved her. She could see it in his eyes, and she loved him even more for standing in the place of her spouse during the ceremony. That was love. It didn't have conditions or boundaries. That's what made it perfection. They respected each other as individuals, as Illuminists.

"Welcome to the Order, Janette Lawley. Turn and be recognized by your peers."

Her mother stood watching, a gold pin on her lapel too. Professor Yulric applauded with more force than his frail arms looked capable of, while Galene dabbed at her eyes with a lace-edged handkerchief.

"Happy?" Darius asked her softly.

"Beyond my wildest dreams, husband."

He sent her a promising look that made her smile before she walked back to her seat. She was going to ensure he made good on his promise, too.

About the Author

Mary Wine is a multipublished author in romantic suspense, fantasy, and Western romance. Her interest in historical reenactment and costuming also inspired her to turn her pen to historical romance with her popular Highlander series. She lives with her husband and sons in Southern California, where the whole family enjoys participating in historical reenactment.

Lessons After Dark

by Isabel Cooper

Author of *No Proper Lady,* a *Publishers Weekly* and
Library Journal Best Book of the Year

A woman with an unspeakable past

Olivia Brightmore didn't know what to expect when she
took a position to teach at Englefield School, an academy for
"gifted" children. But it wasn't having to rescue a young girl
who'd levitated to the ceiling. Or battling a dark mystery in the
surrounding woods. And nothing could have prepared her for
Dr. Gareth St. John.

A man of exceptional talent

He knew all about her history and scrutinized her every move
because of it. But there was more than suspicion lurking in
those luscious green eyes. Olivia could feel the heat in each
haughty look. She could sense the desire in every touch, a
spark that had nothing to do with the magic of his healing
abilities. Even with all the strange occurrences at the school,
the most unsettling of all is the attraction pulling her and
Gareth together with a force that cannot be denied.

For more Isabel Cooper, visit:

www.sourcebooks.com